W9-CBA-342

BEYOND GONE

BEYOND GONE

Douglas Corleone

This first world edition published 2020
in Great Britain and the USA by
SEVERN HOUSE PUBLISHERS LTD of
Eardley House, 4 Uxbridge Street, London W8 7SY.
Trade paperback edition first published
in Great Britain and the USA 2020 by
SEVERN HOUSE PUBLISHERS LTD.

British Library Cataloguing in Publication Data
A CIP catalogue record for this title is available from the British Library.

ISBN-13: 978-0-7278-8985-0 (cased)
ISBN-13: 978-1-78029-680-7 (trade paper)
ISBN-13: 978-1-4483-0384-7 (e-book)

All Severn House titles are printed on acid-free paper.

Severn House Publishers support the Forest Stewardship Council™ [FSC™],
the leading international forest certification organisation.
All our titles that are printed on FSC certified paper carry the FSC logo.

Typeset by Palimpsest Book Production Ltd.,
Falkirk, Stirlingshire, Scotland.
Printed and bound in Great Britain by
TJ International, Padstow, Cornwall.

In loving memory of Edward G. Modica,
Norman J. Civensky, and Michael Kennedy

One can be the master of what one does, but never of what one feels.

Gustave Flaubert

PART I
A Corpse in Cape Town

ONE

I had been in Cape Town roughly six days when I discovered the body. She lay naked, face down, on the single bed, no immediate sign of trauma to the back, neck, or rear of the head. I checked for a pulse, but it was just a formality. I'd been watching Isabel for nearly seventy-two hours and had only lost her late the night before last. The woman I'd been watching was fair-skinned and pencil-thin; the corpse, however, was already swollen, discolored, and smelled to high hell. I wondered how no one, even in this tumbledown four-story hotel, had reported the stench.

Or maybe someone had. Maybe someone downstairs had been paid to ignore it.

Before I could bring the thought to its logical conclusion, I heard the sirens. They bleated from the west and were approaching at a decent clip. I had two minutes, three at most, and felt myself woefully unprepared for this. I'd entered the room in search of evidence, something that might lead me to the whereabouts of Isabel's ten-year-old son. I hadn't come in search of a corpse.

Like it or not, Simon, now you have one.

I moved toward the window but found it nailed shut. The window looked down on a wide cobblestone alley that dead-ended to my left. To my right, two blood-red dumpsters rested side by side near the mouth of the alley. The dumpsters were closed, and, anyway, too far to reach with even the most generous jump, which meant smashing the window would be useless.

I turned back toward the room, which was smaller than most walk-in closets and seemed to be getting smaller, as though the urine-yellow walls were closing in. I glanced toward the toilet, but it offered no suggestions. If you want out of this room, it said, you're going out the way you entered, through the front door. And you'd better hurry, because those sirens are only a few blocks away and you're not nearly as fast at forty-four as you were at thirty.

All that from a toilet.

No time to wipe the room of my prints. And I doubted that it would matter. Whoever placed me in the frame today was no amateur. Fingerprints wouldn't make or break the case either way. My only hope was to get the hell out of there, find a fortress of solitude, and get to work figuring out who the hell had set me up and why.

I opened the door on to an empty hallway and quickly took measure. Could either run down four flights of stairs or take a lift roughly the size of my future prison cell. Downstairs, the first police cars shrieked to a halt behind the hotel. Neither the lift nor the stairs would do; I needed a third option.

There weren't many cars parked in the lot outside and the vacancy sign was lit, meaning the hotel wasn't booked to full capacity. So if the clerk downstairs *had* been paid off to keep quiet about the smell, maybe none of the other rooms on the fourth floor were occupied.

I crossed the puke-green carpeted hallway to the door standing diagonal to Isabel's room. No time to pick the lock, so I lifted my right leg, aimed just below the door handle, and kicked with everything I had.

The door flew open and I breezed through the unoccupied room and went for the window. Not nailed shut; in fact, it was wide open. The stench of cigarette smoke hung in the air and I figured I had a smoker to thank for this pearl of luck. No doubt the maids were airing the room out, readying it for its next guests.

No Cape Town police vehicles were visible from my vantage point, so I lifted a leg over the windowsill and stepped on to the ledge. As my other leg followed, I spotted the filthy green awning below. I aimed for a spot relatively clear of bird shit and dropped from the ledge.

My ass hit the awning, and to my pleasant surprise, the green fabric didn't rip but bounced me off and dumped me on to the circle of blacktop that fronted the hotel. I tucked and tumbled and came to a stop at the feet of a teenage bellboy.

As I pushed myself up, I pulled a pair of crumpled South

African rand notes from my pants pocket, handed them to the astonished kid, and said, 'Thanks,' while placing an index finger to my lips.

The kid bowed his head and I took off up the street in the opposite direction to the sirens.

At the next intersection I lifted a young woman off her black Vespa and set her down on her feet.

'Sorry,' I said to her as I straddled the scooter. Then I accelerated into the intersection, ignoring the red light and accompanying orchestra of horns, a single thought at the forefront of my mind.

If the kid isn't with his mother, then who the hell is he with?

I abandoned the Vespa along Western Boulevard and walked to the bus stop at Green Point. It was nearing the end of the day and public transportation was crowded. When I boarded thirty seconds later, I pushed my way through to the far end of the bus, where I spotted what looked to be a wealthy American tourist dozing off with a full shopping bag between her legs. I stood near her, trying to eye what was in the bag, and when I spotted a tie box, I bided my time until the next stop. There, I casually lifted the bag with my fingers and stepped out the rear door with the rest of the weary commuters.

I ducked into the public toilet I'd scoped out earlier and locked myself in a stall to change clothes. Inside the bag I found a pewter Giorgio Armani shirt and a pair of charcoal trousers by Dolce & Gabbana. The pants were a bit wide in the waist, but it didn't matter because the American had purchased a fine-looking men's black leather belt made by Prada.

After removing the tags, I transferred the contents of my old pockets to my new, then stuffed the old clothes in the bag and set the bag down next to the toilet.

I looked down at my new attire, oddly impressed. All I was missing were the shoes. For the time being at least, mine would have to do.

I stepped out of the stall and surveyed three men standing in front of sinks. Of the three, two were wearing hats, one a wool baseball cap, the other a dark Stetson fedora. I approached the one with the fedora.

'I like your lid,' I said to him, plucking another twenty-rand note out of my D&G pants pocket. 'How much?'

He looked at me strangely, but I couldn't tell whether it was because he didn't speak English or just thought it preposterous that a man dressed in such pricey apparel would be hat-shopping in a dank public men's room when just down the road stood some of the finest boutiques on the continent.

'*How much?*' I said, pointing to his hat.

When he didn't respond, I shoved the twenty rand in his hand and snatched the hat off his head.

By the time he finally composed himself enough to speak, I was already out the door.

TWO

As I headed toward the University of Cape Town in the rear of a taxi, I tried to reach my client back in New York on a burner I'd bought in Cape Flats. The call went straight to voicemail. But I wasn't going to leave a message telling him his ex-wife was dead and his ten-year-old son Brady was missing. Either I'd reach him later and tell him directly or he'd find out from someone else.

Then again, Ryan Cochran claimed not to know anyone else in South Africa.

And I was inclined to believe him. Ryan Cochran was a grammar school teacher in Staten Island. Had been for the past decade according to his employment file with the New York City Board of Education. He lived about a half-mile from the school at which he worked, in a two-bedroom townhouse that couldn't have been worth more than two or three hundred thousand. Before speaking directly with Cochran, I'd gotten my hands on a copy of his credit report, courtesy of my friend Kati Sheffield, a former FBI computer analyst. The Experian report showed that he had a mortgage and several low-limit credit cards from banks like Capital One and First Premier. And that he didn't always make his payments on time. His credit score was a hair under 600. Sounded a lot like the life of an American public-school teacher to me.

Yet when I asked him for ten grand in cash for a retainer, he put up no fuss whatsoever. I had the money in my hands twenty-four hours later. That didn't mean much, of course. Your kid gets taken by your ex in the middle of the night and flown overseas in violation of your US custody order, you find a way to pay the guy you think can get your kid back, plain and simple. You do whatever it is you have to do. Beg, borrow, steal; at that point it doesn't matter. Not to him, and certainly not to me.

I know what it's like to lose a child. To have your heart ripped from your chest, your lungs crushed, your guts spilled. My six-year-old daughter Hailey was abducted from the back-yard of our Georgetown home fourteen years earlier. As a result, my wife Tasha took her own life with a vicious stew of prescription pills.

I'd only recently found my daughter in London, and the psychological damage she'd sustained was even worse than I had expected. For now she was convalescing back at our new home, a four-room cottage in a small village in the former Soviet republic of Moldova, being expertly cared for by my better half, the former Warsaw lawyer Anastazja Staszak.

The taxi dropped me in front of the university, and I paid the driver in cash. I was arriving unannounced and hoped that I could get in to see one of the professors, a woman who had been an international exchange student at American University twenty-some years ago when Tasha and I attended.

I wasn't even sure Jadine Visser would remember me.

Fact was, I didn't operate much in South Africa because it was a country that remained in full compliance with the Hague Convention, a multilateral treaty on the civil aspects of inter-national child abduction. This, however, was a unique case. Ryan Cochran didn't have the wherewithal to go through the proper channels, and a fellow at the US State Department told him his best bet was to contact me. After speaking with Cochran and learning the circumstances surrounding the abduction, I couldn't help but take the case.

Of course, several days ago when I spoke to the client, the case sounded fairly straightforward. Now that Isabel, the child's mother, was dead, things had become rather complicated.

I hoped Jadine Visser could help.

'How did you track her to the hotel?' Jadine asked in her melodious South African accent.

She glanced at the clock above my head for the third time in as many minutes.

Maybe she has a meeting, I told myself. *Maybe she has a class or office hours scheduled for later this afternoon.*

'Her car,' I said. 'Or at least the vehicle she'd been using.

A beige 2008 Toyota Corolla registered to a large international law firm headquartered in the States. I spotted it in the hotel parking lot less than thirty-six hours after I lost her. The parking pass was hanging from her rearview mirror. It listed her room number on the fourth floor.'

We were seated in Jadine's cramped office in the main administration building. Books cluttered every available inch of space. All of the books related to politics or geopolitics, most of them focusing on the African continent and various African countries' relationships with other nations.

'And you haven't seen the ten-year-old boy since you arrived in South Africa?'

'Not once.'

'You checked out the ex-wife's family?'

'First thing I did when I got here. Both of her parents are deceased. She has a sister who lives in Cairo. An aunt holed up in a nursing home in Johannesburg. I paid the aunt a visit; she doesn't even know her own name.'

'And the ex-wife's friends?'

'According to my client, all the friends she had here moved away and lost touch with her years ago.'

'Maybe this Isabel doesn't have the boy,' she said. 'What's his name again?'

'The boy's name is Brady. He Skyped his father when he first landed in Cape Town. He told his dad he was safe and with his mother. But that he was frightened and wanted to come home.'

'Are you sure? Have you seen the recording?'

'The father sent it to me.'

'Skype doesn't record calls. You need to install additional software. You said Brady's father is a schoolteacher? Why does he have that kind of software?'

'For classes,' I said. 'And parent–teacher conferences when both the parents work and can't make it to the school for parent–teacher night.'

She looked at me skeptically.

'I vetted him,' I said. 'Believe me, I'm not in a position to take chances.'

Kati Sheffield, the former FBI computer analyst who now

cared for her three children and performed side work for investigators like me, was thorough in her search. She knew I was at risk and had always been extremely diligent.

'Was there anything in the background of the call that could give you any idea of the boy's location?'

'No,' I said, 'there was a thick maroon curtain set behind him. Brady said his mother insisted on it. And there were no sounds on the recording other than the kid's voice.'

'And why does the father think the boy is in danger?'

'He says Isabel is extremely violent. He sent me Emergency Room records for two separate incidents within the past year. As well as a psychiatric assessment that was admitted into evidence at Brady's custody hearing. Isabel suffers from something called intermittent explosive disorder.'

'I've never heard of it.'

'It's a behavioral disorder that inhibits the person's ability to control aggressive impulses. She suffers explosive outbursts of rage disproportionate to the circumstances. The father said she becomes violent over the slightest transgression, like if Brady tracks mud into the house after a baseball game or uses the wrong sink to wash his hands.'

'The wrong sink?'

I shrugged. 'Apparently, the bathroom sink is for washing because it's ceramic. The kitchen sink is stainless steel and therefore tougher to clean.'

I watched Jadine's eyes, to see if they'd return to the clock. But no, this time they went to the floor. Specifically to the bottom of the door.

Instinctively, I followed her gaze and that's when I saw the shadows. Not just below but through the shade covering the door's large square window.

I jumped from my seat, but I knew any attempt at escape was futile. Unless I could somehow find a way to jump into the pages of one of Jadine's hundreds of books, whoever was on the opposite side of the door was about to have me in their custody.

I looked at Jadine and instantly knew. If she hadn't set me up personally, she'd certainly played along.

How could you? I almost said.

But then I realized how ridiculous I would have sounded. This was my own damn fault. I'd broken one of my most fundamental rules.

I'd come to Jadine Visser for help when I barely even knew her anymore.

THREE

The agents didn't identify themselves. They were dressed in ordinary street clothes and showed absolutely no respect for the Armani shirt and Dolce & Gabbana pants I'd lifted off the American woman on the bus.

When the last of them stepped out of Jadine's office and tried to close the door behind him, Jadine caught it in her hand.

'I'm coming with him,' she said.

'Sorry,' the agent told her, 'but those aren't our orders.'

'They better damn well be, because James promised me I could come along. It's the only reason I agreed to this charade in the first place.'

As we continued walking through the atrium, one of the agents liberated his cellular phone from his pocket and made a call. He dropped back so that I couldn't hear what he was saying.

Meanwhile, my only thought was of escape. There were six agents and Jadine. The agents were armed with handguns. But they hadn't cuffed me. Which, given my history, seemed to me to be rather foolish on their part.

Outside the administration building, the sun struck us hard, but I didn't attempt to take advantage of the opportunity because three of the six agents were wearing mirrored sunglasses.

In front of the building stood a large black van, its engine idling. I waited for one of the agents to toss a hood over my head, to shock me with a Taser, hit me with a blackjack. But none of that happened. The sheer uneventfulness reminded me of my arrest in Paris a few years ago – an arrest that quickly led to a serious ultimatum.

I took a seat in the van. Jadine climbed in next to me.

'What the hell is going on?' I asked her.

She glanced at me but didn't answer.

I stared at her profile. She was stunning in the sunlight.

The overhead fluorescent lights in her office hadn't done her justice. Her short black hair framed a perfectly proportioned face. Her sienna skin remained as flawless as it had been in college. Her dark brown eyes contained that familiar amber twinkle.

The side panel slammed shut and we soon began moving.

Jadine and I had spent three weeks together when I first arrived at college for my freshman year, and I couldn't help but flash back on those precious days now. She was a year or two older than my eighteen years and delightfully more experienced. I tried to remember why in the world I would have dumped her, but quickly came to the conclusion that I'd been lying to myself about our break-up for the past two decades. She'd obviously dumped me.

Then, by rights, I should be the one seeking payback, not her.

So why the hell was she doing this to me?

Another man. I should have guessed.

But not just any man.

We arrived at a safe house off Somerset Road and walked up the concrete steps. When the door opened, two agents ushered me past the living room, which was crowded with suits, and into the dining room where one tall man stood in the center of four others.

He caught my eye. 'Ah, Mr Fisk, how good of you to come,' he said. 'You're a difficult man to find.'

'Apparently not difficult enough,' I said.

He offered his hand. 'James Coleman, but you may call me Jim.'

'I think I'd prefer Mr Secretary if it's all the same to you.'

He displayed the winning smile I'd seen in so many newspapers over the past few months. First at his nomination, then at his confirmation hearings before the Senate. And finally once he took the oath of office as only the second African American male to become the United States Secretary of State.

Coleman was seventy-four but looked a good decade younger despite a head of hair more salt than pepper.

He glanced over my shoulder and bowed his head. 'Jadine, it's wonderful to see you again.'

I wished I could have said the same.

As I watched the exchange, I noticed something pass between them and realized that Coleman and Jadine were something more than friends. Or had been at some point. Jadine Visser had spent many years in Washington following college. And Coleman, of course, was one of DC's indigenous species – a lawyer, a former US Congressman, a two-term US Senator, a lobbyist, a US Senator again, a presidential candidate, a vice presidential nominee, and finally Secretary of State.

He'd traveled a long road to get from the US Capitol to the Harry S. Truman Building at 2201 C Street NW. Especially considering it was just a three-mile walk for the average citizen. A ten-minute drive in DC traffic.

'Let's go upstairs, Simon,' he said, 'where we can speak in private. Jadine, why don't you join us.'

On the second floor, we stepped into what was probably designed as a master bedroom. It now served as a conference room, complete with a long marble table and several upholstered chairs. Jadine and I sat on the left side, Coleman and his deputy on the right.

Coleman folded his arms on the table and said, 'First, allow me to apologize for the ruse, Simon. Our original plan was to meet you in Moldova, but you have a habit of moving around without notice, and the locals must like you because they protect your privacy better than my well-paid staff protects mine – present company excluded, of course.'

I said, 'Let's not just gloss over this part, Mr Secretary. Let me see if I have this right. First of all, the woman I was following for three consecutive days is not Isabel Cochran.'

'No, she is a South African intelligence agent, and a very fine one if she was able to give you the slip.'

'I take it she's still alive?'

'Very much so.'

'And the body?'

'Borrowed. From the morgue. Again, with the help of our friends in South African intelligence.'

'And the boy in the Skype video?'

'A charismatic young actor, who clearly has a bright future

in front of him. In fact, he's beginning a run on Broadway this fall.'

'And the father?'

He chuckled without joy. 'The father is very real, Simon. We knew you were smart, knew you were extremely careful, especially following everything that transpired in the UK. We knew you'd vet the prospective client, so everything you learned about him is real.'

'Except for the custody issue.'

'Right, Simon. The family law attorneys you were in contact with were playing along. The custody order is real enough, including the psych evaluation and the boy's hospital records. Fortunately, however, the order hasn't been violated.'

'I wasn't speaking directly to the schoolteacher then, was I?'

'No, that was actually one of my interns. A very smart young man, from your alma mater, if I'm not mistaken. Again, I apologize.'

I leaned back in my chair, expressionless. 'What do you want from me, Mr Secretary?'

Coleman turned to his deputy, who leaned over and lifted a laptop computer on to the table.

As he opened it, the Secretary said, 'I'd like you to watch this brief video, Simon, which was posted to YouTube just last week.'

The Deputy, who'd not said a word since we entered the room, turned the monitor to face me.

'I believe the scene requires no set-up,' Coleman added.

I stared at the monitor. Not only did the video not need a set-up, but Coleman didn't need to play it. I hadn't seen this particular video before, but I'd seen one like it. And one was more than enough.

The setting was the African bush. One tall dark man with a long black beard and flowing robes stood over a single female, propped up on her knees, sobbing beneath a black hood.

The man uttered several sentences in a language I couldn't identify, let alone understand.

Then he removed the hood, revealing a beautiful dark-skinned African girl, no more than fourteen or fifteen years of age.

I was about to demand they turn the video off, but my voice caught in my throat as the tall bearded man bent over and lifted a machete from the dirt.

I closed my eyes but couldn't shut my imagination to his placing the blade to the girl's throat. Couldn't silence the girl's frantic screams as they drowned out whatever prayer the killer was intoning.

While the video played, I thought about the day I learned Hailey had gone missing. Thought about the dozens of law enforcement officers who had camped out at our home over the next several weeks. About all the leads, all the wishful thinking. I thought about the war room I later created at my studio apartment on Dumbarton. About all the photographs and flyers and news articles. The radio and television appearances in which Tasha and I offered a reward and begged for our daughter's safe return. I thought of the twelve years I spent searching the globe in the hope of finding evidence of Hailey's continued existence.

I thought of all this and wondered who, if anyone, searched for the girl in the video. Of what that search entailed. Of how it ended. I wondered if anyone who loved this girl was still alive, still in the dark about what exactly had happened to her. I wondered how one abducted girl could be so blessed and another so cursed, merely by virtue of where in the world she was born.

After forty-five of the longest seconds of my life, the girl's screams finally ceased. I waited another half-minute, thinking by then the video had to have ended.

But when I finally opened my eyes, the bastard was holding the girl's severed head up for the camera.

I jumped from my chair in search of a wastebasket.

For the first time in years, I was sick to my stomach.

FOUR

'No doubt you've heard about the mass abductions in northern Nigeria over the past several years,' James Coleman said. 'Hundreds of girls, maybe thousands, *taken* from their schools in broad daylight, *stolen* from their beds in small villages in the middle of the night. Their parents and teachers shot dead, their brothers butchered, their houses and schools burned to the ground.'

I told him I had.

'Thanks to the subsequent protests and international social media campaign, most Americans know about the Chibok schoolgirls kidnapping several years ago. Nearly three hundred girls snatched from their beds in their dormitories in a midnight raid on the campus of the Government Girls' Secondary School. The hashtag BringBackOurGirls didn't succeed in bringing back our girls, but it did embolden Rusul Alharb's leader, who proudly claimed responsibility and trumpeted his resolve to continue kidnapping girls who, according to his ideology, shouldn't be wasting their time in schools.'

A knock on the door, a pitcher of ice water and four thick glasses set on the table between us, one poured for Secretary Coleman, one for Deputy Jeffries, one for Jadine, the last for yours truly.

Coleman took a swallow and continued speaking as the server hotfooted from the room, gently closing the door behind him. 'What few Americans know – given that Kim Kardashian and Ashton Kutcher aren't Tweeting about the issue all that much anymore – is that more than a hundred girls, ages eleven through nineteen, were abducted from the Girls' Science and Technical College in Dapchi two years ago. Or that a similar raid on a lesser-known institution in Adamawa State resulted in the kidnapping of an additional ninety-six girls earlier this month.'

'Christ,' I said.

'There's been no Christ yet, not in Nigeria, Simon.' He lifted his glass again, gave it a hard gaze, then set it down without stealing a sip. The Secretary suddenly appeared ill, so sick to his stomach that even water might have triggered his guts to expel their contents. 'Rusul Alharb has been around since 2002, but their slaughters didn't really begin until 2009. They've since killed somewhere between thirty and forty thousand civilians. Displaced more than three million. And *enslaved* an untold number of school-age girls.'

I shifted in my seat but said nothing.

'I won't go into too much detail right now; if you accept my terms, you'll of course be fully briefed by my staff, including my deputy, Mr Jeffries, seated to my left here. But I *will* tell you the militants' revolting motivation since it's as simple as it is insane, and because I hope it will make your blood boil as much as it does mine.'

I knew their motivation, but I sat silently and allowed the Secretary to continue.

'Rusul Alharb is opposed to the so-called Westernization of Nigeria. In short, they are opposed to modern civilization. Particularly secular education. And they're willing to die for their cause. The name Rusul Alharb, in fact, means "Messengers of War." They don't have global ambitions. They're not even intent on attacking Western interests. Which is why the United States and our Western allies refuse to do anything about them. They are Nigeria's problem. But Nigeria isn't equipped to handle a problem of this magnitude. Few African countries are.'

I nodded but said nothing.

'Why are they so hellbent on wreaking havoc on Nigeria? Because they claim that Nigeria is run by a group of corrupt and false Muslims. And so they waged war against them. Their objective? To create a pure Islamic state ruled by sharia law.' He leaned back in his chair and crossed his arms over his chest. 'Sound familiar?'

'Of course,' I said.

'ISIL, ISIS, the Islamic State, *Daesh*, whatever the hell we're calling them these days, they share the same DNA as Rusul Alharb, and Rusul Alharb has since pledged their allegiance to them, going so far as to adopt the name, Islamic

State in West Africa, or ISWA. The United States pledged to eradicate the Islamic State terror organization, and they've nearly succeeded in Iraq and Syria. But the Middle East has oil. Lots of it. Northeastern Nigeria, hardly any; nearly every drop is in the south of the country. And conveniently enough, ISIL has overtly expressed an interest in attacking Western targets, including the US homeland. That perfect combination is what afforded my friend, the President, the political where-withal to send troops back to the Middle East to "degrade and destroy" the Islamic State of Iraq and Syria.'

I said nothing.

'Meanwhile, Rusul Alharb – or the Islamic State in West Africa – has operated with virtual impunity. More than twenty thousand children have been prevented from attending school in the past decade. The death toll keeps rising. Just last month yet another bomb went off in Kano, killing more than a hundred people, at least half of them women and children. And from the accounts of the girls who have managed to escape Rusul Alharb's bloody clutches, the ones who die are the ones who are getting off easy.'

I stole a look at Jadine, whose eyes were locked on the table in front of her.

'The kidnapped girls,' Coleman continued, 'they can only pray for death. Those who were Christian have been forced to convert to Islam. They've been beaten and raped, turned into cooks and sex slaves, even suicide bombers. Many have been forced to marry members of the terror group. The bride price is said to be somewhere around twelve dollars fifty US. Some of the girls have reportedly been taken across the border to either Chad or Cameroon. The rest are said to be hidden deep in the forests of northeastern Nigeria. Despite the heat, the girls are made to dress in dark hijabs and long chadors. If they refuse, they are tortured.' He paused. 'All of this in the name of Allah.'

'Haven't there been attempts to get them back?' I said.

'Ill-conceived, half-assed attempts, sure. The President met with the leaders of Israel, Britain, and France at an emergency summit in Paris. And their main conclusion was that no deal should be struck with the terrorists. Canada, China, even Iran, have all offered use of their intelligence services and special forces. But nothing has been done, because every plan that involves force also runs the risk of severe collateral damage. The terror organization is prepared to kill each and every one of those girls if they see an attack coming.'

'Forgive me, Mr Secretary,' I said, 'but I still have no idea why I'm sitting here. Why I've been lured here. Why I've been taken away from my family, including my nineteen-year-old daughter who until only recently I hadn't seen in twelve years. She *needs* me.'

'And *I* need you, Simon. As I mentioned, the most recent mass abduction occurred in Adamawa. Militants, posing as Nigerian security forces, infiltrated the village of Lawaru, a Christian enclave in the predominantly Muslim state. One that had long been suffering from disease, hunger, poverty. One that the United States Peace Corps had been helping. With government, with technology, with agriculture, with the environment. And most of all, with education.'

Jadine finally raised her eyes, said, 'Tell him, Jim,' and a cloud magically lifted before me, exposing the first real hint of the Secretary's motives.

Coleman nodded to me as though I, rather than Jadine, had just spoken. 'I do regret having to bring you here under false pretenses, Simon. And it gives me no pleasure whatsoever to hold over your head either the body at the hotel on Western Boulevard or the Red Notice issued by Interpol for the crimes you are charged with in Great Britain. I sincerely hope that any further mention of those issues won't be necessary. But as you know more than most, Simon, a *desperate* man will do just about anything. And I am a *desperate* man.'

I looked him squarely in the eyes and saw that desperation spring forward.

He continued. 'Because one of the victims of the Lawaru kidnappings is a Peace Corps volunteer posing as a Sudanese aid worker with no ties to the United States. That's the only reason she's been kept alive this long. She's been using the name Adaku Oni, and her papers comport with that identity. Her *real* name, however, is Kishana. Kishana Coleman. And she is my sixteen-year-old granddaughter.'

FIVE

'The girl you saw in the video, Simon, she was the daughter of a minor Nigerian official – a *nobody* in the geopolitical arena. If Rusul Alharb discovers Kishana's true identity, they will *behead* her and they will record the decapitation, and they will post it on the internet for all the world to see. Including my daughter.'

'What you're asking of me, Mr Secretary, is impossible.'

He ignored my comment and continued his plea. 'How long, Simon, before one of the other girls – in order to prevent being raped or beaten – gives away the fact that they are holding the granddaughter of the highest-ranking member of the cabinet of the President of the United States?'

'I'm not questioning whether her life is in jeopardy, Mr Secretary.'

'How long, Simon, before the media discovers that my granddaughter is missing? That she is with the Peace Corps, assigned to that tiny village in Nigeria. Do you think *they'll* keep silent? Do you think they'll be able to restrain themselves for more than two *hours*?'

'I don't.'

'How long until Pakistani or Iranian intelligence learns that Rusul Alharb is holding my granddaughter? What happens then, do you think, Simon?'

'I don't know.'

'You *do* know. We *all* do, goddammit. Look, my daughter has been through enough in her life. The death of her mother when she was just a teenager. The loss of her stepmother less than a decade later. A father who was married to his career in Washington. An unplanned pregnancy. Sixteen years of living as a single mother. She will not be able to withstand the murder of her only child. There's not just one life at stake here, Simon. There are two. And those two young women –

my daughter and my granddaughter – constitute my entire family. They are all I have left in the world.'

For the next several seconds we sat in complete silence as an aggrieved heat rose in my chest. The play was clear: either I take on a terrorist organization ten thousand men strong and search for a single girl among hundreds or Coleman's people turn me over to South African authorities who would immediately extradite me to Great Britain for crimes allegedly committed in the search for my daughter. Every part of me wanted to tell him to go to hell. And I think the Secretary saw that in my eyes.

He held up his hand. 'Wait, Simon.' He turned to his deputy and said, 'Mr Jeffries, would you please take Ms Visser downstairs for some refreshments while Mr Fisk and I speak in private?'

'Sir, I don't think that's a good idea. Mr Fisk has a history of—'

'Of extreme violence – yes, I know. That's why he's here. Now, please.'

Coleman's deputy slowly stood from his chair and walked to the door. Held it open for Jadine and then stepped through, reluctantly closing it behind him.

James Coleman folded his hands together on the table in front of him and appraised me. 'If you are at all familiar with my work, Simon, then you know that I much prefer to use the carrot rather than the stick. Make no mistake; I'll *use* the stick when I need to – most of us will. But only as a last resort.'

'What are you saying, Mr Secretary?'

'I'm saying I don't give a damn about what occurred in Glasgow the winter you went searching for your daughter. And I don't give a damn about what happened in Dublin either. That your daughter killed some limey private investigator in the middle of an Irish pub full of drunkards is of no consequence to me.' He tilted his head so that he could glance over his shoulder, then turned back to face me. 'And it's of no consequence to my friend, the President, either.'

I held his gaze despite the fluttering building in my chest.

'I've spoken in depth with the President about this,' he said. 'And he and I are in full agreement. Look, you are free to leave, Simon. You will *not* be detained by South African authorities. You were able to get here under Interpol's radar, so I assume you'll be able to return to Moldova without triggering any red flags. In any event, Interpol will *not* be advised of your presence in South Africa by me or my people. You may even keep the ten thousand dollars you were paid for your troubles. All we'd ask for is your silence concerning anything discussed at this meeting. If you stand up and march out that door, you may proceed as if none of this ever happened.'

I considered standing. I considered marching. Coleman's implication that his granddaughter's life meant more than the life of any other girl taken by Rusul Alharb was enough to have me reaching for the wastebasket again. Yet I hesitated. And Coleman continued speaking.

'I'm removing the stick, Simon. Instead, I'm offering a carrot. Specifically, this: if you were to save my granddaughter from these savages, you and your daughter Hailey would be given the opportunity to restart your lives with a clean slate.'

He raised a palm as I started to ask a question.

'I've anticipated most of your concerns, Simon, if not all of them. First and foremost, this has already been cleared with the prime ministers of both Ireland and Great Britain. You complete this mission and you and Hailey may have your lives back. You may bring that beautiful Polish lawyer you appear to be so in love with and live peacefully in the West, whether it's in the District of Columbia, Rhode Island, London, or someplace else entirely.'

'And my daughter, what—'

Coleman raised his palm again. 'Hailey will receive the best psychiatric counseling in the Western hemisphere. She'll have tutors and teachers who will offer their undivided attention to get her up to speed so that she may have her high school diploma. After that, she may attend the university of her choice. Harvard, if she wants. Princeton, Yale, Stanford. Oxford or Cambridge. Perhaps somewhere more modest, like your alma mater. Or maybe she'll choose a party school like UC Santa Barbara or the University of Florida or Penn State. Entirely up to her, and you, of course. Paid in full – tuition, housing, books, meals, everything. Courtesy of the United States Government.'

My mind spun with the possibilities. Over the past several months I'd finally come to accept that Hailey would never have the life Tasha and I had so wanted for her. Despite her intelligence, she'd be limited in every way, including geographically. Now, with so many doors potentially about to open for her, I didn't know what to say. Which was all right because James Coleman wasn't finished talking.

'If Hailey decides she wants to continue her education after college, we'll cover that too. Law school, medical school, Juilliard. The possibilities are limitless.' He cleared his throat. 'And you, Simon, if you wanted to return to the Marshals or begin an entirely new career with the federal government, you'll be welcomed with open arms. We'll set you up in a house, someplace considerably larger than your DC studio apartment on Dumbarton, and you can relax and raise your family full-time, if that's what you'd prefer to do.'

I pictured Hailey going off to college.

I imagined Ana twirling in amazement in Times Square. Only after visiting Hollywood, of course.

I even allowed myself a small taste of a new life – not working with the Marshals or relaxing with a blended drink in a blue-and-white three-story home, but having the freedom to take on whatever cases I wished, regardless of the client's financial circumstances.

I stood and said, 'You have a deal, Mr Secretary.'

We shook, he thanked me, and said, 'Before you receive your intelligence briefing, I'd like you to go downstairs and make nice with Jadine. Because the only reason she agreed to help me meet you is that I promised her that when it came time for the mission, you'd agree to have her along.'

SIX

After fifteen and a half hours and brief stops in Johannesburg and Nairobi, Jadine Visser and I finally touched down in Abuja, Nigeria's capital city. Although we'd been squashed together in coach on the long Kenya Airways flight (commercial so as not to draw any unnecessary attention), we'd engaged in little conversation. Jadine spent most of her time onboard sleeping, a simple action that would likely prove brilliant in the following days. I, meanwhile, studied the jumble of supposedly classified documents on Rusul Alharb and the series of kidnappings that had spawned the #BringBackOurGirls movement on Twitter and, sadly, little else in the way of rescue efforts.

As we disembarked on to the hazy tarmac at Nnamdi Azikiwe International, Jadine turned to me and said, 'Don't be lulled by the relative quiet of the capital. Even though it's ethnically neutral, it's been a target. Just last spring more than seventy people were slaughtered in a jihadist attack. A few months later a bomb blast at the Wadud Plaza shopping mall killed at least twenty-one. Keep vigilant anywhere you see people gathered.'

I didn't comment on the fact that we were right now following a sizable crowd into the terminal.

'The man we're meeting,' I said quietly to Jadine, 'you've met him before?'

'Once or twice.'

As we trekked through the airport, my mind wandered back to Moldova. Only I no longer thought of it as Moldova but *home*. A concept with which I had never been genuinely familiar. I was born in London and to this day spoke with a subtle British accent. I suppose that as a child I considered England home, but shortly after my fifth birthday I was abruptly removed by my father, Alden Fisk. He and I relocated to Providence, Rhode Island, where he re-established his medical practice and I honed my skills fighting in schoolyards. It wasn't so much that I missed London itself, but rather my mother and to an even greater extent my slightly older sister named Tuesday.

Only within the past few years had I discovered that my mother, Tatum Fuller, was dead and Tuesday wasn't my biological sister and had abandoned the name Tuesday Fisk altogether. She was now living in London under the name Zoey Carlyle. I still loved her, of course, and she was pivotal in helping me find Hailey after a grueling twelve-year search. But Tuesday, or rather Zoey, no longer represented home.

New England never felt like home either. Given my relationship with my father, Rhode Island had long felt like a prison, with Alden Fisk as its hard-ass warden. Only after high school did I finally make my escape, not back to London, but to Washington, DC, where I matriculated at American University. It was at American that I met Jadine and, soon after, Tasha, the woman I fell in love with and later married. After our wedding, we moved into a house four sizes too large, a 'gift' from Tasha's parents, the incorrigible Mr and Mrs Dunne of Richmond, Virginia.

Because I resented our colossal house in Georgetown, it too never felt like home. Until, that is, Tasha gave birth to our beautiful little girl, Hailey. It was Hailey, my lovely little princess, who finally made our house a home. Only it was a home I never managed to spend much time in.

Shortly after Hailey was born, I found myself feeling increasingly restless, bored and unchallenged, at the US Marshals' DC field office, so I requested an assignment that frequently took me overseas. While I chased US fugitives abroad, Tasha and Hailey remained home alone in DC. And it was during one of my overseas trips to Romania that Hailey was abducted, in broad daylight, right from our backyard, with Tasha standing no more than twenty feet away in our kitchen chatting with her mother over the phone.

Georgetown never felt like home again.

For the next twelve years I maintained a studio apartment on Dumbarton in the District of Columbia. But I was rarely ever there. Following Hailey's abduction I walked away from

my career with the US Marshals and became a private investigator, specializing in parental abductions, cases in which a
non-custodial parent had taken a child in violation of a court's
custody order and transported the child overseas, often to a
country that doesn't recognize US custody decisions.

I'd arrive in the foreign country with as much information
as the client could provide. Then I'd locate my subjects, both
the non-custodial parent and the child. I staked out their resi-
dence, took note of their routine. When I determined I had
enough information, I made my move, often in the dead of
night. The child was often cooperative. But not always. Some
of the retrievals went easy; others became quite difficult.
Numerous times I was arrested. Eventually, though, I'd get
the child home, no matter what the cost.

The 'return specialist,' a grateful father once dubbed me.
And today that was the term whispered into the ear of a frantic
parent looking for answers from the State Department. Those
whom I trusted routinely referred cases to me, usually by
handing the potential client an ordinary white business card
that read: *The Return Specialist*, along with an email address
for my encrypted Hushmail account.

As we waited in the endless line for Customs, a uniformed
figure emerged. 'Sir, madam, this way, if you please.'

I glanced at Jadine, but she was already lifting her carry-on.
We followed the short gentleman to a corner near the gate.

'Americans, yes?'

Jadine nodded. She apparently held dual citizenship with
the US and South Africa.

He dipped into his pocket and pulled out a stamp. 'I can
pass you through, no problem.' He held out his left hand and
Jadine held out her passport.

The little guy looked at it as though she were passing him
a small pile of dog shit.

I gently pulled back her arm. Reached into my pocket and
handed him a pair of twenty-dollar bills, US.

His face brightened. He took Jadine's passport and stamped
it, then mine. As he handed them back to us, he said, 'My name
is Rashidi. Anything you need, I can get for you. Anything.'

I nodded. Jadine appeared slightly offended, which made me wonder how often she traveled north of Cape Town. Clearly, she was unaware of how business was conducted in countries rife with corruption. But that was all right; I had enough experience for four lifetimes.

I handed Rashidi another bill and said, 'We need a ride.'

'Taxi?'

I shook my head. 'No taxi.'

I had no intention of leaving a trail of breadcrumbs. Not for a foreign intelligence service, not for a pair of dogged investigative journalists, and certainly not for Rusul Alharb.

'Where to?' Rashidi said.

I motioned forward, said, 'We'll tell you once we get into your car.'

As our guide navigated us through the airport parking lot, he explained that Abuja was quiet on the weekends.

'All the better,' I said.

'Here in the city,' Rashidi continued, 'there is not so much to do. So tourists scurry to Lagos or some other southern city. In Lagos, very busy. Very, very busy.'

I placed my arm around Jadine's shoulders and told him, 'The lady and I appreciate our alone time.'

When Jadine shot me a dirty look, I raised my brows in a way that said, *Hey, you're the one who insisted on coming along.*

'Where are you staying?' he asked once we were in the car.

'For now, just take us to Mama Cass.'

'Which one?'

'A few doors up from the Salamander Café.'

'You are meeting someone?'

I narrowed my brows in the rearview. 'It's a restaurant,' I growled. 'Maybe I'm *eating* someone.'

His lips parted, revealing a mouthful of curved yellow teeth.

When I didn't smile back, Rashidi took the hint and kept silent for the remainder of the ride. Which served both of us well. I didn't have to shoo away his questions and, in turn, he was rewarded with a generous gratuity on the State Department's dime.

SEVEN

'We're seeking commercial property,' Jadine said once we stepped into the small real estate office two blocks up from Mama Cass. 'Is there anyone who can help us with that?'

'For what kind of business?' the clerk asked.

Jadine smiled. 'Monkey business.'

'Yes, I see. Please follow me.'

'Monkey business?' I whispered to Jadine as we walked. 'Really? Can I assume you use your birthday as your PIN?'

'Sorry, Simon, I obviously don't live the life of mystery and intrigue that you do.' Jadine looked up at me as we passed through a series of doors in the rear. 'But if you're interested in obtaining my PIN, why not call Kati Sheffield?'

That was enough to silence me. Coleman and his people had clearly done a deep dig on me, but when – and *why* – had they shared this intelligence with Jadine? They couldn't have even been sure that I'd run to her following my discovery of the dead body.

We entered an office that looked much like the rest of the interior. Snot-colored walls lousy with cracks and holes, cheap and unmatched furniture that clearly preceded the birth of Nelson Mandela. Posters that might well have been rejects from a motivational poster company:

> I am *not* a product of my circumstances;
> I am a product of my decisions.

A curious sentiment given that millions of Nigerians were born into extreme poverty; that Nigeria's wealth disparity ranked among the most unconscionable in the world; that fifty percent of Nigerian youth remained unemployed despite the country's having one of the world's highest rates of economic growth.

Seemed to me that the vast majority of Nigerians were indeed products of their circumstances; that most impoverished Nigerians were victims not of their own poor decisions but of decisions made by wealthy pricks greasing the palms of corrupt politicians. Seemed to me that poverty here, as in so many places, was a prison and that said prisoners couldn't simply *decide* to unlock the door and set themselves free. Seemed to me that the postulation conveyed by that poster was a load of horseshit. Like something my father would say to a server at one of his country clubs.

Then again, maybe the poster was meant to be ironic. Or perhaps it was simply covering up a particularly large hole in the Sheetrock.

A slim young man dressed in a Tom Ford navy suit and stylish Cartier specs rose from behind his sizable desk. I pegged him immediately as CIA or Nigerian intelligence. Which made the real estate office little more than a front for, let's say, monkey business.

Jadine made the introductions. The real estate (*cough*, intelligence) agent identified himself as Ndulue Balogun and invited us to take a seat in the pair of well-worn orange client chairs in front of his desk.

Secretary Coleman's deputy, John Jeffries, had already briefed us on Rusul Alharb's strategies and goals, on their key alliances. Provided a PowerPoint presentation on their organizational size and structure, tactics and techniques, defensive capabilities, and weapons and equipment. He enumerated their methods of recruitment and retention, of financing, of waging informational warfare utilizing surprising social media savvy. Balogun would now advise us on their last known locations and most recent troop movements, as well as what could be expected of the Nigerian security forces.

'Rusul Alharb continues to be strongest in Nigeria's three northeastern provinces,' Balogun said with a notable African accent. 'Those are Borno, Yobe, and Adamawa. Military operations conducted by the Nigerian government have successfully pushed most of Rusul Alharb's fighters into the Sambisa forest and Lake Chad region. From those locations, they continue to launch attacks such as raids, assaults, and ambushes, primarily – but not exclusively – against soft targets, including civilians deemed collaborators or critics. They also target security personnel, politicians and religious leaders, critical infrastructure, and banks and businesses.'

According to Deputy Secretary Jeffries, their attacks on banks and businesses were for the purpose of resupplying money and other survival resources. Additional Rusul Alharb objectives included punishing and intimidating civilians, breeding distrust of the government, and defeating the counterinsurgency.

'Unfortunately,' Balogun continued, 'they have also found safe havens in three of our four border countries: Niger, Chad, and Cameroon. So bear in mind that your quarry may not even be inside Nigeria.'

Interestingly, Jeffries had assured me that my being Caucasian on this mission on the African continent would prove to be an asset rather than a liability. 'If they spot you, they won't see you as a predator,' he said without a hint of humor. 'They'll see you only as prey.'

A comforting thought.

Balogun said, 'Military sources inform us that Rusul Alharb also has hideouts in the Gwoza Hills and Mandara Mountains.'

He pulled out a map and unfolded it in front of us on his desk. Jadine and I rose from our seats in order to get a bird's-eye view.

Studying the map, my eyes widened of their own volition. Nigeria itself was a large country – roughly twice the size of California. Add to that the neighboring countries of Niger, Chad, and Cameroon, and you were looking at a total surface area *six times* the size of Texas.

Which meant it would be exceedingly premature to go online and order a hooded Harvard sweatshirt for Hailey. By the time I located Kishana Coleman, Hailey could well be of retirement age.

Which would make me somewhere around . . . dead.

Any optimism I might have had leaving Cape Town melted around me as I stared at the expansive map.

Six times the size of Texas.

What the hell was I thinking accepting this assignment? I'd have had an easier time beating the murder rap.

EIGHT

Coleman's people had reserved us a pair of rooms in a boutique hotel not far from Balogun's real estate office. We checked in without any hassle or even having to provide our real names and addresses. I considered the possibility that this hotel was just another front for an intelligence organization. Perhaps even Great Britain's.

Abuja wasn't just the fastest-growing city in Africa; it was one of the fastest-growing cities in the world. Nigeria's burgeoning role as a geopolitical influencer in regional affairs made Abuja a critical administrative and political center for the African continent as a whole. Meaning, in addition to being a mecca for lawless businessmen and politicians, the city was crawling with professional spies.

All my favorite people.

Aside from the rampant corruption, however, Abuja wasn't truly representative of the rest of Nigeria. The capital was clean and quiet, full of artificial light once the sun went down. Crime and terrorism had driven out any tourist industry, and the locals who lived and worked in the city tended to leave for different parts of the country whenever they could, often rendering the capital a virtual ghost town.

'Where do we begin tomorrow, Simon?' Jadine asked as we entered my room.

'Quid pro quo,' I said. 'I'll answer your question when you answer mine.' I locked on her body language for hints of deception. 'What's your true interest in this case, Jade?'

'Jade, wow. No one has called me that in a *long* time.' She sat down on one of the two double beds as I searched the room for bugs – of any sort. 'Jim Coleman is my friend.'

'He's a little more than that, I think. Who are you to Secretary Coleman anyway? Was he your mentor? Your employer? Your lover? All three?'

'Honestly, Simon, what does this have to do with finding Kishana?'

'Plenty,' I said calmly. 'You're going to slow me down. You're going to put this mission in jeopardy. I have a hard enough time keeping my own ass alive on these missions. That's why I work alone. Protecting yours as well is, frankly, stretching me a bit too thin.'

'Look, I'm the one who recommended you, Simon.'

'Well, then, I suppose I *owe* you.' Much less calmly now. 'After all, over the past decade I've only had the privilege of taking on the Polish mob, Ukrainian sex traffickers, a Colombian drug cartel, and the entire government of Venezuela. All in good fun, to rescue a couple kids I'd never met. Ever since, I've felt maddeningly unchallenged. *This* case, though – taking on a fucking terrorist organization – I have to admit, it takes my business to a whole new level. Now that I'm involved in this case, I can die happy. Which is lucky since it seems unlikely that I'll live much past the next twenty-four hours.'

'There is a teenage girl's life at stake.'

'I'm not questioning the stakes. But there isn't only *one* girl being held hostage by Rusul Alharb. There are *hundreds*.'

'You don't have to worry about anyone except Kishana.'

I stopped what I was doing and looked her in the eyes. 'Oh, I don't, do I? And what makes Kishana's life worth more than the lives of the hundreds of other girls who've been snatched from their beds? Am I supposed to make a distinction simply because she comes from a wealthy and powerful American family?'

'No one said Kishana's life is worth any more than the other girls'. But she *is* worth more to you. She gives you an opportunity – to retake control of your life.'

'My life in Moldova is just fine.'

She rose from the bed and met my glare. 'Don't bullshit me, Simon. We both know damn well that your life clock stopped the day Hailey was taken *and* that it hasn't started again. Not yet. And it *won't*. Not until Hailey's well. Not until you've cleared your name on three continents. Not until you, Anastazja, and Hailey are back in a First World country with all the privileges and opportunities you were born with.' She paused, huffed. 'I know you hate yourself, Simon. I know you blame yourself for what happened to Tasha. But I don't expect you to do this for yourself. I expect you to do this for *Hailey.*'

I made like her tirade rolled straight off my back. Turned, opened the closet door, and pulled out one of the duffle bags Coleman's people left for us. 'How do you know so much about me?' I said, setting the duffle on the bed.

'I'm not without my resources.'

I unzipped the bag and stared inside. Considerable fire power for two people, one of whom had likely never fired a gun. Necessary, though: according to Jeffries, the terrorists had successfully captured untold weapons and ammunition during attacks on Nigerian military facilities. Heavy weapons and equipment, as well as small arms. Additionally, Rusul Alharb had access to a 'robust' arms-smuggling network, especially now that they had aligned themselves with ISIL.

Jadine gazed at me, her right eyebrow slightly twitching just as it had back in college whenever she was livid with me. Which, come to think of it, was plenty often those three weeks we were an item. She said, 'Why are you so *hostile* to me?'

It was a quirk I suddenly remembered about Jadine. When she did something that she knew was wrong, she was like a Jedi in her ability to somehow turn it around on you. Usually by getting mad at you for getting mad at her for her transgression. And when you called her on it, you only made things worse for yourself. By the end of the argument, you were on your knees apologizing, begging for her forgiveness.

'Hostile?' I countered. '*Me?* Jade, if you think *I'm* hostile, wait until you come face to face with ten thousand zealots who'd just as soon burn you alive as look at you.'

Shit. Tears in her eyes. For me, watching a woman cry was a weakness second only to hollow-point bullets.

Still, I wasn't sure in which direction to take this. If I apologized, we might go right back to where we started, with Jadine believing we were a team like a full-metal-jacket Dr Watson and Sherlock Holmes. If I let her cry, or, better, continued to rile her, she might just walk out of this room and tell me I'm on my own. She'd hate me, maybe forever, but at least she'd be safe, at least she'd be alive, regardless of whether I made it back to South Africa in one piece.

I decided. Rest for me would have to be put off for at least another few hours. I needed to wait for Jadine to fall asleep, so I could sneak out without her being any the wiser. I'd leave a note. Maybe. A simple one, short and sweet, even semi-apologetic.

Then I could go off and find the (*girls*) girl.

'I'm tired, Jade,' I told her. 'Cranky. I need some sleep. Why don't you go to your room, we'll each get some shut-eye, and start fresh, you and me, early tomorrow morning.'

She fixed me with a cold glare. 'No. I'm not leaving this room. Not without you.'

I half smiled. 'I appreciate the sentiment, Jade, but I have a significant other, and – if you know as much about her as you do the rest of the people in my life – you're aware that she's plenty jealous.'

'There are two beds.'

'There are two *rooms*. Conjoining no less.'

'I don't trust you, Simon.'

'You don't, do you? Well, you sure as hell could have fooled Secretary Coleman, because he placed his granddaughter's life in my hands, presumably based on your word that I am good at what I do, that I am a man of integrity, that I am someone who won't run back to Moldova the moment I'm let off the leash.'

'I know you'll do your job, Simon. Of that I have *no* question. But I'm not going to allow you to leave me behind.'

I said nothing.

'*Where* are we starting tomorrow morning?' she asked, stripping off her clothes for bed.

I swallowed hard, averted my eyes, read the *In Case of Emergency* evacuation procedures displayed on our side of the hotel room door.

'So?' she said, climbing into bed. '*Where?*'

She left me no choice.

I typically started my investigations at the scene of the crime, the site where the abduction took place. But this was no ordinary kidnapping. Not only did we know *who* took Kishana Coleman but *why* and, to a certain extent, even *where*.

I'd already given plenty of thought to where I'd begin my search for Kishana Coleman. There was no shortage of intelligence on the group that seized her. Rescue efforts fell short simply because the enemy was entirely too dangerous. Not only to the rescue teams but to the hostages. That was why Secretary Coleman tapped me. This was one of those rare occasions when armies failed where a single man might succeed. The Nigerian military had tried the buzz saw; the US Secretary of State was now employing me as a scalpel.

Based on the intelligence, including Balogun's briefing, the Nigerian military had forced the kidnappers into the Sambisa forest and Lake Chad region. I needed to clear those areas before focusing my attention outside of Nigeria, before attempting to locate the terrorists' safe havens in the border countries of Niger, Chad, and Cameroon.

Even if I couldn't find the girl in northeastern Nigeria, I was certain to find at least one faction of the terrorist organization which was, after all, a confederation comprised of hundreds of individual groups with autonomy to make most day-to-day decisions. If I could grab one of the bastards and get him away from his camp, I could interrogate him. I'd use the carrot, the stick, and anything else that was handy.

In my experience in this business, you rarely hit the long ball. Instead, you had to work station to station – slapping singles into the outfield, putting on hit-and-run plays, stealing bases, belting sacrifice flies – like a Major League Baseball team short on power.

'Well, Simon?'

'I'm going next door to phone Ana,' I said. 'Get some rest. Tomorrow morning, sometime before dawn, be ready to enter the forest.' I opened the door to the adjoining room and turned back to her. 'Though it'll be damn hot out there during the day, I strongly recommend you wear one of the hotel's complementary bulletproof vests.' I grinned mirthlessly. 'Who knows? If we damage them up good enough, we may even get to keep them as souvenirs.'

NINE

We rose before dawn and were driven via taxi back to Abuja's Nnamdi Azikiwe International Airport, where we boarded a British SA-342 Gazelle helicopter, courtesy of the Nigerian Air Force. The chopper was making its usual seven a.m. run from the capital to Borno State and would, therefore, be unlikely to attract unwanted attention.

Onboard, Jadine and I changed into fatigues (atop Kevlar vests), readied our go-bags, and otherwise prepared for the drop. I'd expected from Jadine a strenuous objection over our method of entering the forest, but she assured me that she and a pair of her American University friends took several skydiving lessons 'just for kicks' following college.

'Besides,' she said over the fierce whirring of the blades overhead, 'we'll be hovering at a fairly low altitude directly over our drop point in Damboa. The jump should be a piece of cake.'

'Cake,' I agreed, hoping to refrain from vomiting before I reached solid ground.

I considered confessing to Jadine that I wasn't particularly fond of heights but held my tongue. If Jadine was as much of an adrenaline junkie in college as she was now, I'd surely boasted to her that I came from a long line of distinguished British mountaineers (which was true) and that my father and I had reached the highest peaks of New Hampshire's White Mountains (which wasn't). My father had indeed tried numerous times to take me climbing in New England, but on each occasion I'd refused to exit the car, telling him in no uncertain terms to piss off. 'If you want to die at six thousand feet,' I'd said, 'be my guest. Just be sure to leave the housekeys here with me at sea level.'

To my recollection, I'd always suffered from acrophobia (the fear of heights), or, perhaps more precisely, basophobia (the fear of falling). Whether some unpleasant event from childhood had triggered the phobia I didn't know. All I knew was that I strongly preferred to keep both feet on earth.

I forced back a sudden surge of panic and focused. Logic dictated that this jump would be no more hazardous than it would have been a few years ago while my daughter was still missing. And as much as I hated heights back then, I had never once hesitated doing what needed to be done, not only in my search for Hailey but in my search for all the kidnapped children I'd been tasked with returning.

I cleared my mind to the best of my ability. But Roger Murtaugh's words in the *Lethal Weapon* films rung in my ears the remainder of the flight.

I'm getting too old for this shit.

Or at least that's what I wanted badly to believe – that after this mission it might just be time for me to finally hang up the spurs and step lightly into the warm bath of retirement.

Unless you characterize my disquiet over heights as an event, the jump itself was uneventful and, as always, far more of a rush than I'd ever admit aloud. The sensory overload that comes with skydiving creates a kind of ecstasy not so dissimilar to sex. Seeing the planet from a completely unique point of view – specifically, *coming at you.* Hearing the loud yet peaceful rush of wind you could only otherwise enjoy in a Category 3 hurricane. Smelling air as crisp and pure as that atop one of the world's tallest mountains. And, of course, feeling that tingling up and down your skin as the temperature rises, as the air pressure falls, as you slowly build up speed, hurtling toward the earth, until it's time for the moment of truth, time to pull the cord, open the chute – and then, finally, the rare satisfaction that accompanies the knowledge that you're somehow going to arrive back on solid ground without busting up every last bone in your body. Some even go as far as to dub the climax an 'air-gasm.'

Jadine and I each glided gracefully into the bush and touched gently down on the ground already running. We disconnected our unmarked chutes and slowed to a power walk as we entered the forest.

Reams of intelligence suggested that, despite the Nigerian military's repeated claims that the terror organization had been fully flushed out of the Sambisa forest as a result of recent aerial and ground bombardments, a number of Rusul Alharb's camps remained. Only six months earlier, one of the victims of the Chibok kidnappings had been rescued near Pulka village in Borno. The rescued girl told authorities she'd been held captive in the Sambisa forest for years. She'd only been removed from her camp when the fighter who purchased her to be his bride became too ill and injured to fight. According to her, at the time she was taken from the forest, more than a hundred girls still remained. Making it clear that, notwithstanding the Nigerian military's efforts (or claims), the Sambisa forest persisted as a Rusul Alharb stronghold even today.

Prior to the last decade, Sambisa had been a game reserve. For nearly forty years, the vast forest was used exclusively for safaris. Before the terror group's invasion and takeover, Sambisa maintained a large population of leopards, lions, elephants, and hyenas, along with baboons, patas and tantalus monkeys, red-fronted gazelles, roan antelope, and dozens of species of rare African birds.

Even before the jihadists made Sambisa their own, however, the forest had come under attack from poachers, from energy companies felling trees for fuel, even from human agriculture. When Rusul Alharb arrived, they massacred most game-reserve management and caused any remaining staffers to flee. They then proceeded to collapse cabins, destroy safari lodges, and capture a training camp fitted with military facilities. Said site was codenamed Camp Zero.

Located in the heart of the 40,000-square-mile Sambisa forest, Camp Zero was developed during Nigeria's military era to serve a special security force loosely titled the 'national guard.' Due to public outcry, the dictatorial military regime that had been erecting the camp was forced to halt construction. The already-mismanaged facilities subsequently fell victim to neglect and abandonment and never lived out their purpose. Sadly, at the time construction was halted, the military installations were so far along that they weren't demolished, but instead left to languish in the bush. When Rusul Alharb invaded the forest, Camp Zero became their natural headquarters.

Thus, during this trek through the Sambisa, Camp Zero would be our first target.

Amped on espresso and adrenaline, I initially felt as though I were taking a stroll through Yellowstone National Park. *That*, I knew, would soon change. For now, however, all we could do was march onward and upward. Sweat in the early-morning sun. And, like Pooh's buddy Tigger, think, think, think.

I replayed last night's phone call to Moldova over and over in my mind because I so missed hearing her voice.

'Did you find the missing boy?' Ana had asked with her lovely Polish accent.

'Not exactly.'

'What does this mean, *not exactly*?'

'Means I was set up, Ana. I now have a new mission, not in Cape Town but in Nigeria.'

'Nigeria?' She could be heard rapidly tapping keys on her laptop. 'Where in Nigeria, Simon? Your US Department of State urges Americans to "reconsider travel."'

'Yeah, well, the *head* of that same department says that this particular American doesn't *dare* reconsider.'

'What do you mean? The website declares it is unsafe to travel there "due to extensive crime, terrorism, civil unrest, even *piracy*."'

'Well, we don't need to worry about piracy, baby. The area I'm heading to is landlocked.'

'*Where*, Simon?'

I considered lying. But now that we were together, Ana had every right to know where I was going, what I was doing. If something happened to me, I didn't want her to spend the rest of her days wondering what that something was and whether I was dead or alive, as I did for twelve brutal years following Hailey's abduction.

'The northeast,' I told her.

She gasped. 'The website says that this is the *worst* place you could go. Borno, Yobe, and Adamawa State – all these areas are far too dangerous. "Terrorists," it says, "continue to

plot and carry out attacks on security forces and infrastructure."
They target malls, markets, hotels, churches, restaurants, bars,
schools, even the public transportation.'

'Yeah, well, I'm not going to any malls, Ana. And it's been
years since I've set foot inside a church. Not since my time
in Caracas.'

'Simon, this is not a time for the joking.'

Her English was improving daily, but I continued to find
her rare miscues endearing.

'I can't get into this over the phone, Ana. I'm sorry. Just
know that I'm doing this for a noble cause, and if for any
reason I can't make it back, promise me you'll take care of
Hailey.'

'Simon, you never speak like this. I am scared.'

'I'm a bit scared too, frankly. But fear's healthy, isn't it?
On all my missions, all those years Hailey was missing, I
never once felt *true* fear, because I genuinely believed I had
nothing to live for. But now, knowing that you and Hailey are
waiting for me in Moldova, I'm shitting goddamn bricks.'

'What does this mean, to shit the bricks?'

'Is Hailey doing all right?'

'Do you want to speak with her?'

'No. Brief my little girl on a need-to-know basis. She's been
through enough. Tell her I love her and that I'll return home
soon.'

'And if you don't?'

'Cross that bridge when we come to it.'

'Easy for you to say, Simon; you will not be around to cross
this bridge with me.'

'Hey,' I said, lowering my voice to a whisper. 'Truth is, if
this mission is successful, it's going to drastically change our
lives for the better. I've got guarantees from the United States
Government. Any existing criminal charges against me or
Hailey will be dropped by the US and its allies. In other words,
we'll be able to come out of hiding. We'll be able to live
anywhere we want, be able to visit anywhere and everywhere
on earth.'

'Even Hollywood?'

'Even Hollywood, baby.'

'I don't understand. How—'

'I can't get into the details now, but trust me, life for all three of us is about to vastly improve.'

'*If* you live through this mission.'

'Well, I sure as hell ain't here to die.'

Silently marching up an endless hill with Jadine striding right behind me, I again rewound the previous night's conversation in my head, wishing I'd cautioned Ana not to get her hopes *too* high. After all, even though *I* wasn't in the forest to die, I strongly suspected ten thousand or so jihadists might have other, uglier ideas in mind.

TEN

Hours later, I suggested we rest.

'You're in awful good shape for a college professor,' I said.

Jadine set down her pack and sat up against a tamarind tree, just out of sight of the dirt path we'd been following.

'Not slowing you down too much then, am I, Simon?'

On the contrary, if it wasn't for her presence and my pride, I'd have rested two or three times already. I strongly started to suspect there was significantly more to Jadine Visser than it seemed.

'Been to Nigeria before, have you?' I asked her as I twisted open my canteen.

'I've been all over this continent.'

'Funny,' I said. 'When you appeared surprised by the bribes at the airport yesterday, I thought you'd never been to Abuja before.'

'I'm just outraged by the rampant corruption, as usual.'

I took a taste of water. 'Abuja seems fairly modernized.'

'Compared with most areas in Nigeria, it is. Outside of the major cities, it's still the late nineteenth century here.'

I shook my head slowly. 'I take it the influx of oil money has somehow failed to trickle down to the masses?'

'To say the least.' She shifted her lithe body like a cat; even in a Kevlar vest, she was graceful. 'Civilians in urban areas could live reasonably comfortably in this country for just one thousand US dollars a year. Seven hundred bucks a year for folks in the rural areas. Yet three-quarters of the Nigerian population earn under those amounts, and more than half of *those* people earn less than a dollar and a quarter a day.'

'And I thought life in DC was tough.'

'Life in the States *is* tough. Not to the same degree but for the same reasons. The Nigerian government gave businesses and corporations more than two *billion* dollars in tax waivers last year.'

'While politicians simply mutter the mantra, "We've got to compete globally."'

'Same, same,' she said, before finally indulging herself with her own canteen.

Somehow, over the decade-plus I was searching for Hailey, I felt sure the constant fog of melancholy surrounding me would dissipate were we ever to be together again. And the day I found her, a dark cloud indeed lifted. But as much as the state of Simon Fisk had changed, I quickly realized that the state of the world remained the same. I'd seen too much ugliness over the years to simply dismiss it.

Over the subsequent weeks and months in Moldova with Ana and Hailey, I recognized that this angst – this undefined dread about the human condition – would be with me until I became ashes. There was plainly no escaping it, not in the twenty-first century when suffering halfway across the globe remained merely a few clicks away.

You couldn't close your eyes anymore.

Not without it weighing heavily on your conscience.

In truth, I now realized, this angst had *predated* Hailey's abduction. It existed the day I left the Marshals' DC field office to hunt fugitives overseas. It was present the day I left for Romania.

It hadn't always been there, though. Wasn't there in college. Wasn't there when I first married Tasha. And it certainly wasn't around when Hailey was born. Which meant that this dread had enveloped me sometime during the six-year period between Hailey's birth and Hailey's abduction.

Once I'd narrowed it down, I searched for an even more specific time period – and suddenly the date came aglow with dozens of neon arrows aimed directly at its center. It wasn't just *my* date, as it turned out; it was a date all the world knew well. A date we'd all (but a few heartless of us) be deliriously happy to forget.

Namely, the eleventh of September 2001.

Nearly twenty years had passed since the September 11 attacks, yet that dreadful day remained as fresh in my head as this morning's breakfast. I awoke that dawn to my usual alarm and snoozed once. Outside, it was shaping up to be a beautiful Tuesday, a real gem in the DC area. Lying naked next to me was my wife Tasha who, with just the right nudge, woke wanting to make love before we got out of bed. After sex, I teased her about her ability to return to sleep while I jumped into the shower for work, and she retorted in her standard manner, reminding me that ever since baby Hailey was born, I'd kept the same hours while she'd been on-call 24/7.

I, of course, had no retort to that because it was merely an astute observation.

In the months since Hailey was born, Tasha had proved herself to be an amazing mother. Her instincts were incredible, her attitude remarkable, and she exhibited an extraordinary amount of patience. Meanwhile, to borrow a cliché, Tasha and I were a young, happily married pair, a white upper-middle class couple who had never known tragedy and never expected it. Certainly not there, in our big, luxurious Georgetown house, paid for in full by the illustrious Mr and Mrs Dunne of neighboring Virginia. I had hated the house simply because of the way we obtained it, which was admittedly unfair to Tasha and her parents, if not the house itself. My father had had wealth and it never did anything useful for him (quite the contrary), so I simply wanted no part of that world – not the mine's-bigger-than-yours, not the dressing to impress, not the country club bullshit – for my family.

On promising days such as that one, I ate a quick breakfast of blueberry toaster waffles and a double shot of espresso. I kissed Tasha and Hailey goodbye, then stepped into the garage, clicked the opener, and mounted my motorcycle, a modest-yet-kick-ass late model Kawasaki Vulcan. The ride to my office in Crystal City, Virginia, took roughly twenty minutes at that early hour. I arrived at work a little after seven and immediately made myself sit down at my desk to execute a boatload of paperwork I'd been putting off since early summer.

I was happy in my job. Proud to be part of the long and storied tradition that was the United States Marshals Service. The Marshals had been formed in 1789 by the First Congress and signed into law by none other than President George Washington, making us the oldest federal law enforcement agency in the nation. We were responsible not just for conducting fugitive operations but serving arrest warrants, protecting officers of the federal judiciary, managing criminal assets, transporting federal prisoners and, something few people knew, operating the United States Federal Witness Protection Program.

Like any big kid, I was ecstatic to become part of the same cop shop as Wild West legends Wyatt Earp and Wild Bill Hickok. After all, it was Wyatt Earp who, with his brothers Virgil and Morgan and his buddy Doc Holliday, gunned down Billy Clanton and the McLaury brothers at the O.K. Corral in Tombstone, Arizona. Other famous marshals included the escaped-slave-turned-activist and author Frederick Douglass, Bat Masterson, Cal Whitson, and the 'Three Guardsmen' – Bill Tilghman, Chris Madsen, and Heck Thomas – who came to prominence for their relentless pursuit of such notorious outlaws as the Dalton Gang and the Wild Bunch in the Oklahoma Territory.

Shortly after eight fifteen on the morning of September 11, as I proofread a twenty-page report detailing a multimillion-dollar criminal forfeiture, I heard from across the room a woman's gasp. I rose from my desk to learn the source of her astonishment and found a half-dozen colleagues doing the same. In the next few moments, as we approached her desk, we learned that a Boeing 767 carrying ninety-two people had been hijacked over central Massachusetts. Immediately following the hijack, the American Airlines flight had apparently hooked northwest, then turned south, placing it on a collision course with New York City.

We eventually went back to our desks, but few of us got anything done.

Thirty minutes later, there was another gasp, another exodus to the front of the room to discern what had happened. Anxiety among us sharpened and escalated as we digested the news that a second American Airlines flight carrying sixty-seven people was hijacked above northwest New Jersey. This Boeing 767 had briefly continued southwest, then looped back to the northeast, also heading toward the Big Apple.

Like everyone else in the country, my colleagues and I watched the horrendous events play out on television as news trickled into our office from official sources. Just before nine, we were advised by the FBI that another plane was hijacked above southern Ohio. By then, we already knew we were under attack, as Flight 11 had just crashed into the North Tower of the World Trade Center.

We'd barely had time to catch our collective breath before the unthinkable happened again, when Flight 175 struck the south face of the Trade Center's South Tower.

'We're at war,' friend and fellow agent Chris Wicker said solemnly.

Around nine thirty, we learned that yet another plane – United Airlines Flight 93 – had been hijacked above northern Ohio before curving sharply southeast.

Fewer than ten minutes later, we were jolted by an explosion as Flight 77 crashed less than half a mile away from our office. The jet had been deliberately flown into the western side of the Pentagon, igniting a violent fire.

Several agents and I immediately rushed down the stairs to do whatever we could to help the victims in Pentagon City. Only by the time we got to the garage, all roads had been closed by DC police.

Roughly, I grabbed Wicker's right arm and told him, 'I rode the bike in today.'

Breathlessly, he said, 'Let's try it.'

Minutes later, we jumped on to my bike and – zigzagging past DCPD roadblocks – turned right on to South Clark, left on to 12th Street South, right on to Army Navy Drive, heading toward South Eads Street. From there could see thick clouds of black smoke rising from the Defense Department's iconic headquarters.

Unable to drive any further, we leapt off my bike and hoofed it toward the massive black hole where a concrete wall, five stories high, had stood just minutes earlier.

'My *God*,' Wicker said, the words barely heard over the blaring sirens.

After running a couple of hundred yards, we were stopped and permitted to go no further. We displayed our badges and were allowed inside the outer perimeter to assist shaken-up survivors, but we couldn't go anywhere near the blaze. Which was just as well since there was nothing more we could have done.

'Who the hell did this?' Wicker said ten minutes later, as his eyes welled from the pervasive smoke and heat, maybe even a trace of emotion.

I remained silent, because all I could do was speculate. But a single thought reverberated in my head like a deafening roar in a desolate cavern.

This can only be the work of fucking al-Qaeda.

ELEVEN

Jadine and I were already deep into the Sambisa forest when the sun began its fade from the orange Nigerian sky. Not for the first time in the past few years, my age was playing havoc in my muscles and bones. Jadine, on the other hand, appeared none the worse for wear. Except for a bit of red dirt on her face and fatigues, she looked as fresh as the hour we entered the forest.

Despite the infuriating itch, it wasn't until we settled down in a clearing that I noticed the hundreds of insect bites up and down my arms and legs. I resisted the immediate urge to scratch the hell out of them and instead ducked my hand into my go-bag and retrieved my medical kit. Quietly, I fished around for the tube of anti-itch cream. Before I could uncap it, Jadine threw her hand up.

'What are you doing?' she said.

'Hydrocortisone,' I told her. 'For the bug bites.'

She shook her head. 'We may be downwind of one of their camps.'

'We're hunting terrorists,' I said, 'not a pack of bloodhounds.'

Although I cracked wise, I knew she was right, and I immediately got on myself for nearly making a mistake that could have cost us our lives.

'Use an ice pack,' she said.

That was the first time I realized how lucky I was to have her along. I replaced the tube in the med kit and removed an ice pack. I knew it wouldn't be as effective as the cream, but it was either the ice pack or scratch myself raw.

Fortunately, the itch was my only worry when it came to insect bites. Since I never knew where a mission might lead me, I had seen my regular doc in Moldova days before flying to Cape Town.

'Where in Africa are you going?' he asked me.

I told him, 'Just give me the works.'

So I was caught up on my immunizations: hepatitis A, hep B, meningococcal meningitis, rabies, typhoid, even yellow fever. The doc also boosted my tetanus, diphtheria, and measles vaccines. That's right, *measles*, if you could believe it. Eradicated in the States at the turn of the century, yet, twenty years later, First World children were dying from the virus all over again. All because an elaborate fraud – perpetrated by a doctor stripped of his medical license – had gone viral on social media. Today, thanks to him and a few vacuous celebrities, you needed to be cautious not only in the wilds of West Africa but on the streets of Seattle, Des Moines, and Tampa.

When I ran down the list of vaccines I'd gotten from the doc, Ana had nodded her head slowly and said, 'Do not dare to come home with a venereal disease either.'

We'd both chuckled but her eyes had remained deadly serious.

During last night's call, I hadn't mentioned my need to bring Jadine Visser along. What I'd told Jadine earlier was true: Ana *was* jealous, and her blood could run as hot as lava. And since I had met Ana herself during a mission in Warsaw, she was particularly suspicious whenever I went abroad on a job. I wouldn't lie to her, of course; when I returned home (*if* I returned home), I'd inform Ana I worked with a female partner in Nigeria. But, for reasons of self-preservation, I *might* forget to mention that Jadine and I dated during our first few weeks in college.

'We'll rest in shifts,' I said to Jadine. 'I'll take first watch.'

'How are you at climbing trees?'

Perplexed, I said, 'I was OK climbing them as a ten-year-old kid in Rhode Island. Since then, not all that much practice. Why?'

'We need to maintain a deep respect for this forest. The area isn't as crowded with wild animals as it was when it was a game reserve. But there are still a few fantastic beasts that we need to watch and listen for.'

'Such as?'

'Our main concern should be lions. *Large* ones.'

'Lions,' I said flatly. 'Large ones.'

Her face suggested she wasn't pulling my leg.

'Jade, have I properly thanked you yet for involving me in this case?'

'Lions tend to be nocturnal,' she said, ignoring my sarcasm, 'and they're highly opportunistic. They hunt after dusk. So, if you hear anything unusual – and I mean *anything* – wake me straightaway. We won't have much time to scramble up into the trees.'

I reached into my go-bag. 'I love lions as much as the next guy, but . . .' I pulled out the Glock 19 provided by Coleman's people. 'Forgive me if I don't chance my life on my tree-climbing skills.'

'If you fire a weapon, Rusul Alharb fighters will be on us in a heartbeat.'

I swallowed hard. It had been a long time since I thought I was in over my head, but this was the second mistake I'd made just since we sat down. Not to mention the second time Jadine saved both our asses. And to think that less than twenty-four hours ago I had been set on leaving her behind at the hotel in Abuja.

You don't know your enemy well enough.

That realization caught me by surprise. Technically, I'd been in the fight against jihadists since the day I was sworn in as a US Marshal. Only one month earlier, FBI officials had determined there were al-Qaeda terrorist cells operating in the US homeland. Raids on suspected terrorists commenced shortly thereafter.

As a US Marshal, I was tasked with managing the criminal forfeitures in connection with the arrests. The more I learned, the greater I judged the threat. It wasn't just the *amount* of money involved (though that was mindboggling in itself), it was the *source* of the funds that I found utterly terrifying.

Then, in the first week of August of 1998, Dr Ayman al-Zawahiri warned that a 'message' was on its way to America. 'A message,' he said, 'in a language that Americans will understand.'

The following day, the American embassies in Nairobi, Kenya, and Dar es Salaam, Tanzania, were bombed, almost simultaneously.

Between the two attacks, 224 were killed, nearly 4,600 injured. As the investigation into the attacks continued, President Bill Clinton was apprised of evidence that Osama bin Laden was currently attempting to purchase weapons of mass destruction. President Clinton subsequently ordered a strike on a suspected al-Qaeda camp in Afghanistan. Unfortunately, the US strike just missed bin Laden, and the following year he was added to the FBI's 'Ten Most Wanted.'

In the subsequent twenty-four months, intelligence gathering continued. As did al-Qaeda attacks. More than a hundred pounds of explosives were intercepted at the Canadian border at Port Angeles, Washington State. The perpetrator, who was a known member of al-Qaeda, confessed that his intended target was Los Angeles International Airport.

Soon after, several US flight schools fell under investigation because Italian intelligence agents had picked up phone conversations that specifically mentioned using commercial airliners as missiles.

In late 2000, the USS *Cole* was attacked, an incident clearly linked to Osama bin Laden.

Then, in early 2001, the FAA – the Federal Aviation Administration – cautioned airlines and airports that terrorists might attempt to hijack or destroy American aircraft. Months later, National Security Advisor Condoleezza Rice was warned during an intelligence briefing that an al-Qaeda attack on the homeland was, in fact, 'highly likely.' By August 2001, the FAA had specifically warned airlines and airports that terrorists might use weapons modified from everyday items (for example, boxcutters).

The point: we had plenty of warning. And I'd been involved from the very beginning. Although my role had been significantly limited, the job had worked up my curiosity enough for me to seek out classified intelligence. In the years immediately preceding the September 11 attacks, I learned as much about our enemy as I could.

Hence my reaction to Wicker's 'Who the hell did this?'

Yet this evening, despite a pair of intelligence briefings just this morning, I felt woefully unprepared for a night in the Sambisa forest.

Or am I just scared?

Was I making stupid mistakes on account of my fear?

Or am I just getting old? Becoming slow. Losing the edge that kept me fueled these past twenty years.

'Get some sleep, Jade. I'll wake you if I see or hear anything.'

As I said it, the shrill cry of a large bird carried along the wind.

I scanned the coarse trunk of a nearby tree, noting the thickest branches and various footholds.

I rose to my feet. 'I better go take a leak before you fall asleep.'

'Just be careful,' she said as I headed into some low-lying bushes. 'The bushes in this area appear to have thorns and some of them are probably poisonous.'

Great, I thought as I unzipped my fly. *Now I'll need to return to Moldova and somehow convince Ana that I caught a sexually transmitted disease simply from pissing into an overly amorous shrub.*

TWELVE

Quite pleased to report that the night passed without a lion attack, Jadine woke me at dawn and we devoured our scrumptious morning rations, a choice between a gourmet strawberry porridge and a Wolfgang Puck-inspired Capri Sun pouch of a pork sausage omelet and beans.

It's no wonder the lions didn't attack us, I thought. *We don't have any food.*

'Let's get an early start,' Jadine said immediately after we ate.

Overnight, mosquitoes had drained me of roughly three pints of blood, so I was happy to get moving again.

Well, *happy* may be a bit of an overstatement.

'Ever married?' I asked Jadine as we traipsed through the forest a half hour later.

'Never.'

'Kids?'

She shook her head.

'Pets?'

'Two cats.' She glanced at me. 'Let me guess. You're a dog person and you despise felines.'

'I've got no problem with cats,' I told her. 'Granted, that could change dramatically if we find ourselves face to face with a lion this morning.'

Truth was, I'd never had a pet. I'd wanted one as a child; dog or cat or guinea pig, it didn't matter. But my father, of course, always refused. 'They're filthy goddamn things,' he'd say. 'I won't have an animal running around this house.' In college, it was simply impractical. After college, when I married Tasha and we moved into our Dunne-financed DC McMansion, I was told Tasha's parents would frown on our bringing a dog into our brand-new abode. 'We should give it a couple years, at least,' Tasha had said, uncomfortably yet inflexibly. 'Once we have children, we can justify it to Mom and Dad. Now it'll just feel frivolous.' But once we had our hands filled with Hailey, we decided we'd wait until our little girl asked for a furry companion and let her choose the type of animal. By six, she hadn't yet mentioned a pet. I often wondered whether the dog I'd wanted to get years earlier would have barked and alerted Tasha that someone had come to the backyard fence the day Hailey was taken.

I followed Jadine along the path, feeling vulnerable; as much as we'd wanted to continue wearing our bulletproof vests, the heat this morning made it impossible.

About an hour later, she halted and placed a finger to her lips. 'I think we're coming up on one of their former camps,' she whispered.

Jadine went into her go-bag and removed what at first glance looked like a twentieth-century sat phone. We'd each packed our own bags from the duffels left us by Coleman's people back at the hotel in Abuja. In addition to my weapons and ammunition – including armor-piercing and incendiary rounds – I'd packed a small multipurpose tool kit with a heavy-duty metal hole punch; a compass; an LED squeeze light; a fire-starting kit; a water storage device and purification tablets; electrolyte tabs; a signal light; a thermal blanket; steel wire; duct tape; Kevlar thread; a magnifying lens; waterproof note paper and ink pens; a lockpick; a universal handcuff key; and, of course, the previously mentioned med kit that included everything from moleskin adhesive patches to malaria pills and antibiotic ointments.

She pressed a discreet button on the odd-looking device and a small screen came ablaze.

'Looks like something out of *Star Trek*,' I said quietly. 'Like a tricorder.'

'Not so different actually. It's a radio-frequency sensor that detects and identifies trace quantities of explosive materials.'

'It detects IEDs,' I said.

'Exactly. The militants plant IEDs around their camps to warn themselves of intruders and to make sure none of their hostages flee.'

'Hasn't the Nigerian military already cleared this area?'

'Supposedly.' The sigh that followed contained a definite

note of condescension. 'So, if you trust in the competence of the Nigerian military, please do feel free to run on ahead, and I promise to catch up.'

Despite her arrogance, I took a hard pass on the invitation.

'So what exactly does that device detect?' I asked.

'Chemicals such as ammonium nitrate on the particle level.'

'Looks highly sophisticated.'

'And ultrasensitive,' she said.

'A gift from Secretary Coleman?'

'On loan from an intelligence agency.'

I raised a brow. 'And you learned how to use it in just the past few days?'

She performed an about-face that halted me in my tracks. 'Simon, I don't like being given the third degree.'

'And I don't like searching for a terrorist stronghold while being kept in the dark about things like IED detection systems.'

'It's just a precaution.'

'A fairly important one, isn't it? Tell me, Jade. What if something had happened to you and I was on my own? I would've dug that thingamajig out of your go-bag and tried to make a goddamn phone call with it.'

'I'll teach you how to use it next time we rest.'

'If I'm not already resting *in pieces* by then.'

'*Quiet*, Simon.' She stopped. Her little doojigger had detected something. When she finally spoke again, she said, 'We need to navigate *around* this next clearing.'

Carefully, I continued to follow her, doing my absolute best to keep my temper in check. And to step directly into the boot prints she left in her wake.

The camp was surrounded by a dilapidated five-foot clay wall with an opening the size of a door. Inside the wall, the burned-out remains of huts (made of mud, dung, bark, and browned grass) stood as silent reminders that Rusul Alharb and their hostages had been there. On the ground lay busted clay pots, plastic buckets, and the occasional pool of dried blood staining the earth. Although the bodies were gone, the area still smelled of death, of smoke and gunpowder, of piss and shit and burning flesh. The morning's rations curled in my stomach.

'According to a ten-year-old girl found in the area,' Jadine said, 'she was held here for more than eleven months. When she was discovered, she was coughing and wheezing and had a bulging stomach indicative of severe malnutrition. She had no food, no water, no clothes. There was no one else around for miles.'

'Who found her? Nigerian soldiers?'

A tilt of the head, though I wasn't sure she actually heard me; her eyes were fixed strongly on the visual evidence of destruction and death.

She said, 'When the army approached their camp, the fighters thrusted their hostages forward as human shields. The girl only escaped after a bullet buzzed over her head and took out the child rapist who'd made her his wife. She didn't know who was friendly and who was the enemy. So she hid in the bush for days before soldiers finally discovered her.'

I felt myself overheating with anger. Then I asked a question I knew I didn't want answered: 'What did she say about her time *at* the camp?'

'When she wasn't being raped or beaten,' Jadine said, 'she was in the forest with her captors foraging for food, trying to be mindful of landmines. Even though she'd been a Christian forced to convert, she told rescuers she'd looked forward to her daily Islamic prayers, since it was the only time she and the other women and children knew anything resembling peace. Outside of prayer time, the girls lived in constant fear. Over the eleven months she was held at the camp, she watched fourteen of her friends grow thinner and sicker until they finally died. Near the end, she was just waiting for her turn.'

For a time, neither of us spoke.

'You all right?' I finally said as my finger caught a tear gliding down Jadine's smooth cheek.

'Let's look around.' She motioned with her head. 'You search counterclockwise in concentric circles. I'll search clockwise.'

'Yell if you come across a lion,' I said.

'You going to save me, Simon?'

'No,' I told her, 'I'm going run like hell.'

We shared a bleak smile before setting off in opposite directions. It barely made sense to split up, I thought, as I started my search. The camp wasn't large, couldn't have held many more than a hundred people, counting hostages. It wouldn't take long to comb the entire interior. But Jadine seemed to want to be alone, out of sight. My best guess was she didn't want me to see her so vulnerable.

There's something she's not telling you.

I rounded the first hut and spotted the leg of a baby doll, blackened by fire. Near it lay a plastic two-gallon jug, probably used for drinking water. The jug was empty and overturned but not burnt, which seemed strange among all this fire wreckage.

According to intelligence, the terrorists routinely set their camps on fire as soon as they detected Nigerian forces near the perimeter, for the primary purpose of destroying any strategic plans or clues as to their brothers' locations. Like Wall Street bankers shredding documents as feds arrived in unmarked vans with bouquets of search warrants in their hands.

How does one plastic jug survive the incineration?

I stepped around the next hut and spotted in the dirt a pair of empty shells from an AK-47. Here, the smell of fire was more pungent. *Fresher.* But I could only smell burning wood, not mud and dung and clay and grass. Growling, my stomach alerted me to something else as well. Something that smelled like . . .

Meat.

Suddenly, my Simon senses were tingling. I reached back into my go-bag for the Glock.

But it was too late.

Before me stood an emaciated child of roughly twelve. The picture of innocence except for the assault rifle aimed at my chest.

'Hands up! Hands up!' he shouted.

I reached for the sky. And remembered briefly doing the same for a little boy at Hailey's fifth birthday party in the backyard of our house in Georgetown. He'd been holding a Super Soaker I'd purchased over Tasha's objection specially for the occasion.

Over the past decade and a half, I'd had at least a dozen real guns trained on me at point-blank range. But I had never been more frightened than I was now. And it wasn't just because I needed to make it back home for Ana and Hailey. No. My panic was heightened because when I searched this boy's eyes, I found no humanity left in them. His face appeared carved in stone, while his index finger darted in and out of the trigger guard like a serpent's tongue tasting the air. *All he knows about guns is how to fire one*, I thought. *All he knows about life and death is survival: his own.*

And hatred. He clearly knows how to hate.

Zealots taught that subject well.

Over his shoulder I spotted the source of the smell. He'd been cooking meat over an open fire now dwindling to nothingness. I couldn't make out the origin of the meat because I'd never smelled it before. My visual suggested that the boy's lunch had once been some sort of monkey. Tantalus maybe. The adorable one with a jet-black face and long tail. A monkey that might have once graced the cover of *National Geographic*. But then, could I truly begrudge the boy for eating?

'My name's Simon,' I said gently.

'Why here? Why here?'

'Searching for a friend,' I told him.

'Devil got *no* friend!' he shouted, as his finger continued to dance inside the trigger guard.

I had no move. If I went for his gun, I'd be full of holes by the time I got to him. Superficial wounds could be treated using the med kit. But when I opened the kit this morning, I spotted no spare organs or surgical tools. If this child decided to fire, I was a dead man.

In the distance I caught movement. My first thought was that I was about to face a second child soldier. But this individual wasn't carrying an assault rifle, just an automatic handgun, glinting hard in the harsh West African sun. I quickly set my eyes back on the boy, hoping I hadn't given away her presence and location.

She wouldn't shoot the boy, would she?

I suddenly felt terror for *him*. I'd been tasked with rescuing a teenage girl, not snuffing out the life of a twelve-year-old boy. But I also realized Jadine's options were limited. If she attempted to distract him, he might well pull the trigger before turning around. Little doubt he had been trained to do just that.

Or he would spin and fire at Jadine. She stood slightly farther away, but the boy wouldn't need much aim with an AK-47. One spread and he'd probably get lucky.

She could shoot him in the leg, I thought, but in the forest a shot leg would leave him as good as dead. And Jadine, I knew, wouldn't abort our mission to rush him back to Abuja for medical treatment.

'*Wannan abokina ne!*' Jadine finally shouted.

The boy smartly swung the rifle toward the ground before turning around. I made the snap decision to disarm him. I reached him in ten steps; in fewer than six seconds he was immobilized on the ground.

'Sorry, kid,' I said, tossing the rifle out of reach and relieving him of a large knife that hung on his belt. 'No one dies here today.'

He struggled under me but oddly seemed far more fascinated with Jadine, who approached slowly, her weapon lowered but ready.

'You speak Hausa?' I asked her.

'Just a few phrases.'

'What did you say to him?'

'I told him you were my friend.'

'That's a bit ambiguous, isn't it?'

She said, 'It was the closest I could come to "Drop the gun." Somehow, "Where is the restroom?" seemed inappropriate.' She examined the boy's face with sadness. 'Besides, it wasn't my words he responded to. It was my voice.'

'You sound my motha,' the boy said emphatically. He glared at Jadine as though she were a ghost.

Tears fell from his eyes as I lifted him to his feet, and I was instantly struck with an uncomfortable mix of contempt and pity.

I said, 'Tell me, kid. Where are the other members of the band?'

Jadine repeated a version of my question in Hausa.

Unfortunately, the boy clammed up like Cosa Nostra. And despite whatever this child had seen and whatever he had done for the cause of Rusul Alharb, he was far too young for me to rough up.

Finally, forty minutes later, after eating half our lunch rations, the boy confided he was alone. He had split off from his unit a week earlier to remain with an injured friend. The friend had died a couple of days ago. By then, however, the boy figured it was too late to catch up to his unit, so he came to the only place he knew – his former camp.

'You are soldiers,' he said, eyeing our fatigues.

'Not soldiers,' I said. 'We're private eyes. We're in the forest looking for someone.'

He eyed me suspiciously. 'Who-who?'

Jadine swallowed hard and said, 'A young girl who was kidnapped in Adamawa State around the start of the month.'

The child displayed a lopsided smile, neither happy nor sad but matter-of-fact.

'What?' Jadine demanded of him. 'What do you know?'

Slowly, the boy shook his head, but his eyes never left Jadine's.

'*What?*' she repeated.

Finally, he shrugged his bony shoulders and parted his lips. 'All them bitches be dead-dead,' he said.

THIRTEEN

The boy's name was Danjuma, a Hausa name that simply meant 'born on Friday.' He was eleven years old, nine at the time he was recruited by Rusul Alharb fighters. Although he insisted his enlistment was voluntary, the circumstances surrounding it suggested otherwise: Danjuma joined Rusul Alharb on the day the terror group burned down his village, on the day he watched his mother raped and his father shot point-blank in the head with a .45. In sum, his ability to make life-and-death decisions just might have been compromised.

Amidst the chaos in the burning village, Danjuma had thought to run but remained frozen. Undoubtedly in shock, the boy was even unable to cry as he witnessed the wholesale slaughter of friends and family. That stoicism in the face of such carnage did not go unnoticed by the commander of the fighters responsible for the wanton destruction of Danjuma's village. The commander, a ruthless and charismatic Nigerian known as Papa Truelove, 'heroically' prevented the boy's execution just as a teenager named Ekong was about to squeeze the trigger of the handgun pressed hard against the back of Danjuma's skull.

'From today forward,' the commander announced, wrapping his arm around Danjuma's angular shoulders, 'we shall call you *Dutse*.'

Dutse was the Hausa word for 'rock.'

Although child soldiers were by no means exclusive to Africa, roughly forty percent of child soldiers across the globe were located somewhere on this continent: in Algeria, in Angola, in Burundi, in Chad, in the Central African Republic. Meanwhile, the use of child soldiers was deemed *endemic* in the Congo, Liberia, Sudan, and Sierra Leone. The number of child soldiers continued rising and, as a general rule, as the number of child soldiers *increased*, the recruiting age of children *decreased*. All told, hundreds of thousands of child soldiers between the ages of seven and seventeen were currently being used in African armed conflicts by rebel and terrorist groups, as well as official government forces.

The motivation to recruit children like Danjuma was obvious: the boys were vulnerable, expendable, replaceable, and cheap to maintain. That child soldiers were physically weaker and generally inexperienced in combat was by no means ideal. But those disadvantages were far outweighed by favorable boyhood traits such as fearlessness and a willingness to accept the most dangerous assignments. And, of course, children were easier to deceive, to indoctrinate, to influence and control. In addition to corporal punishment, they could be manipulated using some combination of starvation, thirst, drugs and alcohol, voodoo, sexual assault, and extreme fatigue.

Meanwhile, the global proliferation of light automatic weapons made child soldiers nearly as effective on the battlefield as adults. And, whereas their fathers and uncles might demand monetary compensation, children could often be convinced to fight for intangible incentives, such as prestige, honor, duty, and revenge. Many children simply had nowhere else to go. Blights such as poverty, disease, and war had historically forced children into *all* types of labor, fighting included. And many countries in modern-day Africa – including Nigeria – continued to experience all three torments in the first two decades of the twenty-first century.

I thought again of that poster on the wall of Balogun's real estate office.

> I am *not* a product of my circumstances;
> I am a product of my decisions.

Yeah, sure. And I'm the fucking Easter Bunny.

The decision to trek through the Sambisa forest with Danjuma as our guide fell somewhere on the scale between incredibly reckless and downright stupid. Yet the vote between Jadine and me came out two to none, in favor of.

From there we shared a stark difference of opinion. I

reasoned that while the boy might be able to lead us to active camps not discoverable on our maps, he could also lead us straight into a variety of ambushes or booby traps. All he had to do was shout out at the right moment, and Jadine and I would be immediately captured or killed.

Still, Jadine insisted we not cuff or gag him.

'Why not just give him back his rifle?' I said in protest.

Jadine shrugged. 'As long as it's unloaded, I'd have no problem with that.'

Danjuma had agreed to accompany us of his own accord because he was obviously afraid of remaining alone in the forest. But once we discovered a unit of thirty or so Rusul Alharb fighters, I pointed out, that rationale would smash straight out the proverbial window as fast as a bullet through gray matter.

Although I felt strongly that the boy should at least be gagged, I fell short of insisting upon it. Only minutes later, as we continued our march through the bush, did I realize what that inaction actually signified: for the first time in fourteen years, I'd conceded control of the mission to a civilian.

As we walked, Jadine and I continued to converse, partly out of our extraordinary fear and partly out of straight-up boredom. Odd, I thought, how the two could go hand in hand. But then, I'd never been a soldier deployed in the mountains of Afghanistan or the deserts of Iraq. I'd a feeling many in the military knew the fear–boredom union much more intimately than I ever would.

'You know a hell of a lot about me,' I said to Jadine as we squeezed through a pair of rubber trees, 'but I still don't know much of anything about you.'

'I told you – never married, no kids.'

'All right, then. That tells me you're *not* a wife or a mother. But it doesn't tell me much at all about who you *are*.'

'You found me at the university, didn't you?'

'OK. So, how long have you been in Cape Town?'

She pushed past a thicket of bushes. 'About six years.'

'That leaves a good decade and change *blank* then, doesn't it? Before your time at American, you lived with your mother in Johannesburg and attended university there. So start with graduation. What did you do after college?'

'Law school.'

'Where? South Africa?'

'In the States. My father's alma mater.'

'Which is?'

'Now we're venturing into territory we already explored in college.'

'Over a period of *three weeks* at the start of my freshman year! And we spent a good deal of that time getting loaded.'

'*You* were getting loaded. I was nursing my drinks and babysitting you.'

'You're telling me you remember *everything* about *my* first eighteen years?'

'Everything you *told* me.'

'And I suppose you didn't need to brush up while you were conspiring to lure me to South Africa with Coleman.'

'Not a bit.'

'Three weeks,' I repeated with an incredulous shake of the head. 'Three.'

'They were memorable weeks,' she said, then added, 'At least for me.'

That line made me give it a good, hard think.

'Wait,' I said moments later, 'your parents were divorced, right? And following the divorce, you adopted your mother's maiden name because you didn't want anything to do with your father. Because . . .' I searched for it. 'Because he cheated on your mother.'

'Top marks, Simon.'

'But then you went to his alma mater. Can I assume you've since mended fences?'

'To an extent.' Then she threw me a bone. 'The law school I attended is Georgetown.'

'And *after* law school? You remained in DC?'

'Across the Potomac, in Arlington, Virginia.'

'That's where your father's originally from?'

'Close. Bethesda.'

'Maryland,' I said. 'That's right. You were an Orioles fan. What did you do while you were in Arlington?'

'Just a boring government job.'

Something caught in my throat, but I finally managed, 'You were in the DC area on nine/eleven, then.'

'Yes.'

A deep sigh emerged from my lungs as I readjusted my go-bag. 'That day's been replaying in my head ever since our impromptu meeting with Secretary Coleman. It was that goddamn video that triggered it. That sense of complete helplessness to change the outcome. An invasion of the US mainland seemed unthinkable until that first plane struck the North Tower.'

'It had happened before.'

'Yeah, in the War of 1812. A little before my time.'

In the days and weeks following 9/11, I halfway expected things to return to normal. Instead, normal itself underwent a drastic transformation. And by the time the dust settled around the Pentagon, something else had taken its place: a headful of impenetrable fog, present even on the clearest, brightest day; that bizarre melancholy I had carried like an albatross these past two decades.

Why, though, did it hit me so hard?

Maybe it was the age I was at the time: still young and invincible with so much ahead of me. Before the attack, life was so good I didn't know what to feast on first; it felt as though the sky were the limit and there was nothing but my own fears to keep me from climbing. Following 9/11, the fall from that cliff was a cruelly long one.

Maybe the attack hit me particularly hard because I was so physically close to Pentagon City, so entrenched in DC by then that it was difficult to separate the nation's capital from home.

Then again, maybe it was the constant news coverage, the utter saturation in all forms of media. Whether the level was appropriate was beside the point; the point was you couldn't escape it. Turn off the news, open an email, and it was there. Close the email, step outside for fresh air, and you found yourself in a jungle of American flags. Flags hanging on houses, on balconies, on cars, even displayed horrifically on the back of black leather jackets. Then everyone with a bloody tie pin, and if (God forbid) you left yours at home, you needed to call the wife, have her drop it off at the office so that you weren't made to feel like a heartless, unpatriotic prick on the side of the terrorists.

I remember thinking, where was all this patriotism on September tenth? Just how long is this sudden love-of-country going to last?

Then there were the thousands upon thousands of disquieting flyers. The pictures and descriptions of the missing. Most of whom, we all knew, were more than likely dead.

All that love in the days immediately following 9/11, and then hard on its tail, all that hatred. Of Muslims, of Arabs. Even of Sikhs, since people with that much hate in their hearts were too stupid to know the difference.

In the wake of the boundless tragedy, a them-or-us mentality sprung from the airwaves. Only we hadn't been attacked by a state actor. We weren't at war with another country. We'd declared war on a tactic, on a relatively small group of people with a warped ideology. Twenty years later, some still failed to fully comprehend that.

True, it was beyond frustrating to feel powerless to avenge the 9/11 dead. Which made altering reality for the sole reason of striking back at 'someone' seem – admittedly even to me – somehow fair and equitable at the time. But nearly twenty years later, we continued to reap the consequences. And I, for one, was so goddamn tired of it.

In late 2001, I was mad as hell with the rest of them. Because of my federal law enforcement experience with the Marshals, however, I recognized our enemy early on: a militant Sunni organization with a small but unknown number of men.

Cruel men.

Evil men.

Men who were better to the world dead.

Finally, two decades later, these were the type of men I was hunting in Nigeria's Sambisa forest. Men who butchered entire villages. Men who raped women and children. Men who strapped on suicide vests and planted explosives in the ground where any innocent child might step on them.

It took almost twenty years, but as I traipsed through the

forest, I felt as if I finally had an enemy to avenge for the events of September 11. Inexplicably, I discovered, I still thirsted for revenge.

Fortunately for me, I could reason taking this vengeance because there were lives to be saved.

'This way, this way,' Danjuma shout-whispered back to us before running on ahead.

Jadine and I hurriedly followed him toward a clearing. As we ran, Jadine broke out her IED detection system. The moment she turned it on, the device lit like the Christmas tree at Rockefeller Center.

'Wait!' she shouted at Danjuma.

He either didn't hear her or he didn't care. Danjuma just kept running.

FOURTEEN

At some point I decided it was too late for Danjuma and tackled Jadine to the ground, so as to avoid an additional casualty. Jadine and I hit the dirt so hard that it took us a moment to realize the boy wasn't exploding. And yet Jadine's device continued to warn us that we were in the midst of a garden of landmines.

Danjuma turned back to us with a questioning look.

'IEDs,' I called to him and pointed at Jadine's particle detector.

The boy smiled. 'Trick you, yeah, yeah.'

'Trick us?'

Danjuma mimed spraying the clearing with some sort of liquid. Maybe ammonium nitrate, which by itself was fairly harmless; in fact, it was predominantly used in agriculture as fertilizer. Rusul Alharb was obviously up on technology and far more cunning than I initially thought.

As I helped Jadine to her feet, I noticed tears in her eyes.

'You all right, Jade?'

'I'm going to get one of you killed,' she said.

I suspected her concern was less for me and more for Danjuma.

'Nonsense,' I told her. 'If anyone's getting anyone killed, it's the fault of Rusul Alharb. And possibly Secretary Coleman.' Saying his name aloud had me wondering again. 'Just what *is* your relationship with him anyway?'

'This again?'

'I think I've earned the right to know.'

She stepped past me.

I said, 'I don't care if you're sleeping with him. I just—'

'Don't be disgusting,' she snapped.

I followed her. 'Disgusting? What's that for? He's not a bad-looking man.' I shrugged. 'Maybe a little old. But then, my views on age and sex lately tend to evolve every twelve months or so.'

'You marry?' Danjuma asked, pointing to each of us as a pair.

I winked at him. 'Nah, we just fight like we are.'

He waved us forward with a bemused grin. 'Come-come.'

We followed Danjuma to a point on the opposite side of the clearing. Between two tremendous tallow trees, he stooped to the ground, planted his hands in the soil, and furiously began digging.

My immediate thought was, *He has a firearm buried here.* In the next moment, I made my third questionable tackle of the day, my second of the boy.

'Jade, check the ground for a weapon,' I said over my shoulder as I held him down.

She moved cautiously to the area where Danjuma was digging. She lowered herself to her knees and picked up where he had left off.

'Let him up,' she said after thirty seconds.

I lifted the boy to his feet and asked Jadine, 'What did you find?'

Slowly, she raised her eyes to mine.

'We found a door,' she said.

We lowered ourselves down the ladder: me first, Danjuma second, Jadine bringing up the rear.

'It's a super-bunker,' I said, firing up my flashlight.

Jadine frowned. 'The Nigerian military must already know about this. We're only a few klicks south of Camp Zero.'

'If Rusul Alharb have the money to build this, they have the money to bribe a few dozen poorly paid soldiers.'

I followed the narrow white corridor that seemed to stretch on forever, shining my torch back and forth.

'How long has this bunker been abandoned?' I asked Danjuma over my shoulder.

'No long.'

I ducked into one of the rooms off the corridor. Found an old desk, an ancient computer missing its hard drive. A torn Rusul Alharb flag on the wall.

Only a matter of time before they're all wearing flag pins, I thought.

These days, flags, in my opinion, divided far more than they united.

In recent years, toxic tribalism had infected the States and many countries of Europe. Virtually everywhere I had traveled over the past two decades, I'd found a growing pack mentality. You were either on the dark side or the side of light, depending on your worldview, religion, your political party, even your stance on a single social issue, no matter how inconsequential in the grand scheme.

Wasn't it Thomas Paine who said, 'The World is my country, all mankind are my brethren, and to do good is my religion'?

Thomas Paine. Dead more than two hundred years.

Ahead of his time.

Ahead of *our* time.

I realized at that moment that I *did* love my life in Moldova. In a small village, isolated from nearly everyone but Ana and Hailey, and a handful of people whose names I couldn't yet spell or even pronounce properly. Why would I want to return to the States? Why would I want to return to the West? Wouldn't Hailey have a happier life in Moldova? With a computer, she could not only attend school, but she could do just about any decent job she could do in an office building in New York or London. She could do good for the worst-off without living among the worst of humanity.

Suddenly, I felt short of breath. Was it the thick layer of dust blanketing the floor and furniture? A rare spell of claustrophobia. Or something worse? A heavy pressure weighed on my chest. Then sweat. Dizziness. Confusion.

'Are you OK, Simon?'

Will I ever see Hailey again?

I realized then that I wasn't doing this for Hailey and never had been. I'd tricked myself into believing I was. Yet Hailey wouldn't want me to take this tremendous risk. Chances I would survive this mission *and* accomplish the objective Coleman laid out were just about nil. So why was I doing it? Why was I here? As much I still desired it, it wasn't for revenge for September 11. It certainly wasn't for Ana or our relationship. It wasn't for Jadine or Secretary Coleman. Wasn't even for Kishana Coleman. At least, not *only* Kishana Coleman.

That video. That fucking video is why you're here. That video is why you're committed to seeing this through.

The execution.

The beheading.

The cries of pain and terror emanating from the laptop's tiny speakers.

If provided an opportunity to prevent that from happening to other girls, I had a *duty* to take it, didn't I? How else could I lay my head down on a pillow every night?

No, I wasn't deluding myself into believing I was some kind of hero. There was nothing special about me, certainly nothing gallant. My steadfastness was merely mankind's natural instinct at work. My resolve to safeguard the innocent was simply what it meant to be human, what it had *always* meant to be a member of humankind. A willingness to set aside selfishness and to make sacrifices. A yearning for some semblance of justice. The capacity to care for the welfare of others, even strangers half a world away.

'Simon,' Jadine called from another room. 'You need to come and take a look at this.'

When I reached her, Jadine held out a calendar, the names of the months (*Janairu, Feburairu, Maris*) and days of the week (*Lahadi, Litinin, Talata*) set out in Hausa. Each day of the *current* month was crossed off, with the exception of the present week.

Which meant Rusul Alharb fighters left this facility recently. In just the past few days.

'Why *now*?' she said.

'Heat,' I told her. 'Looks like they made a preemptive break for it.'

'You think they were warned?'

'That,' I said, 'or they had some *other* reason to believe a state actor might be about enter the arena.'

Although we'd dismissed out of hand Danjuma's suggestion concerning the fate of the girls, we couldn't dismiss the distinct possibility . . . that Rusul Alharb had discovered Kishana's identity and anticipated an American-led rescue mission or strike.

Jadine's voice fell off. 'If they did learn who she is, do you think they have already killed her?'

'Depends on what's more valuable to them,' I said softly. 'A fortune in ransom. Or sending a perfectly blunt message to the entire Western world.'

FIFTEEN

Generally, by this point in the mission, I'd have discovered a trail of breadcrumbs. This time, however, there was no trail to follow. All we could do, it seemed, was search the entirety of West Africa, clearing areas one at a time until we found the girls. And hope against hope that we found them in enough time.

Whether Kishana Coleman was dead, as Danjuma suggested, was no longer a factor in determining whether to proceed. Even if she was murdered, Danjuma confirmed what we'd already suspected: that there were countless other girls still being held captive. We might not be able to save all of them. But there was a good chance we could save some.

Unless we got ourselves killed before we found them.

There was a good chance of that too. But it wouldn't help to dwell on it.

For the next ninety minutes, we silently searched the entirety of the underground super-bunker. Only after an hour beneath the earth's sweltering surface did we finally realize just how vast the underground network of tunnels really was. The tunnels led all the way from that nondescript clearing that sent Jadine's IED detector into fits to Rusul Alharb's former nerve center, the notorious Camp Zero.

As the Nigerian military had reported, Camp Zero was thoroughly destroyed. Although the Nigerians hadn't provided any photographic evidence of the camp's dismantling, it didn't take a practiced eye to confirm there were smoldering ruins where the fortress once stood. Yet the tunnels and bunker directly below the camp remained in first-rate condition. Given the numerous entryways from the camp to the underground facilities, it was clear why no photographs of the camp's ruination were included in the intelligence reports. Clearly, Nigerian soldiers had been paid to ignore anything below the surface.

At first glance, the ground below Camp Zero had also been

abandoned. But on closer inspection, the bunker relinquished her secrets. Carefully, so as not to cause a cave-in, Jadine and I dug into the walls with the small tools we carried in our go-bags. Hidden behind those walls was an arsenal to rival an army's. Assault rifles, general-purpose machine guns, rocket-propelled grenade launchers, and enough ammunition to kick off World War III.

We also discovered enough materials to construct dozens of suicide vests. Not only the fabric and explosives but the ball bearings, nails, screws, bolts, and other items that served as shrapnel in order to maximize carnage.

Yet the true find for me was behind a different wall altogether. A wall that opened on to a large area serving as a garage. A garage that housed a few dozen motorbikes that looked as if they had arrived here in a time machine. And I don't mean from the future.

'Even if we can't drive the bikes any faster than fifteen miles per hour, we'll still be able to cover five times as much ground,' I said to Jadine, trying to contain my excitement. 'And we'll conserve a considerable amount of our own energy.'

There was plenty of gasoline available. Enough, it seemed, to burn the entire Sambisa forest to the ground.

'What about the noise from the bikes, Simon? What about the fact that we may drive right over an IED and get blown to smithereens?'

'Look, there are risks either way.' With sweat streaming down my forehead and stinging my eyes, I pointed at the rocky ceiling above our heads. 'The longer we're out there in the forest, the more likely we'll be seen. With the motorbikes, we can cut that time down with a hatchet. And no offense, Jade, but it's not like your IED detector has been a lifesaver. Three-quarters of the time it was stuffed inside your go-bag. And once it finally did go off, we were promptly informed by an eleven-year-old that we'd been duped by a group of backward fanatics.'

'And just which way do you propose we go with these bikes?'

'We continue northeast,' I said. 'I suggest we scour the villages of Borno State, then Borno's capital, Maiduguri.'

From there, I proposed that we head to Lake Chad, which bordered all three of Nigeria's neighbors on the edge of the Sahara.

Following a rigorous debate over what to do about the arsenal below Camp Zero, we concurred that we needed to defer any action until after we completed our mission.

'What about Danjuma?' Jadine finally said quietly.

I glanced back at the boy as he studied the motorbikes with childlike fascination. 'We bring him along.'

'Can we trust him?'

'Of course not,' I said softly. 'But I *do* think we can buy a kernel of loyalty by hiring him as a translator and guide.'

After completing our search of the super-bunker and its tunnels, Jadine and I walked our bikes up the ramp, then moved them a safe distance from Camp Zero. In a small clearing just to the north, we paused and shared our lunch rations with the boy, who devoured them as though they were *filet mignon* as opposed to a poor excuse for chicken and penne.

Once Danjuma had determined we were no threat (and after I offered him a job that would earn him more in a week than most Nigerian adults earned in a year), Danjuma started talking. And talking.

As he spoke, I thought, *How could I have missed the humanity in those eyes earlier?*

Prior to the daytime raid on his village, Danjuma told us, he had never even handled a weapon. The charismatic Rusul Alharb commander, Papa Truelove, made certain that fact changed by nightfall.

'*Dutse*,' he said, 'you will make one fine soldier someday. You want to make one fine soldier, yes?'

Danjuma, still in shock, could only bow his head in tacit agreement.

'A soldier's first duty,' Truelove told him, 'is loyalty to his commander. If you remain loyal to me, I will remain loyal to you. But if you are disloyal, *Dutse* . . .' He turned his thumb and index finger into a gun and pressed the latter against the boy's forehead. 'If you are disloyal, I will have no choice but to put you down like a sick dog and leave your wretched body to rot in the sun.'

After threatening to murder him, Truelove handed the boy his first taste of alcohol even though it was forbidden by the religion Rusul Alharb was supposedly fighting for. That night, Danjuma and several other male children taken from the village imbibed like a pack of first-year frat boys.

Unsurprisingly, the next morning, Danjuma went to Truelove with an excruciating hangover. Truelove provided him a handful of cheap opiates called Tramadol to ease the pain, along with a gram of cocaine to drive off any accompanying fatigue.

That night, he gave Danjuma tranquilizers to help him sleep.

The following day, Danjuma saw his first action as a soldier when his unit teamed with others to assault the town of Baga, a ten-thousand-person fishing community near Lake Chad. Only a few years earlier, Baga had been the target of another Rusul Alharb assault that killed nearly two hundred civilians and destroyed more than two thousand homes.

During the present assault, termed the Baga Massacre in our intelligence packets, Danjuma and several other child soldiers served as an integral part of the support element. Traveling in a convoy of trucks, motorcycles, and armored personnel carriers previously stolen from Nigerian security forces, Rusul Alharb fighters rushed the Baga military base serving as the headquarters of the Multinational Joint Task Force. Although the task force was also comprised of troops from Chad, Niger, and Cameroon, only Nigerian soldiers were manning the base at the time of the assault.

Utilizing RPGs, IEDs, and small arms, Rusul Alharb militants swiftly captured the base, sending Nigerian security forces fleeing for the bush, along with hundreds of unarmed civilians. Meanwhile, a *civilian* joint task force attempted to repel the attack, primarily using handguns and machetes. Heavily outmanned and outgunned, the civilian task force ultimately fell, granting militants free rein to slaughter residents and loot and burn down any remaining homes, churches, and businesses.

Over the next several days, Rusul Alharb fighters went from

home to home, executing young men, kidnapping young women, and chasing small children and the very elderly from their towns. According to local sources, as many as two thousand people were killed in the assault, yet the Nigerian government insisted casualties numbered under two hundred. Some Nigerian officials had the audacity to deny the massacre had taken place at all. Satellite images obtained by Amnesty International, however, clearly showed that at least sixteen towns, villages, and settlements in the area were leveled during the five-plus days of hell.

When the assault proved successful, Danjuma and his fellow child soldiers were rewarded with an unholy mixture of cane juice and gunpowder. Danjuma felt like Superman and apprised Papa Truelove that he wanted to raid the next village on his own.

'In time,' Truelove told him. 'In time.'

Later that night, Papa Truelove summoned Danjuma into his hut.

'If you want to eat,' he said, slowly lowering his pants, 'you must also treat.'

The boy shared this last bit reluctantly with a stream of tears while Jadine was off relieving herself in the forest. Had I not personally witnessed so much evil over the previous two decades, Danjuma's story might well have broken me. Instead, his tale would likely fester in my head with the rest, until they one day plunged me into absolute madness.

After consuming our lunch rations, we mounted the bikes, Danjuma on the back of mine, and headed in the direction of Maiduguri.

Predictably, Jadine Visser knew how to ride better than most motorcycle enthusiasts I'd met over the past quarter century. Although I had previously promised myself that I wouldn't be shocked to see her demonstrate a skill your average college professor wouldn't possess, her sheer adroitness at handling the bike over the rough terrain of the forest left me gripping my jaw to keep it from tumbling to the forest floor.

There's more than a little she's not telling you.

Meanwhile, despite the constant rush of adrenaline, my

mind couldn't catch a break. Being around Jadine caused me
to think constantly of college, and thinking of college caused
me to think constantly of Tasha. Of making out on the bed in
her dorm room because (according to her) my freshman roommate, Terry, smelled like feet. Of eating Sloppy Joes across
from her in the college cafeteria while she looked on with
revulsion in front of a bowl of Romaine lettuce. Of playing
frisbee with her in the quad, assiduously counting our consecutive catches like a pair of score-obsessed children. Of sitting
next to her in the movie theater, contemplating the smoothness
of her neck while she sat silently, plucking overly buttered
popcorn out of a king-size bucket, completely engaged by the
picture. Of Tasha as a frosh, Tasha as a sophomore, Tasha as
a junior, as a senior, as my fiancée, my wife. As the mother
of my daughter. As the only other person in the world who
could truly comprehend the limitless anguish of losing Hailey.

Of Tasha's suicide.

Of her funeral.

Of her gravestone just outside Richmond, Virginia.

Watching my wife's coffin being slowly lowered into the
ground was the last time I feared death – until now. Because,
I discerned, we don't profoundly fear for our own lives, not
really. We fear only leaving our loved ones behind. We fear
for *their* lives and our role in them.

Without love, I decided, fear didn't exist.

With love, however, fear was veritably infinite.

The decision to ride north toward Maiduguri rather than east
toward Gwoza wasn't made without a great deal of trepidation
on my part. Based on the intelligence we'd received from
Secretary Coleman and Deputy Secretary Jeffries, my initial
instinct had been to exit the Sambisa forest near the Gwoza
Hills, where Rusul Alharb was known to possess key hideouts.
Although the Nigerian army claimed to have retaken the area
from the terror organization, there were recent reports of Rusul
Alharb militants fleeing the forest on motorcycles and entering
the Gwoza villages of Goshe, Attagara, Agapalwa, and
Aganjara.

My worry was that I had chosen to avoid the Gwoza Hills

out of this newfound fear. Roughly five years earlier, the local government district known as Gwoza had been the site of the Gwoza massacre, an event in which Rusul Alharb militants dressed as Nigerian soldiers invaded several predominantly Christian villages and slaughtered hundreds of civilians. With its rocky, hilly terrain that included the Mandara Mountains on the Cameroonian border, it was particularly difficult for Nigerian forces to penetrate Rusul Alharb's defense elements in the Gwoza Hills. Although intelligence had confirmed that Rusul Alharb maintained strongholds in the mountainous region, the heights – some 1,300 meters above sea level – prevented any serious military action. From caves in the Mandara Mountains, Rusul Alharb fighters would have spotted the Nigerian army the moment troops exited the forest.

Jadine and I would have made a significantly smaller target but a target, nonetheless – in an area in which, if we were to come under heavy fire, there was nowhere to run and certainly nowhere to hide. The destruction of local roads and bridges had isolated the territory from the rest of Nigeria, and the high ground of the mountains provided fighters a clear view all the way to the Sambisa's tree line.

From everything I'd read, there was a better chance that Rusul Alharb had hidden the kidnapped girls in the Gwoza Hills and Mandara Mountains than somewhere north of Borno State's capital, Maiduguri. But that didn't necessarily make heading in that direction the optimal strategic move to rescue them. After all, if Jadine and I were shot and killed on our approach to the hills, who would come for them? Some had been held hostage for more than five years. Some had been forced to wed and give birth and were too ashamed to head home to their families on their own, even if escape were possible.

I didn't want to think of the team of Visser and Fisk as the last hope for Rusul Alharb's most vulnerable victims, but if history was any indicator, Jadine and I *were* indeed just that. And I couldn't simply bury that fact.

SIXTEEN

R oughly ten miles from the edge of the forest, we shed
our fatigues, stashed our go-bags, abandoned our motorbikes, and set out on foot in secondhand earth-toned
civilian clothes. Less than two hours later, we stepped out of
the bush and into our first northeastern Nigerian village, a
community known as Konduga.

Located roughly fifteen miles southeast of Maiduguri,
Konduga possessed a population of just over ten thousand,
though it was unclear to me whether that number included the
thousands of refugees who had fled here from even smaller
surrounding communities. The entirety of northeastern Nigeria
had now been under siege by Rusul Alharb for more than a
decade. And their presence showed in just about every fathom-
able way.

Although I'd reviewed all available intelligence about the
impoverished village, I still wasn't prepared for the sight of
Konduga. In recent years, I'd visited the worst of the worst
slums in countries all over Eastern Europe and Central and
South America. I'd seen poverty and its consequences up close
and met its victims, the most vulnerable of whom continued
to visit me in night terrors. But I'd never been to a village
quite like Konduga: a flat, red-dirt region that could well have
served as the backdrop for those old Save the Children
commercials with Sally Struthers. The ones with infants and
young kids who tugged at your heartstrings so hard they
nearly snapped. Images of toddlers, sick and malnourished,
sitting alone in the dirt, wearing only a diaper while flies
sauntered across the whites of their eyes. The ones with tooth-
pick arms and bloated bellies, whom you could save 'for the
price of a cup of coffee.' If only you were willing to sacrifice
your morning fix of caffeine.

According to our intel, Konduga had recently been attacked
by a pair of female suicide bombers who detonated their

explosives at the entrance to a refugee camp, killing dozens and injuring hundreds. The attack occurred as a nongovernmental organization (what's known as an NGO) provided refugees badly needed assistance in the form of potable water, food, and medicine. Humanitarian aid workers – not unlike Kishana Coleman and the US Peace Corps – were frequent targets of extremist groups like Rusul Alharb. Regrettably, the 'toughest job you'll ever love' sometimes came with life's steepest price tag. More than three hundred Peace Corps volunteers had made the ultimate sacrifice in the program's sixty-year history.

Although I didn't boast many soft spots, I possessed one for the Peace Corps. Back in college, Tasha had a close friend named Aubrey Lang, a farmer's daughter from Ames, Iowa, with dreams of seeing the world. Without the means to leave the Hawkeye State on her own, she became resourceful and joined the Peace Corps. Despite spending years earning an American University nursing degree, Aubrey requested placement in Costa Rica in order to do her part to save the rainforests. When she learned that the Corps' Protected Areas Management program required a degree in a related field, she took out further student loans to enroll at the University of Wisconsin in Madison. There, she took part in local conservation activities while pursuing a second bachelor's in wildlife management. In Costa Rica, Aubrey provided technical training to park staff, including managers, guards, and guides, in an effort to promote community-based conservation while aiding in the development of the country's ecotourism industry. After falling in love with the Costa Rican people, she applied for and was granted an extension of service so she could work with the children of San José's outlying slums, which were becoming increasingly desperate and violent. Years later, when I called on Aubrey for help on a case that took me to Costa Rica, she told me her time in the Peace Corps was the most rewarding in her life and, if given the chance, she would do it all over again.

Jadine and I kept our heads down as we looked around. According to the intelligence, most Konduga residents were illiterate subsistence farmers earning the equivalent of less than twenty bucks a year. A precious few families in the village had access to twenty-first-century necessities such as electricity, plumbing, and drinking water. Several attacks prior to the recent pair of suicide bombings had already demolished much of the village. Most of the remaining structures were simple huts constructed of straw and corrugated metal. Perfect targets for any big, bad wolf looking to huff and puff and blow your house in.

Within one of the after-action reports, Jadine and I had found the name of a middle-aged Konduga resident who told UN investigators that he had been on his way to mosque when the most recent pair of bombs went off, almost simultaneously. He immediately darted in the direction of the blasts to help members of the civilian volunteer force working to rescue the terror attack's most severely wounded victims. Near the site of the suicide bombings, Jadine quietly inquired as to where we might find the gentlemen, whose name was Umar Okafor. After several failed attempts, she was finally pointed in the direction of a small hut that had been singed in one of the explosions.

While Danjuma and I waited in the bush with a pair of military-grade binoculars, Jadine tapped on the corrugated tin door, which moments later opened on an elderly woman dressed in a bright orange traditional African wrap. On her feet the old woman wore a pair of neon green shower slippers, which seemed to be the village go-to in footwear for those who wore anything at all on their feet.

Mic'd up with the sound flowing directly into my earpiece, Jadine spoke to the woman in a language I didn't recognize. The woman responded, then held up a finger and closed the door. The hut apparently comprised of a single room, so if Umar was home, it wouldn't take long for the old woman to find him. Unless, for some reason, he didn't want to be found.

'What language is that?' I said quietly into my mic while Jadine waited for the woman to return.

'Kanuri,' she whispered with a tenderness that caused me to shiver.

Although I had only just skimmed the dozens of pages of history on northeastern Nigeria, the Kanuri people had stood

out, given their connection to the medieval Kanem-Bornu
Empire, which dated all way back to the eighth century CE
and remained an empire for twelve hundred years. In the late
1800s, the region was invaded by an army from eastern Sudan
and ultimately absorbed by the British Empire's Northern
Nigeria Protectorate. Colonialism then continued in some form
until 1960, when Nigeria officially declared its independence
from British rule.

When the elderly woman finally returned to the door, she
wore a thin smile and invited Jadine inside. There, she introduced Jadine to the man named Umar Okafor. Although the
mic permitted me to hear the goings-on in case there was
trouble, for the next half hour I sat in the bush with Danjuma,
unable to decipher a word of what was being said. While I
briefly experienced that peculiar mixture of fear and boredom
again, it dissipated minutes later as I warmly – and somewhat
guiltily – recalled the rare and powerful sensation that rose in
my chest when Jadine whispered that single word – *Kanuri*
– into the earpiece in my left ear.

The name Umar provided Jadine was Harun al-Haggi.
According to Umar, al-Haggi was a Rusul Alharb militant who
had injured his right arm in combat and returned to Konduga
to lie low while he convalesced. Al-Haggi was currently staying
with family in a structure just down the road. Prior to joining
Rusul Alharb, he and Umar had been close friends; in fact,
they'd grown up together.

As we approached al-Haggi's hut, several men and boys
were kicking around a partially deflated soccer ball in a
wide-open space to our left. As much as we tried to remain
inconspicuous, our presence soon caught the attention of a
rail-thin teenager, who promptly pointed us out to a pair of
early-middle-aged men. A moment later, one of those men
tore off in a run.

'There's our rabbit,' I said.

'*Shit*,' Jadine hissed.

'Don't sweat it,' I told her. 'The chase is my favorite part
of the job. And, at the risk of sounding narcissistic, I'm pretty
damn good at it.'

I then shot after our target like the proverbial bat out of hell.

Although I half expected to be tackled, if not shot dead, by my quarry's confederates, the chase went on unimpeded. Roughly ninety seconds later, after zigzagging past a series of single-room huts, I caught up with him in what could loosely be described as an alley.

I snatched him by the back of the neck, spun him around, and threw him to the ground with all the pleasure of a lineman sacking a quarterback on third and ten.

'Your name is Harun al-Haggi,' I said to him.

'Fuck you, motherfucker, fucking devil fuck.'

'Your English is pretty good,' I said with a mirthless grin. 'Learn it from watching *The Sopranos*?'

He twisted his neck and spat in my face as I frisked him on the ground. 'Fuck you, fuck your mother, motherfucker!'

'Yeah,' I said, calmly wiping away the spittle, '*The Sopranos* was a favorite of mine too. I particularly liked it when Tony roughed someone up for disrespecting him.'

I lifted him off the ground and slipped my left arm under his right. I then gripped his right hand just below the fingers and folded it back as far as it would go. With my right, I rammed his elbow forward as hard as I could, tearing the tendons and ligaments in his right wrist.

He screamed as if I was murdering him, so I released his arm and chopped him in the throat to shut him the hell up. He crumpled to his knees, gasping for breath.

'I hope you didn't run because of unpaid parking tickets,' I told him. 'Because if you don't know what I want you to know, I'm going to snap every last bone in your body.'

He was clearly struggling yet determined to get a word out, and I hoped I hadn't damaged his vocal cords so badly that he couldn't speak.

'W–w–what do you want to know?' he finally managed.

'I want to know about kidnapped girls.'

He remained on his knees, hacking. 'W–w–what about them?'

'Where are they being held?'

Jadine, who'd sprinted after me, caught up. 'The ones taken

from Adamawa State,' she threw in as she slid to an abrupt halt, kicking up a small cloud of dirt in front of us.

Instinctively, I shot her a look.

She said, 'I know you want to rescue *all* of the girls, Simon, but we need to be practical here.'

I did my damnedest to hide my irritation with her interruption. It wouldn't do to show this bastard that there was division among our ranks. Still, I recognized now that Jadine and I possessed conflicting agendas. Because the more I learned about Rusul Alharb, the less likely it became that I would be able to leave the African continent while a single girl continued to be held captive by the terrorist group. My conscience simply wouldn't permit it.

'Well?' I said to the guy whose right wrist now dangled from his arm like a dying leaf in a strong breeze. 'How about it, al-Haggi? Where are they?'

He looked faint. As if he might pass out from the pain. Couldn't have that now, could I? Fortunately, I always kept a small vial of smelling salts on my person for just such an occasion. I broke them out now and shoved the ammonia up under his nose. His eyes went cartoonishly wide as he let out another scream that may have been meant to puncture my eardrums.

'You'll hurt your throat wailing like that,' I told him.

'They will *kill* me if I t–t–talk,' he cried.

'*I'll* kill you if you don't. At least with them, you'll have a bit of a head start.'

He glared at Jadine, said very assuredly, 'You won't kill me. You are American.'

Squeezing his chin, I turned his head to look at me. 'I don't know what the hell kind of fairy tales you've been listening to,' I said, 'but you're about to experience the shock of what's left of your short-ass life.'

I grabbed him by his faded and torn black T-shirt and prepared to introduce him to the Glasgow kiss.

'Simon?' Jadine said, motioning to the mouth of the alley where a group had gathered to watch the fireworks.

'Well,' I said to her, 'you have any better ideas?'

Slowly, she bowed her head. 'As a matter of fact, I do.'

SEVENTEEN

Jadine Visser's 'better ideas' would have sounded startlingly familiar to anyone who had read the US Senate Intelligence Committee's report on the CIA's use of torture during the War on Terror. While I would never be mistaken for a pacifist, reading that report (as I did when it was published years ago) shook me to the core. It detailed how detainees – some of whom were later discovered to be victims of lying informants or mistaken identity – were: force-fed anally; subjected to rectal rehydration; violently raped; subjected to mock executions; made to play Russian roulette; kept awake for more than one full week; locked in coffins for eleven straight days; forced to stand for hours on a pair of broken feet; made to shit in a bucket, unless being punished, in which case even the bucket would be taken away; and, of course, repeatedly waterboarded to the point of becoming completely unresponsive, very nearly drowning. All occurring while intelligence officials misled the United States Congress and the American public as to the effectiveness of these so-called 'enhanced interrogation' techniques.

'This isn't a black site,' I protested when Jadine unholstered a revolver and suggested our prisoner 'spin to win.'

We were now in friendly territory (though just *how* friendly I wasn't sure) in Borno State's capital, Maiduguri, where we had been met by Deputy Secretary Jeffries and a Nigerian intelligence agent who set us up on the second floor of a safe house that appeared none too safe.

'No, it's not a black site,' she countered. 'It's a lawless nation that allows its children to be kidnapped and converted, turned into child soldiers and sex slaves.'

I scanned the empty room, wondering if any of the hundreds of bugs crawling up and down the dilapidated walls were listening devices. In the adjoining room, our prisoner was shackled to a rusted radiator that I feared he could break with his hands. Well, *hand* singular since he only had one working hand left.

'Give me more time,' I told her. 'I'll get the information we need.'

'There *is* no more time, Simon. We just chased down a Rusul Alharb fighter in the middle of Konduga and drove him here in an ancient military Jeep with hundreds of people watching. Do you *really* think he's the only militant in Maiduguri right now? Do you *really* believe word isn't already on its way to the leadership that you and I are tracking the kidnapped girls?'

I sighed. 'All right. Good cop/bad cop, then. But let me play the bad cop so I can control just how far this interrogation goes.' I paused, muttered, 'Besides, the violence I did to that poor bastard's wrist should give my threats an added air of authenticity.'

'Be my guest,' she finally said. 'But if you don't get what we need quickly, we're employing more serious measures, up to and including waterboarding.'

I could almost *see* her setting the clock in her head and knew I wouldn't have long – and that I wouldn't receive any two-minute warning.

We stepped into the next room, where Harun al-Haggi was kindly waiting for us from his spot on the filth-covered floor.

'S–something, please, for the pain,' he said, motioning to his right wrist.

'Answer my questions,' I told him, 'and I'll personally guarantee you all the ibuprofen your stomach can handle.'

'Tramadol,' he pleaded. 'I need Tramadol. It's the only thing that . . .'

Unsurprisingly, the unfortunate son of a bitch was addicted to opiates. Epidemics like opiate addiction heeded no geographical boundaries; discriminated against no race, no religion, no socio-economic class; took no sides in war. As much as it might trouble me later, I wouldn't hesitate to use his burning need to our advantage, if it became necessary. It'd be more humane than placing a gun in his mouth for a forced hand of Russian roulette. More compassionate than simulated drowning, rectal rehydration, or whatever other methods of torture Jadine had hidden up her sleeve.

There's a lot she's not telling you, Simon. And it may well be information that's going to get you killed.

I wasn't sure why I continued tiptoeing on eggshells around Jadine. I'd always hated being left in the dark. Especially while I was in the middle of a heated search for a kidnapped child. Had any other client held out on me, I'd have returned any payment and severed the relationship in a heartbeat. But then, Jadine wasn't technically the client. In truth, I wasn't sure what she was or how she fitted into this puzzle. All I knew was that, even after all these years, I still harbored deep feelings for her. Maybe I was afraid that hearing the whole truth from her this far into the investigation would send me packing for a return trip to Moldova. Maybe I was afraid of having to leave Jadine, of having to dump this perilous mission solely in her lap.

Jadine lowered herself to one knee on the threadbare silver carpet in front of our prisoner. 'Listen,' she told him, 'Simon here wants to feed you to the Nigerian military when we're done with you. You know what happens then, don't you?'

He bowed his head. Al-Haggi knew all too well that the Nigerians would immediately execute him with a point-blank shot to the back of the skull.

'You want Tramadol?' she said. 'We'll give you as much Tramadol as you can carry. The Nigerian army keeps stores of it here in Maiduguri. Answer all our questions and we'll put you on a plane to any place on the continent. We'll set you up with enough currency to start a new life. If you have family here, you can send for them.'

'Rusul Alharb will *kill* my family,' he said.

'We can protect them,' Jadine said. 'Answer our questions and we'll send an exfiltration team for them straightaway. Understand?'

Although he nodded his head, he clearly – and rightly – remained suspicious. If Harun al-Haggi cooperated, it wouldn't be for money, drugs, or his family. It would be to avoid being immediately turned over to the Nigerian army. And even relying on *that* meager promise from Jadine, I was sure he realized, was one hell of a gamble.

Less than an hour later, the three of us – Deputy Secretary Jeffries, Jadine, and I – gathered downstairs around a small table in the semi-dark. Danjuma, who'd reluctantly driven with us to Maiduguri, was now in a safe house down the road, where he was being fed and examined by a pediatrician and a dentist. From there, he'd be flown to the US Embassy in Abuja, where he would apply for (and presumably be granted) political asylum in the United States.

Deputy Secretary Jeffries opened his laptop and punched in the intricate web address given us by Harun al-Haggi. We had no idea what to expect; al-Haggi insisted that he had no knowledge of the site's contents, only that it contained audio, video, and print information deemed top secret by Rusul Alharb leadership. When I asked him how a low-level terrorist currently on the disabled list came to learn about this top-secret web address, he didn't hesitate. He said that ever since he'd been sidelined from fighting with the arm injury, he'd been acting as a courier between Rusul Alharb commanders in Borno State and the Lake Chad Basin.

Didn't he realize that his curiosity would likely cost him his head? Did he fuck. He hadn't volunteered for the job; he'd been drafted and had assumed all along that the Top-Dog-to-Big-Cheese messenger job wouldn't end well for him. He simply figured that if the position was ultimately going to earn him a bullet to the back of the head anyway, why not try to intercept some high-level information that could potentially be used as currency to buy him safe passage outside the country?

Thinking of the video Coleman and Jeffries had shown me in Cape Town, my insides spun with desperation and dread. In my head were images of Hailey, not safe and content in Moldova with Ana but here in Nigeria in the grasp of the monsters that made up Rusul Alharb. Hailey on her knees, Hailey in a pitch-black hood, Hailey with the business end of a machete pressed against her milky white throat, her blood feeding the blade.

While al-Haggi had indeed sung to us in return for our promise that he wouldn't be turned over to the Nigerian military, his song was trapped like lethal toxins in my stomach and lungs. I felt ill in a way I hadn't felt since finding Hailey. And Jadine, from all appearances, was faring no better.

'The girls at Adamawa,' al-Haggi had said, 'we take many. But we want only one.'

Upon hearing those words, Jadine had staggered. I'd caught her just before she sank to the floor.

'You all right, Jade?'

'Just a little lightheaded,' she said. 'Too much sun.'

The girls at Adamawa, we take many. But we want only one.

'All right,' Jeffries said as he tapped in the lengthy password Harun al-Haggi had given us. 'Everyone prepared for this?'

The girls at Adamawa, we take many.

When neither of us answered him, Jeffries looked up from his screen. Jadine and I each offered a subtle nod of the chin. Jeffries lowered his gaze back to the screen and touched a single key. 'I'm in.'

But we want only one.

Jeffries' eyes remained locked on the monitor for what felt like an eternity. Finally, he dropped his elbows on to the table and buried his head in the palms of his hands.

'Oh, dear God,' he murmured. 'Oh, dear God, no.'

The image frozen on the screen was of Kishana Coleman.

'The girls from Adamawa, we take many,' Harun al-Haggi had said. 'But we want only one.'

'One?' I'd asked.

Over the lower portion of Kishana's face was an arrow inside a circle.

'Hit the play button,' Jadine said.

Jeffries ran a trembling finger over the mouse and led the pointer to the play button. Reluctantly, he tapped it and the image of Kishana Coleman sprang to life.

'Why one?' I'd said.

Al-Haggi swallowed hard. 'Because she is the daughter of one of our men.'

As Jadine and I stood over either side of Jeffries' shoulders, the girl in the video began to speak.

'My name is Kishana Coleman,' she said in American English, 'granddaughter of the US Secretary of State James Coleman. I am a volunteer with the United States Peace Corps, assigned to a humanitarian mission to aid refugees in Yola, Adamawa State, in northeastern Nigeria.'

She wore a black hijab that exposed only her face. A large Islamic State flag hung on the wall directly behind her.

'My father is Ahmad Abdulaziz,' she continued flatly, 'former professor of Islamic Studies at Maiduguri University and a loyal member of Rusul Alharb. My father was recruited by the US Central Intelligence Agency and Nigeria's National Intelligence Agency nearly two decades ago, shortly after the group was founded by Mohammed Yakubu in the name of Allah, most gracious and merciful.'

I stole a glance at Jadine, whose lower lip was now trembling. I reached around her waist and pulled her to me as Kishana resumed speaking.

'My father today makes it known to the people of the world that his faith and loyalty cannot be sold to the highest bidder.' Her voice faltered but only for a moment. Then: 'And neither can mine.'

Jadine looked on with watering eyes as my head filled with countless questions.

'Our allegiance is to Allah,' Kishana said, 'to Rusul Alharb – the Islamic State's West African Province – and to its leader, Abubakar Shagari, who cannot die except by the will of Allah.' She blinked. Once, twice. 'Very soon, my father and I shall prove our allegiance. And together, we shall ascend into Heaven, while the faithful rejoice, and the infidels in this earthly realm stand around, counting their dead.'

PART II
The Dead Heart of Africa

EIGHTEEN

The drive along the A3 highway from Maiduguri to the Lake Chad Basin was brief but treacherous, leaving us little choice but to ditch the Jeep for a ride in the trailer of a heavy-duty truck carrying humanitarian supplies for basin residents uprooted by the ongoing conflict with Rusul Alharb.

Our ride had been procured by Deputy Secretary Jeffries with the cooperation of the Nigerian intelligence official, whose name now somehow escaped me. Huddled next to Jadine in the claustrophobic space, surrounded by towering stacks of unmarked brown boxes, I refrained from asking her for the name, choosing instead to wrestle with every last word and image I'd sponged during the past week. Christ, how could I not remember the name of someone I met less than an hour earlier? Was my short-term memory yet another casualty of my mid-forties? Or was I simply tired and subconsciously conserving headspace?

No, the name was important. Why it eluded me while names from the years-old Lindsay Sorkin case – even the names of minor players like Dietrich Braun and Karl Finster – were just a thought-click away baffled me, perhaps even frightened me a little. Particularly since I'd recently received word that my father was suffering from an aggressive form of dementia. I couldn't imagine the ramifications of being struck with such a disease this early in life. Would I lose even those precious six years of memories I had of Hailey as a child?

Little Hailey, bouncing in her baby swing, listening to me read Dr Seuss, watching with mild bemusement as I sang obnoxious songs about her head, shoulders, knees and toes, knees and toes?

Little Hailey, dousing herself in ketchup when I had hoped to keep secret from Tasha our stopping at Arby's and splurging on an extra-large order of curly fries?

Little Hailey, coming off the bus from kindergarten, sporting a paper crown for a classmate's birthday, with a smile as wide as a five-lane highway?

I cleared my head, told myself the name of the Nigerian would come to me if I just quit thinking about it. Being stuffed into this tight space was having an unusual effect on me. Although I'd never been particularly claustrophobic, my guts curled the more I considered what a helpless position we had put ourselves in. To distract myself I turned to Jadine and asked if she was enjoying the ride, which thus far had been hot, jolting, and otherwise hellish.

'She was clearly reading from something behind the camera,' Jadine said, circling back to Kishana Coleman's apparent martyrdom video.

'I don't dispute that,' I told her. 'But that doesn't necessarily mean her statement was involuntary.'

'I'm *telling* you it was involuntary.'

Her tone left me an opening and I seized on it. 'No offense, Jade, but I'm not sure where this certitude comes from.'

'It comes from years of practiced observation.'

'Of whom? Your students? Determining whether they're speaking off the cuff or using index cards? Just tell me, Jade. How can you presume to know this girl's state of mind?'

Finally, with a starburst of exasperation, she grasped me hard by the shirt and stated, 'Because she's my *daughter*, Simon.'

For all my suspicions, her words struck me like a semi. I'd merely been pushing Jadine to admit that she *knew* Kishana Coleman. Not that she'd *birthed* her. All I'd hoped to gain was better insight into Jadine's relationship with the Secretary of State, so that I could make some sense of her role in this mission. I'd suspected they were ex-lovers or old friends or that she'd worked for the Secretary while he was in Congress. I wasn't in the least bit prepared for this, and my gape undoubtedly betrayed my utter astonishment, even in the wee light poking through the trailer door.

'Which,' I said as slowly and as delicately as possible, 'would make *you* James Coleman's . . .'

'Daughter.'

Doing my damnedest to tamp down my emotions, I turned

away from her. As much as I felt for Jadine at that moment
– as a friend, as a former lover, as someone who'd also lost
a child – I couldn't excuse the position she'd put me in. I
thought of Vince Sorkin's request to accompany me in Paris,
of Edgar Trenton's suggestion that he meet me in South
America. 'I work alone,' I'd told them both. Which was true.
And when I *did* have help, it derived from friends like Aubrey
Lang or the German private detective Kurt Osterman. Never
had I sought help from a client. The job was precarious
enough without such a profound and unpredictable emotive
element at play. Because if I'd learned anything at all over
the past fifteen years, it was that a parent would do absolutely *anything* to rescue their child. Regardless of whether
the risks they were taking made any objective, rational sense
at all.

Having a parent along jeopardized the mission. Jeopardized
the child's life, to say nothing of my own. Of course, it was
pointless to make this case to Jadine, since she already knew
the entire argument; otherwise, she would have come clean
before I ever accepted the assignment.

Take it easy on her, Simon. Who would you *have deceived
to get Hailey back all those years ago? Who would* you *have
manipulated? Who would* you *have flat-out used?*

Anyone. Everyone.

Jadine, Aubrey, the feds Rendell and West, private investigators, civilian volunteers.

Truth is, I would have risked the life of every last man,
woman, and child I knew if I thought it might help me get
Hailey back unharmed.

As we continued toward Lake Chad, I remained silent,
casting aside thoughts of Jadine's duplicity and searching my
fogged head for the name of the Nigerian intelligence official
we'd left in Maiduguri. Again my thoughts turned to my father
and his illness and its dreadful consequences, of what it would
be like to lose the few memories I had of Hailey's childhood
to disease or even to decades of regular wear and tear on the
mind.

Little Hailey, hovering over me as I did ab crunches while
watching the news, asking 'Are you t'inking what I'm

t'inking?' which invariably translated to 'How about we turn that frown upside down and put on some cartoons?'

Little Hailey, cutting the crust off her pizza one day, consuming *only* crust the next.

Little Hailey, refusing to get in the bathtub, then minutes later refusing to leave it.

Little Hailey, making funny faces at the kitchen table, wanting to make us laugh when she sensed the slightest bit of tension in the room.

Little Hailey, sneaking out of bed and sitting up with me watching Hitchcock movies when I couldn't sleep because of jetlag or just plain old nerves.

Little Hailey.

As I pictured my little girl dozing next to me on the sofa while I half watched *The Birds* (sound off, subtitles on), the truck we were in gently slowed, then rolled to a stop.

I glanced at Jadine as we listened to the first snaps of commands being shouted at our driver. Seconds later, several pairs of boots could be heard marching along either side of the trailer.

'*Bude shi!*'

'What are they saying?' I asked Jadine in a whisper.

'They're ordering the driver to open the back of the trailer.'

NINETEEN

More clipped commands as the driver methodically undid the latches on the rear of the trailer. They were ordering *him* to open the doors in case this was an ambush. Thankfully, from the look on Jadine's face, the driver wasn't telling them about us; he wasn't giving us up. Not yet anyway.

Of course, there was the slim possibility that the truck had been stopped by Nigerian security forces. Although we'd been told there were none currently positioned in the area, these soldiers could well comprise a secret detail that not even what's-his-name knew about. If so, what would they do once they found us? Kill us? Take us prisoner? Let us go? And if we were lucky enough for the latter, could they be trusted – not the troop as a whole but each individual soldier? Following this, would we be crazy to go on as planned, without altering so much as our mode of transportation? If we simply remained in the back of this truck, would we be greeted by a half-dozen armed-to-the-teeth Rusul Alharb militants when we finally arrived in Lake Chad? It would take only a single traitor to send word to the enemy.

Regrettably, just before the trailer door rattled open, my worry over the trustworthiness of the Nigerian security forces became moot. Because Jadine had just heard a turn of phrase that left no doubt in her mind that our truck had been stopped by Rusul Alharb.

'Can't *talk* our way out,' she whispered.

'Can't *shoot* our way out,' I whispered back.

There it was again, that fear, like a living thing lodged somewhere in my digestive system, seeping into my blood, poisoning every part of me. It was no secret that pronounced fear greatly impaired decision-making. In the years following Hailey's disappearance, as I traveled the globe retrieving *other* people's children, I'd attributed my failure to act decisively in those early days to the sheer terror I experienced when I first learned my daughter had been abducted. After Tasha committed suicide, after the national news media moved on, after the feds packed up their gear and went home, I began to think more clearly. By then, I'd lost just about all hope of finding Hailey, and with that hope went the constant worry, the bottomless consternation, that I'd lost my little girl for good. Resigning myself to the mere possibility that I'd never again see my daughter alive unburdened me just enough to work as a private investigator specializing in child abduction cases for the next dozen years. And over those years, I'd like to think I'd done some good.

Jadine (fewer parts crippling fear, more parts laser focus) gripped my arm and spoke into my ear. 'So we either surrender, get dragged to the side of the road and executed—'

'Or,' I said, sliding my free hand into my go-bag, 'we set off a grenade and take as many with us as we can.'

'I don't like either option.'

'Neither do I. But unless your father stashed some magical fairy dust in your go-bag, those are about the only options we have.'

I waited, pondering whether Rusul Alharb could have known about our being transported in this truck. But then, who could have given us up? So few people knew about it: Deputy Secretary Jeffries, the lone Nigerian intelligence agent, the truck driver, who was supposedly a longtime contractor, completely trustworthy and trained by the armed forces.

'All right,' Jadine finally said as though she were settling on an after-dinner drink. 'If we're discovered, pull the pin.'

Only then did I fully register that I was already holding the grenade in my hand. As I wrapped my fingers tightly around its grooved center, I asked, 'Once I release the lever, how long do we have?'

'Three to five seconds, tops.'

The trailer door was now fully raised. Sunlight squeezed past the stacks.

I pulled the pin but held tight to the lever so that if they shot me, the grenade would fall and go off. Since we were situated at the very back of the trailer, we were only a few feet from the fuel tank. The explosion would likely ignite the gas, killing everyone within shouting distance. The thought of which was terribly unsettling. Not only were Jadine and I about to die, but we were about to do so alongside some of the worst humanity had to offer.

The jihadists started to unload the supplies while we sat silently eight towers back. I decided that when they reached the sixth stack, I'd release the lever and blow us all to hell. Not like a suicide bomber so much as a starship captain initiating self-destruct. Capture just wasn't an option here. Capture meant the worst kind of death.

Not that I found blowing myself to smithereens the least bit appealing. In fact, buried deep below my usual unyielding pessimism was the narrow hope that these bandits could carry away only so many boxes. That they'd steal fewer than the three or four stacks directly in front of us and let us on our merry way without Jadine and me ever being discovered. After all, what good would it do them to unload an entire truck of supplies only to have three-quarters of them stolen by fellow marauders because they needed to leave them behind? Their camp couldn't be too close to the road, could it? And surely the largest vehicles they had in this area so near Maiduguri were motorbikes.

Of course, if they were expecting us, this wasn't a robbery at all. This was a search and destroy. Jeffries had assured us that he masked his IP and that Rusul Alharb wouldn't know we or anyone else accessed the website given to us by Harun al-Haggi. But how could we know for sure that the leadership didn't possess superior computer technology? If they had learned that someone accessed the site, it wouldn't have taken them long to figure out that the leak of the web address likely came from the messenger who had carried the top-secret information from the Lake Chad Basin to Borno State.

Once they realized he was the prime suspect, it was just a matter of time before they contacted Konduga and learned that Harun al-Haggi had been carted off to Maiduguri by an official-looking man and woman, the former of whom was white. And if we had the messenger, it was only common sense that we'd deduce that the direction in which the message was carried suggested that the video originated in the Lake Chad Basin. Since there was only a single viable route from Maiduguri to Lake Chad, it wouldn't take a tactical genius to decide where to place the roadblock to search incoming vehicles.

While we awaited our fate (and at least in my head the fate of hundreds of others), memories and thoughts furiously fought their way to the forefront of my mind. What goes through the gray matter when you have less than a minute left to live? How much can one really reflect on forty-four years in fewer than sixty seconds?

In the end, I found nothing at all to contemplate but the permanent cessation of the consciousness of former US Marshal Simon Fisk.

I was unready to die. Of that I was sure.

But tough shit, because I wasn't getting much say in this; very few of us did.

Less than a minute later, the militants had cleared roughly half the stacks between us and them. In my right hand, I held the grenade. In my left, Jadine's hand. Both my palms were as drenched with sweat as a petite woman giving birth to a sixteen-pound baby.

I considered getting into a crouch but thought, *What good would that do?*

Two stacks left.

Three to five seconds, she'd said.

The reverberant pop of a gunshot outside the truck nearly caused me to lose my precarious hold on the sweat-slicked grenade.

The boxes ahead of us stopped moving.

A man called out in Hausa to the men in the rear. There was a brief back-and-forth I couldn't understand. Then it sounded as though the boxes of supplies were being carelessly replaced in the truck. I looked to Jadine, who waited until the trailer was fully repacked and the door latched down.

'Their commander executed our driver,' she said as the engine restarted. 'They've decided to steal the entire truck.'

I vigorously nodded to Jadine as though these events were encouraging, but washing over me was a terrible guilt that our driver's demise equaled our good fortune. But then, I was just about to take him out myself, wasn't I? I hadn't even given the matter a thought. How was that possible? How was it possible that Jadine hadn't thought of him either? Or had she? Had she decided the driver's life was expendable? Or that once Rusul Alharb found us hiding in the back of his truck, the driver was as good as dead anyway? Or had she considered him a soldier in this war on Rusul Alharb, a man who'd knowingly and willingly placed his life on the line for the better good? Or had she thought he betrayed us?

The bullet he took rendered that last scenario extremely unlikely.

In any event, at most this was merely a temporary reprieve. The militants would unload the truck at some point. And then they would discover us.

I slipped the pin back into the grenade with little doubt that I would be removing it again at the conclusion of this hot, jolting, and otherwise hellish drive.

TWENTY

We continued in the direction of Lake Chad. While Jadine was concentrating on our direction and travel time, I busied my mind with the intelligence I'd perused on the Lake Chad region back at the safe house in Maiduguri. Since we were continuing along the same route, it seemed reasonable to assume that was where we were heading. At least as far as we could travel on wheels. Jeffries had promised to have a small boat waiting for us on shore. Unfortunately, he also told us not to expect personnel, so we couldn't now count on a rescue attempt at road's end.

According to experts, Lake Chad was yet another victim in the ever-expanding global calamity known as man-made climate change. Satellite images clearly showed that the republic's namesake, one of the largest bodies of water in Africa, had shrunk by as much as ninety-five percent over the past half-century. The source of food for more than forty million people, Lake Chad was experiencing an ongoing decline in fish production, a grave reduction in its livestock population, and a constant degradation of its pasturelands. In other words, it was a prime location to set up shop if you were a terrorist organization.

Rusul Alharb's attack on Lake Chad five years earlier had been its first assault on the country of Chad as a whole. Launched from northeastern Nigeria, the assault was at least partly in reaction to the Chadian government's decision to intervene in the Rusul Alharb conflict raging in neighboring states. Shortly after the Lake Chad assault, two suicide bombings claimed the lives of dozens of innocent civilians in the Chadian capital of N'Djamena. It was Rusul Alharb's sick way of saying, *Welcome to the war.*

'Want to tell me about Kishana's old man?' I said.

She shook her head without looking at me. 'We shouldn't talk. They might hear us.'

'Not over the rumble of *this* engine, they won't. Besides, I've still got the grenade. Any way you look at it, Jade, we've got the upper hand.'

'Glad you can make jokes, Simon.'

'Oh, you know damn well that the only joke here is on me. And it's one hell of a laugh riot.'

She finally turned and locked her narrowed eyes on mine. 'I have *no* excuse for all the deception, Simon. It was mean, it was dirty, it was selfish – and you know what? I'd do it all over again. And you, of all people, know why. Because I *knew* you were my best damn shot at reaching Kishana alive. And I couldn't risk you saying no. I couldn't even risk your hesitation. And yes, Simon, I studied *everything* someone could learn about you without setting up a tent inside your head. I *knew* you insisted on working alone. I *knew* you would never in a million years consider taking a distraught parent with you on a mission, no matter how much they could contribute to a successful outcome.'

I said nothing; there was nothing to say. Nothing to do except change the subject. No use spending the final hours of your life in a heated argument with someone you deeply cared for, despite everything that had transpired over the past few days.

'How about you tell me about Kishana's old man?' I asked again.

'In order to do that,' she said with an exaggerated sigh of resignation, 'I'm going to need to take you all the way back to *my* old man.'

'Well,' I grumbled, 'as the corn stalk said to the farmer, "I'm all ears."'

James Coleman met Jadine's mother, Thabisa Chetty, in Johannesburg while he was a young, ambitious US Congressman giving a fiery speech to the first General Students' Council of South Africa. Fortuitously, Chetty was the student representative tasked with welcoming the congressman to Witwatersrand University and seeing to the needs of him and his staff during their five-day visit.

Unsurprisingly, host and guest connected immediately. Both

Coleman and Chetty were fiercely opposed to apartheid, and when they conversed on the subject, it was as if they were mind-melding or singing in an ancient alien language only they could comprehend. Thabisa Chetty had never met a man with such a well-articulated ideology of Black Consciousness, and Coleman had never met a young woman with such a flawless blend of beauty, intellect, and passion. They fell for one another within hours and, that first evening, Thabisa stayed in the modest accommodations she'd arranged for Coleman, while his Chief of Staff bunked aboard the small plane in which they'd arrived from their initial stop in Namibia. Thabisa would later describe the following five days as the most electrifying time of her life.

'Let me guess,' I said. 'Your mother never saw him again.'

Jadine dismissed me with a brief head shake. 'Before he returned to Washington, they'd promised to write each other.'

And both were as good as their word, depositing a brief handwritten message in the post on the same day they received theirs, so that said messages arrived like clockwork. There was only *one* break in the relationship's first fourteen weeks of correspondence, and it came when Thabisa most feared it would – in the days immediately following her own message to Coleman revealing that she was pregnant.

For nearly two weeks, Thabisa locked herself away in her dorm room, leaving only to retrieve the mail, which repeatedly betrayed her to the point of tears.

Then one day after returning empty-handed from the mail-room, she buried her face in her pillow and screamed. For nearly forty-five minutes, she earnestly contemplated suicide, only to be interrupted by a heavy knock on her door.

'*What?*' she shouted.

A tall, athletic girl she barely knew popped her head into the room. 'Phone call for you. Asked me to be quick about finding you because he's calling all the way from the States.'

When Thabisa placed the receiver of the payphone to her ear, Coleman instantly abated all her fears, assuring her he was absolutely delighted by the news of the pregnancy.

'Perhaps,' he told her, 'it's a sign from the Lord that we're meant to be together.'

That weekend they spoke over the phone for hours. Making plans, talking baby names, even touching on the subject of marriage.

Following a few weeks of mild debate, they agreed that shortly before Thabisa was due to give birth, she would fly First Class to the United States and deliver the baby in Falls Church, Virginia. The lone caveat, Coleman apprised her, was that they would need to be discreet. Congressmen, after all, came up for re-election every two years, and voters in his highly religious district simply wouldn't tolerate their congressional representative having a child out of wedlock. Nor would they tolerate a quickie marriage to a pregnant woman, let alone a dark-skinned foreigner. He loved their unborn daughter already, he assured her after they learned Thabisa would give birth to a girl, 'but, honey, she's political dynamite.'

Still, Coleman reassured her that he was in this relationship for the long haul, averred that he would be a full-time father to his daughter, and insisted that both mother and daughter would have unconditional love and ample financial support. They just needed to be careful. Because if Coleman's political opponents caught wind of the baby, they'd leak it to the news media, who would start asking questions. Before long, a reporter would deduce that the South African university student Thabisa Chetty became pregnant during Congressman James Coleman's official visit to Johannesburg.

'It would be beyond unseemly,' he told her.

Nevertheless, the congressman gave Thabisa every reason to believe that a more permanent arrangement was imminent once she gave birth to their baby.

'Less than a week after giving birth,' Jadine said, 'my mother realized he'd brought her there *just* to have me. Just so that I'd have full US citizenship.'

Two weeks later, a still-healing Thabisa Chetty returned to Johannesburg with her newborn daughter, a pack of broken promises, and no true means of support.

A few years later, Jadine added, her mother married a man of modest means named Luan Visser, and both mother and daughter proudly changed their last names from Chetty. Luan was a kind but sickly man who treated both Jadine and her

mother well but died a few weeks short of the couple's fifth
wedding anniversary. Thabisa, meanwhile, without having
finished her college degree, worked three jobs to support her
and Jadine by herself.

When I met Jadine at American University years later, she'd
just returned to the US for the first time since she was an
infant. Despite her dual citizenship, she had enrolled as a
foreign exchange student to remain as anonymous as possible.

While studying at American University, Jadine buried the
hatchet with her father, who had for nearly twenty years been
estranged from her. After earning her bachelor's degree in
political science, she grudgingly accepted Coleman's help to
send her to Georgetown Law School. Despite her reservations,
she agreed to keep their relationship secret so as not to harm
Coleman's political career, which he imagined would end with
nothing less than an eight-year stint at 1600 Pennsylvania
Avenue.

'I confess,' she said, 'that, at the time, I was intrigued by
the idea of secrecy and anonymity. I was drawn by the fantasy
of having a father with such power. By the time I applied for
law school, I was so tantalized by the prospect of being the
daughter of a bona fide Washington power player that I all
but forgot about my mother eight thousand miles away, the
woman who worked three jobs in order to raise me on her
own.'

Thabisa Chetty tragically died in a two-car motor vehicle
accident on a rural road north of Pretoria before Jadine ever
had a chance to see her again.

TWENTY-ONE

'After law school,' Jadine said in the gloom of the trailer, 'I went to work for the State Department. As an intelligence officer.'

I narrowed my eyes, already suspicious of the tale she was weaving. 'The State Department doesn't *have* intelligence officers,' I said, 'except maybe in Jason Bourne movies.'

She shook her head. 'That's not entirely accurate, Simon. It's a highly secretive program, which is to say the public isn't aware of its existence. *Congress* isn't even aware of it. But following nine/eleven, the State Department decided it needed its own intelligence officers in the field. So State's Bureau of Intelligence and Research, which at the time employed only a few hundred people whose jobs were strictly analytical, added a counterintelligence and espionage unit with several dozen agents to work in some of the world's most volatile areas, West Africa included.'

'But the bureau's a *civil* intelligence agency. You're telling me the State Department let loose in hot spots around the globe dozens of agents with virtually *no* formal training in espionage?'

'Hardly. The bureau hired a *private* intelligence agency to train us. All our instructors had either taught or trained extensively at Camp Peary.'

Camp Peary, more widely known as The Farm, was a highly classified 9,000-acre military camp near Williamsburg, Virginia. One of the nation's most secret federal facilities, The Farm was essentially bootcamp for agents assigned to the CIA's Clandestine Services Division. Needless to say, the instructors there were some of the best of the best.

'Does the Director of National Intelligence know about this program?' I asked.

'That depends on who the Director of National Intelligence *is* this week. You need to understand, Simon, that the State

Department took a bold but *necessary* initiative here. Four years later, when the Senate Select Committee on Intelligence issued its blistering report on pre-war intelligence on Iraq, only one agency – the State Department's Bureau of Intelligence and Research – was spared the awful performance review that the CIA and other US intelligence agencies received.'

'You knew something about Iraq that the CIA didn't?'

'Of course not. We shared everything one way or another. We all had the same intelligence on WMDs in Iraq. We just came to the correct *conclusions*.'

'So Kishana's father,' I said, circling back to my original question, 'you were what? His handler?'

She sighed, long and deep. 'Not long into the War on Terror, I was assigned to the US Embassy in Abuja. Back then, Ahmad was an academic, a professor of law and religious studies at the University of Maiduguri. I recruited him soon after I arrived at my post after targeting him at a conference on international environmental law in Nairobi.'

No surprise there. Intelligence agencies frequently recruited academics at conferences, even going so far as to host their own. Jadine went on to say that this gathering in Nairobi was the first sham conference staged by the State Department's new intelligence unit. And it was a great success.

'I began the recruitment just as I was taught, with a seemingly random encounter – what we call a "bump." Just a fleeting brush at a brunch buffet in the hotel's most casual restaurant. I had a tray of food in my hand and said something like, "It's not cheating on your diet when you're outside your home country, right?" He smiled at me. He may have even stopped to respond, but I kept walking. A day later, at the same restaurant, he came up to my table and asked me which country I called home. And we just started talking from there.'

'You were ordered to target him?'

She shook her head again. 'As an intelligence officer, you usually choose your own targets. You want someone valuable but not *so* valuable that they're going to be beating away other intelligence officers with a stick. Ahmad was young and relatively unknown. But as a professor at Maiduguri University

– where radicals were preaching religious fundamentalism in the square – he was in a prime position to gain actionable information.'

At the end of brunch that second day, Ahmad asked Jadine if she'd like to have dinner with him. She played coy and suggested something a bit less formal, like going out for drinks. He smiled awkwardly and explained he was a devout Muslim and therefore forbidden to consume alcohol. As she apologized for her presumptuousness, she watched all traces of doubt and suspicion drain from his face. When she met him again for a rather formal dinner that evening, his eyes were filled not only with longing but trust.

'After dinner we went for a walk. That's when I'd planned to make my pitch to him. We were walking by the Nairobi Arboretum when I stopped, turned to him, and said, "Ahmad, I'm from the . . ." I never got the rest of the words out because his lips were on mine. And it was a kiss like none I'd ever experienced before.'

'Present company excepted, I assume.'

She smiled in the darkness. 'You *were* a good kisser, if I remember correctly. But this was different. There was a magic in it that just doesn't exist when you're drunk on Miller High Life in a guy's freshman dorm room.'

'Hey, it's the "*Champagne* of Beers."'

'Plus, your freshman dorm room smelled like feet.'

I allowed myself a chuckle. 'My roommate Terry had a terrible problem with foot odor. Kept him out of medical school, or so I've heard.'

'Anyway, before I knew what hit me, Ahmad and I were in his room back at the hotel and in his bed making love.'

'I guess the sin of fornication doesn't rise to the level of sipping a Heineken.'

'It was his first time, Simon. Ever. And it started him down the path of believing in a modern Islam.'

'I bet it did,' I said, immediately wishing I hadn't.

But she ignored the comment and moved on. 'We spent the next afternoon at Nairobi National Park watching baboons and black rhinos . . .'

She paused as though she hadn't anticipated getting this

deep into the story and had to search her memory for what happened next.

Or to search for another lie.

But, no. Given the circumstances, this was as close as Jadine would come to making a dying declaration. Regardless of her motives, she had no more need to lie. Neither of us did. And, admittedly, it was tempting to cut her off mid-sentence and divulge to her what – and just how much – she meant to me in that moment. In truth, though, I wasn't sure whether these deep feelings were truly for Jadine or for my younger self. My life before Tasha, before tragedy ever struck. Did I really just want to return to that fork in the road and – despite my love for Tasha, despite my love for Hailey – choose the path least likely to result in twelve years of savage pain?

After all, three weeks (which was how long Jadine and I were together) was hardly any time at all. Yet during those twenty-plus days, Jadine and I had shared so many experiences. We'd driven an hour and change on the back of my first bike, a Suzuki RMX250, from American University to Baltimore's Camden Yards to attend a late-season Orioles–Red Sox game. On school nights we watched nearly every classic black-and-white movie we could name (she named many; I named very few). We even spent an entire weekend in a mud-drenched tent at a massive music festival at the Old Latrobe in Pennsylvania, jamming to bands like Green Day, the Chili Peppers, Nine Inch Nails, and Korn. Those three weeks were some of the greatest of my life. Some of the most electrifying, you could say.

Jadine said, 'I finally told Ahmad that night after dinner at the hotel. He wasn't angry – I almost wished he was. I could see the pain of betrayal on his face. Even though we'd only known each other a few days, I'd wounded him, badly. I'd not only lied to him; I'd caused him to sin. I'd corrupted him in the very way the Islamic radicals were telling everyone Western women would, if given half the chance.'

Still, Ahmad loved her and believed her when she said that she loved him. So, following the conference, when they returned to Nigeria – he to Maiduguri University and she to the US Embassy in Abuja – they continued their relationship.

In secret, of course. Jadine already had years of experience with hush-hush relations, thanks to her father who was, by then, the junior US Senator from Maryland.

Over the next several months, Jadine and Ahmad rendez-voused in cities across the African continent, from Marrakech to Abidjan, Cairo to Kampala.

Meanwhile, at Jadine's urging, Ahmad formed a relationship with an emerging Islamic figure named Mohammed Yakubu, who'd found his way to Maiduguri to preach to a group of followers who would, before long, become known around the city as the Nigerian Taliban.

TWENTY-TWO

Mohammed Yakubu, a heavy-set man who dressed in loose-fitting robes and no shoes, had recently begun his own mosque, a makeshift structure set outside his own home. Later, he would use his father-in-law's land to build an entire complex in the Maiduguri neighborhood known as Freeway Quarters.

Although he had little formal education, Yakubu was well versed in Islamic studies and (at least, early on) attracted to his cause intellectuals, including doctors, lawyers, and university professors. So Ahmad's friendship with Yakubu did not ring false.

At least not in the beginning.

Several months into their friendship, however, Yakubu traveled alone to Saudi Arabia for the Hajj, the annual Islamic pilgrimage to Mecca, Islam's holiest city. When he returned, his teachings and beliefs became far more radical.

Over time, as Yakubu's rhetoric grew increasingly extreme, more and more mainstream Muslims distanced themselves from the preacher, leaving Ahmad in a situation fraught with danger.

Before long, Ahmad – the intelligent university professor who preferred life's simple pleasures – had mutated into a man of countless secrets and lies. In Maiduguri, Ahmad Abdulaziz was a devout Muslim dabbling in fundamentalism. Meanwhile, in Abuja, he had secretly married Jadine Visser, a lapsed Christian, who had recently given birth to their secret daughter, Kishana, who'd been conceived out of wedlock.

Knowing that any one of his many secrets and lies could get him killed, Ahmad wanted out.

'I convinced him to stay in,' Jadine said quietly, as tears streamed from both eyes. 'I'm the one who pushed him to continue his relationship with Yakubu because the intel Ahmad was feeding me was making me a fucking *star* at the State

Department. I told Ahmad, "The more radical Yakubu becomes, the more crucial it is to have someone like you on the inside. You're not doing *me* any favors by staying in – you're saving lives." And I truly believed it – at least that second part. And the second part, I figured, was all that mattered. Yet I also knew damn well that I was putting my career before Kishana's father. Ahmad kept his life in jeopardy for years, Simon, solely because I pressured him to do so.'

Today, Jadine had little doubt about the toll the years of constant dread and treachery took on Ahmad's mind.

'So, if he's a terrorist,' she said, 'I *made* him a terrorist. And if my baby daughter dies in a suicide bombing, I might as well have strapped the vest on to her myself.'

Once Yakubu's fundamentalism set him on a collision course with mainstream Islam, he turned away from the intellectuals and toward Maiduguri's poor and aimless youths. Kids who had dropped out of school, become addicted to drugs, or whose futures were otherwise marred.

In a city rife with corruption and soul-crushing poverty, Yakubu's anti-establishment rhetoric rang true, while his charisma was undeniable. Despite his tough messaging and considerable physical size, Yakubu effortlessly came off as warm and inviting. And his message was simple enough for even the least educated to grasp; plainly put, Yakubu and his followers were standing firm against a world that was becoming increasingly evil.

With his cult of personality and anti-government message, Yakubu deftly persuaded the disaffected masses that Nigeria's secular leadership was the cause of their most pressing social and economic problems – and that the only solution to those problems was a swift return to strict sharia law.

'After a couple of years,' Jadine said, 'I could tell that even though Ahmad completely disagreed with the radical messaging, he had become enamored of the messenger and his followers. Yet I still kept him in.'

'Did you sense then that Ahmad was beginning to believe the rhetoric himself?'

'Not at all. Ahmad was – Ahmad *is* – a smart man. And

Yakubu's strict fundamentalism didn't stop at forbidding Western education. He also taught his wildest, craziest beliefs; he was convinced the earth was flat, and he disputed Darwin's theory of evolution. How could any intelligent man with all his faculties actually believe such . . .'

She didn't need to finish the thought. It was a question I had considered often over the past twenty years and never discovered an answer to.

As Yakubu's popularity grew, so did his group of followers, which had come to be known as Rusul Alharb. Radicals around the world took notice. Including al-Qaeda leader Osama bin Laden, the Saudi Arabian terrorist credited with perpetrating the deadly attacks on the World Trade Center and the Pentagon on September 11, 2001. By funneling money through a London-based Islamic charity, Osama bin Laden afforded Yakubu the ability to expand, along with his following.

Meanwhile, for seven years, Ahmad straddled the knife's edge of living a double life.

'Then,' Jadine said abruptly, 'roughly a decade ago, there was an uprising in Maiduguri.'

The chaos started during a funeral procession for Rusul Alharb members who had been killed in a traffic accident.

'Some of Yakubu's followers spotted a fellow mourner being stopped and humiliated by police. Yakubu's followers intervened by stealing the police officers' guns. The police opened fire and wounded at least twenty members of Rusul Alharb.'

Immediately following the incident, a fiery Mohammed Yakubu called for an armed jihad against Nigerian police and security forces.

Hours after the funeral, several dozen Rusul Alharb members rushed a police station armed with military-grade guns and grenades. On-duty officers fled to gather reinforcements in order to prevent the militants from breaking into the armory. Although police were successful in protecting their weapons, police leadership knew they needed to respond – and respond they did, by launching a raid on a shanty town where many Rusul Alharb members were known to live.

A gun battle ensued. In the end, more than fifty were dead and another two hundred had been arrested.

'After the raid,' Jadine said, 'Yakubu publicly stated that he and his followers were ready to fight together and die together. There was such chaos at the time that Ahmad was having difficulty contacting me. By then, I wanted him out, but my superiors pleaded to keep him in for a few more days, at least until the current situation played out.'

In the two days that followed, Rusul Alharb attacked state police headquarters in Maiduguri, as well as a prison and police training facilities.

'Ahmad had previously apprised us that these were possible targets, so, for the most part, security forces were ready. But there was still so much bloodshed.'

Then, on the third day of the uprising, Nigerian security forces sought to crush Rusul Alharb by launching a brutal night-time raid on their mosque and headquarters.

By sunrise, much of the Freeway Quarters neighborhood had been leveled and piles of bodies lined the streets.

Somehow Yakubu escaped.

But his luck didn't hold for long.

After witnessing more than a thousand deaths in less than a week, the Nigerian government had no intention of allowing the man who incited the terrible violence to get away. Within a few days, Yakubu was arrested by heavily armed soldiers in a barn on his father-in-law's property, not so far from his demolished mosque.

He was interrogated by Nigerian security forces, then handed off to police.

'Alive,' Jadine emphasized.

Within hours, Yakubu's dead body lay riddled with bullets in the dirt outside police headquarters.

Accounts of what transpired were inconsistent, to say the least. One Nigerian police official claimed that Yakubu was shot while trying to escape. A second insisted Yakubu was killed in the crossfire during a gun battle between Rusul Alharb militants and Nigerian security forces. Civilian witnesses denied both accounts. In fact, most unbiased reports indicated that Yakubu had been handcuffed, seated on the ground and praying outside police headquarters, when three irate officers opened fire, summarily executing the Rusul Alharb leader without charge or trial.

'Ahmad was one of the witnesses,' Jadine said. 'He watched officers shoot his friend, first in the stomach, then in the chest, then in the head. Ahmad was never the same after that. Not mentally, not physically, not spiritually.'

TWENTY-THREE

T he brakes screeched like a pack of rabid hell hounds, dirt and rocks kicked up against the undercarriage, and the titanic truck carrying us in its belly finally skidded to a stop. My heart pounded hard; my own guts threatened to spill their meager contents. I was dizzy with fear and profoundly loathed myself for it. For the first time in my life, I genuinely felt like a coward.

Ironically, the very idea of being a coward was always one of my greatest fears. It was why I took my beatings in the schoolyard and never breathed a word of them. Why I stood up to the old man, even when he came at me with his belt. Why I wanted so badly to prove myself as a marshal by hunting fugitives rather than sitting at a desk handling high-end criminal forfeitures. Being a coward, in my mind, had historically been unacceptable.

And it still was.

Only cowards gave up, gave in, without a fight. No question, I'd needed to accept innumerable personal flaws over the past twenty years – since Hailey's disappearance, I'd become cynical, vicious, hard, unforgiving – but the one thing I needn't ever accept was being a coward.

I pushed the grenade back into my go-bag.

When I pulled my hand out, it was no longer shaking.

I wasn't going to take my own life to avoid the wrath of a group of fanatics. If they wanted me dead, they were going to have to come at me like soldiers. Let them shoot me, stab me, burn me, hang me. Let them cut my fucking head off.

Whatever happened, I decided, Simon Fisk wasn't about to make it easy for them.

I lifted my assault rifle and motioned for Jadine to do the same. I rose on one knee and parted the two stacks of boxes directly in front of me just enough to create a line of fire. Jadine followed suit. We raised our weapons, put our eyes to

the sights, our fingers inside the trigger guards. And waited
for the trailer door to roll open.

'You think they're going to leave the truck like this
overnight?'

'Not without a good number of well-armed guards, they're
not.' I lowered my rifle and sank my hand back into my go-bag.
'But we're getting the hell out of here while it's still dark.'

From my bag, I produced a twelve-inch tactical survival
hunting knife that I nearly left back in the forest because of
the two pounds it added to my pack.

'That's going to make significant noise,' she said.

'A necessary evil if we're going to see how many are out
there and where they're positioned.'

It had been roughly an hour since we had heard voices
outside, fifteen minutes since the last footsteps. We wouldn't
be alone, but we might not have as much company as I initially
expected. Made sense now that I considered it. After all, who
the hell would have the balls and/or be stupid enough to steal
from Rusul Alharb?

'You sure that knife is strong enough to punch through the
wall of the truck?' Jadine asked.

'I gave the truck a good, hard look before we left Maiduguri.
Not necessarily thinking of stabbing holes from the inside but
hoping the walls were thick enough to stop small-caliber bullets
shot at the truck during the drive. I came away thinking that
if we were hit by anything more powerful than a slingshot,
we were screwed. The frame is made of steel, maybe fifteen
or sixteen inches deep. But the body is nothing but aluminum.
This knife should cut through the wall like warm butter.'

My leg muscles felt as if they were tearing as I pushed
myself off my haunches and stood. 'I'm going to make the
hole at eye level, so we'll be able to duck behind a few rows
of boxes if we take on fire.'

Jadine slowly rose to her feet. 'I'll start clearing a path toward
the trailer door in case we see an opening to run for it.'

In the darkness, I felt around the cool surface inside the
trailer. There were certainly spots that would be easier to punch
through than others, but I couldn't exactly start tapping along

the wall to find them. Once I used the knife, we wouldn't have much time. But as long as I avoided the beams, I doubted I'd hit a snag.

Once Jadine cleared a path to the trailer door, we strapped on our go-bags. The door locked from the inside, not the out, so, aside from the noise, opening the door wouldn't be a worry when the time came. It was questions such as who would greet us and with what level of firepower that were of much greater concern.

We wouldn't know until we had eyes. And we wouldn't have eyes until I punched a hole in the side of the truck.

'Ready?' I said, wiping the sweat from my head and checking to confirm Jadine was in position. 'Here goes.'

The sound of the knife striking aluminum echoed throughout the trailer as though a bomb went off. But there was no audible reaction from the outside, which either meant the noise had been muted by the outer wall of the trailer or we were out here alone. If we were, I was sure we wouldn't be for long.

Rocking the edge of the knife back and forth, I widened the hole. As soon as I was relatively certain there wasn't a gun pressed up against the side of the truck, I put my eye to it.

'We're not at a compound,' I said quietly. 'We hit the end of the road. We're at the edge of the lake. Assuming they're taking the stolen supplies into Chad, they're going to need to do so with boats.'

'See anyone?'

'Not yet.' I placed my ear against the hole. 'But I do hear voices. Faint, far off. Two, maybe three men. I just can't tell which direction their voices are coming from.'

'Raising the trailer door will make a hell of a racket. The old tracks make it sound like a freight train speeding by.'

'Next time, ask your dad to pack us some WD-40.'

'Next time?'

'Figure of speech,' I said. Then, 'We're going to need to create a diversion.'

'With a diversion, we'll be *enticing* them to come to us.'

I tried to play several different scenarios out in my head. In Maiduguri, we'd traded our earth-toned civilian clothes for black tactical gear. From sleek, high-traction Under Armour boots to Blackhawk Hellstorm balaclavas covering most of our head, face, and neck. All but our eyes.

'It's pretty damn dark out there,' I said. 'Best-case scenario: if the diversion is significant enough, we may be able to use the night as cover to get away clean.'

'Get away to where exactly?'

'Looks like a marsh out there to our right. To the left: flat lands, no woods, no cover. Which means we'll need to make for the water and hide in the reeds. They're tall enough. Let's just hope the water's not too deep near the shore.' I turned in her direction. 'You a good swimmer, Jade?'

'What do you think?'

'I think you probably trained with SEAL Team Six.'

'All right,' she said. 'That's best-case. What's worst-case?'

'Worst-case scenario: we're spotted as soon as the door rises and need to pick off the nearest militants with our assault rifles, then book for the water in the hope of reaching it before the arrival of reinforcements.'

Jadine said nothing.

I shifted and said, 'I'm going to need to punch a second hole.'

'What for?'

'So that I can see what I'm shooting at.'

'What *are* you shooting at?'

'There's a pick-up truck out there – an old Toyota Hilux, I think. Painted black and draped with their goddamn pirate flags. We didn't hear any vehicles along the way, so it must have been parked here already. Maybe waiting for the hijacked truck to arrive with the stolen supplies. It's far enough that it would create a genuine diversion, yet close enough that I think I can hit the gas tank.'

'You *think* you can hit it?'

'Reasonably confident.'

'Would that even cause an explosion?'

'Using incendiary bullets, it will.'

'Do you want me to take the shot?'

I looked back at her, hoping she could read my expression in the darkness or at least accept my silence as a definitive answer.

'I didn't think so,' she said. 'I'll get ready to lift the trailer door.'

I stabbed a second hole just above the first one. Twisted the edge of the knife to widen it, then put my eye to it. No good. I stabbed another hole. Widened it. Held my eye to it. It didn't make the world's greatest gun sight, but it would do.

'Ready,' she said. 'I'll lift the door fully as soon as we hear the explosion.'

'Have your weapon ready.'

'No worries there, Simon. I'm locked and loaded.'

'Right, then. On three.' I pressed my eye against one of the upper holes, said, 'One.' Pressed the barrel of my weapon up against the lowest and said, 'Two.'

I love you, Hailey.

'Three.'

I squeezed the trigger.

The resulting explosion was deafening and produced a light show worthy of Pink Floyd or Zeppelin.

TWENTY-FOUR

Jadine leapt from the lip of the trailer and made for the marsh. Currently less a lake and more a seasonal wetland, the freshwater surrounding the expansive maze of bite-sized islands in the Lake Chad Basin ranged in depth from just a few feet to no more than a couple of dozen. Since the water was stagnant, swimming through it wouldn't present a problem. The three bastards running toward the explosion with AK-47s, however, were a different story altogether.

As stealthily as possible, I jumped down and followed Jadine's route to the shoreline. On the other side of the truck, I paused to listen for reinforcements. In the stillness of the night, I was able to hear them perfectly and determined they were much too far away to fire with any accuracy. I poked my head around the corner and looked through my sight to determine the size of their contingent.

Too many. Too close. We'd need to move quickly or risk a bullet to the back.

As soon as I had spun round and started running again, I knew I had been spotted. Kicking up sand, I lowered my head and pushed forward. Just as the bullets began hitting the beach, I ducked into the reeds and vanished in the black water.

While those first shots sounded small and distant, they quickly became louder, closer. I held my breath and ducked my head underwater, pushing myself as hard as I could, hoping to disappear in the pitch before the Rusul Alharb fighters reached the shore. Since there were plenty of islands within reach, Jadine and I could swim in virtually any direction. Which meant that as long as we remained out of sight, once we were farther from the beach, they'd likely need to get lucky to hit us.

Or for us to be unlucky, I supposed.

And we needn't be unlucky just on the Nigerian side of the lake. In the pitch dark, it was impossible to know for certain which islands were uninhabited. The lake region's geography meant it was an ideal spot for smuggling networks to set up shop. And because of its terrible poverty and ever-worsening conditions (including looming food and water shortages), it was fertile ground for Rusul Alharb recruitment. In other words, it was a flip of the coin whether we came ashore on a quiet little fishing village or a quiet little Rusul Alharb hideout.

But staying in the water any longer than necessary wasn't an appealing option either. Buried within the intelligence reports on the Central African lake region was the fact that the Chari River ran through Lake Chad. The Chari was a 900-mile waterway known as one of the few remaining marine habitats on earth of a species called *Dracunculus medinensis*, which roughly translated as 'the little dragon from Medina.'

The name had struck a rather disgusting bell for me. Years earlier, I'd seen former President Jimmy Carter on one of those late-night talk shows. He was publicizing the Carter Center, which had initiated a program to wipe out the guinea worm, a species thought to be near eradication. Only eight countries had failed to earn certification for erasing the existence of the nematode within its borders. All the countries were located in Africa; all were actively engaged in some form of protracted civil war.

Since neither Carter nor the host (nor anyone, I supposed) could adequately detail the sheer foulness of the worm or what it did to the human body, the producer supplied visual aids – without any warnings advising viewer discretion, I might add. Before I knew what was happening, my tired eyes were locked on a video of one of these snow-white guinea worms, some two or three feet in length, being slowly extracted from the skin of a screaming human being.

Jimmy Carter offered the fun facts that the guinea worms were probably the 'fiery serpents' of the Israelites described in the Bible and that the method of coaxing the worm from the flesh by meticulously wrapping it around a stick over the course of several excruciating days was most likely the inspiration for one of my father's favorite emblems, the Rod of Asclepius, the universal symbol of medicine.

How's that for a tie pin?

Carter went on to relay that a person became infected by the guinea worm simply by ingesting the microscopic copepod that contaminated fresh water. Once ingested, the copepod was dissolved by stomach acid and the larvae migrated through the wall of the intestine, where they matured into adults and sexually reproduced within the tissue. Following copulation, the male died while the female migrated to the person's subcutaneous tissue, where it remained for roughly *one full year*. Until, finally, a blister formed on the skin's surface, usually on the lower extremities but occasionally on the scrotum. Only once that blister ruptured could the jolly practice of extraction begin.

I lifted my head from the water and decided I'd come ashore the first piece of land I saw.

Only I couldn't see much at all. I half hoped Rusul Alharb's incoming fire would move in closer to provide a little light. The moon was a sliver and the stars overhead appeared surprisingly dull, considering there was virtually no light pollution emanating from the region.

Moments later, I wanted like all hell to take back my wish. The gunfire was now thunderous against the calmness of the water. I made the mistake of looking back. In seconds, the bullets would reach me unless I became invisible again. I drew a deep breath and went under, kicking my feet as quickly as I could without them breaching the surface.

Underwater, the crackle of gunfire was replaced by the eerie hiss of bullets searching for targets near the lake floor. As I came up for air, I imagined a shot penetrating the back of my skull and nearly flew into another panic before ducking back below.

Worried about losing Jadine, I briefly lifted my head again.

A short distance to my right, I spotted Jadine's head emerge from the water.

She was breathing hard. Nearly as hard as I was.

'This way,' she managed.

As had become my MO since those first hours back in the Sambisa forest, I dutifully and gratefully followed her lead, this time with absolute confidence I was making the right decision.

TWENTY-FIVE

Thirty minutes later we crawled ashore a nanoscopic island in the dark.

'Have we crossed into Chad?' I asked once I was positive the Rusul Alharb militants back on the beach had quit expending bullets on us.

'Impossible to tell for sure,' she said, hands on her knees, catching her breath like I was. 'But due to its shrinking, there's not much of the lake left in Nigeria. So we're likely either in Chad or Cameroon.'

Our destination was Bol on the Chadian side of the lake. Bol, which happened to be the capital of the lake region, was the town where Harun al-Haggi was physically handed the highly confidential message with the web address containing Kishana Coleman's professed martyrdom video. That al-Haggi had received the message less than a half-mile from the local airport suggested that the video was filmed elsewhere, probably somewhere south or east of the Lake Chad region. Although it was unlikely that a flight plan had been filed with Bol's small, low-traffic airport (which consisted of little more than a paved runway), someone in the area had surely laid eyes on the plane and, at the very least, could tell us from which direction it had materialized. If so, we'd acquire that information one way or the other, carrot or the stick; at this point it didn't much matter. Not to Jadine. And not to me either.

'We need a boat,' she said.

'You won't get any argument from me.'

My arms were sore. My legs felt like drenched matchsticks. I was having trouble filling my lungs with oxygen. This job, this mission, was taking more out of me than any that came before it. Neither of us had seen the boat that Jeffries and what's-his-name had supposedly arranged for us. Which, I supposed under the circumstances, was a plus, since it

prevented Rusul Alharb from following us into the lake. But
it did beg the question: Why wasn't the boat at the end of the
only road from Maiduguri to Lake Chad as we were told it
would be? Had someone stolen it earlier? Or had it never been
there to begin with?

'To find a boat,' Jadine said, 'we're going to need to find
people.'

'That proposition,' I admitted, 'is substantially less
attractive.'

Jadine reached into her go-bag and produced her binoculars. First, she peered back at the shore, where we'd last
seen the Rusul Alharb militants. Seemingly satisfied that we
were alone, she redirected her gaze outwardly toward the
lake.

'There,' she said, pointing north. 'In the distance. I see a
contained fire.'

'How far?'

'Here,' she said, handing over her binoculars, 'see for
yourself.'

I refocused the binoculars and peered north, relieved to see
little *but* the fire. Although I wasn't in love with the idea of
getting back into the worm-infested waters, I was at least
mildly relieved that we wouldn't likely be contending with
any larger lifeforms. The shrinking of the lake had all but
eliminated most of the lake region's mighty carnivores such
as its lions and leopards. Given the current shallowness of the
water, we were also unlikely to run into any hippopotamuses
or rhinoceroses. According to the intel, some less lovable
species *had* thrived due to the lake's contraction. Most notably,
rodents. Amphibians and reptiles were still very much present
as well. Crocs, rock pythons, spitting cobras all continued to
call the lake region home.

Minutes later, with our automatic rifles above our heads,
we moved slowly through the water. In most areas, the lake
reached up to Jadine's chin and my neck. Although there
seemed to be very few steep drop-offs, we were careful to
avoid them.

All the while we navigated the island maze, we kept our
eyes fixed on the man-made fire in case it was suddenly

extinguished (and, with it, all hopes of making it through the rest of this night unscathed).

By the time we reached what we'd begun calling Fire Island, we were both exhausted. We collapsed on to the beach to catch our wind, while our hands remained on our rifles.

As we waited, a pair of unarmed teenagers, dressed in T-shirts depicting the wrong World Series champions for the previous two seasons, cautiously approached us. Spoken in Chad were two main languages – French and Arabic – and more than 120 local languages. The teenagers who addressed us spoke unmistakable Arabic, and I was once again grateful to have a linguist like Jadine on my team, despite her withholding this vital information from me earlier.

Once they'd relayed a message, Jadine turned to me. 'They welcomed us to their island. Their village is a short distance from here, and they'd like to take us to meet the village elders.'

'Your call,' I said.

'Let's follow them,' she said, rising from the rocky sand. 'But remain vigilant.'

The boys led us toward the fire, which stood at the center of a diminutive fishing village a short distance away. There, we were immediately greeted by a half-dozen others, including the village chief.

I felt slightly embarrassed to be carrying an infantry assault rifle into their small fishing village but knew that could change in a heartbeat. I'd heard too many stories of soldiers in Iraq and Afghanistan approaching seemingly friendly civilians, only to be overtaken and killed in an ambush. My old friend Chris Wicker's younger brother Steve had been one of them. He'd joined the Marines shortly after the September 11 attacks. Was deployed to Afghanistan and killed in action in the Dai Chopan district in Zabul Province fewer than twenty-four months later.

After several minutes of introductions, we were seated around the campfire, Jadine and I consuming our evening rations as opposed to our host's offering of fresh fish from Lake Chad. We insisted we didn't want to impose, especially in light of the looming food shortage, though our real reason for refusing had much more to do with the risk of becoming infected by the guinea worm. Apparently, Jadine was none too fond of the species either.

After we finished eating, Jadine asked the chief about their island the way one would inquire about an old friend's newly constructed ranch in San Bernardino.

With a weighty sigh, the chief slowly responded in heavily accented English.

'When I was a child,' he said, 'the water off our shore was so deep I did not know if there was a bottom. So many fish, you could not skip a stone on the lake without hitting three. Our island – this island that is now barren – was thick with greens. Which helped our cows to be fat with milk.' He shook his head at the obvious devastation that had overtaken the island. 'Whatever were our problems back then, we at least always had food and water.

'Then, as teenagers, my friends and I, we see that the lake is retreating from our shores. The mainland, once so far away, now looked to be coming right for us. We tell this to our parents, and they tell us, "Do not be so stupid; everything is well." But we have two eyes like everyone else. We see the reeds. We see the water lilies. We see that the trading boats need to use alternate waterways.

'And then, years later, we are afflicted with the drought. We are afflicted with the famine. And they can no longer say, "Do not be so stupid; everything is well." Because why, then, are we so hungry? Why are we sick and dying, the old and young both? Why cannot the medicine man make his medicine?

'We grow up and grow old facing these problems, for thirty years, finding small ways to resolve them. Then, on top of all this – on top of the drought, on top of the famine – we are afflicted with Rusul Alharb. They come to our islands with their guns and their machetes and they take away entire villages. They make our daughters into their wives and our sons into their soldiers. They take our mothers and our sisters and turn them into slaves. For the few who are spared, there is nothing left. They take our fish. They take our cattle. They take our harvest. And because they promise to return, from our own homes our people must run and hide.

'They say they are Muslims and yet they burn to the ground

our mosques. They say they are fighting this fight *for* us, then they behead our families, our friends. They set us on fire, burn us alive. And what can Chad do, as weak as this country is? Just a small army with very few weapons. No match are they for Rusul Alharb. Instead, the government bans our fishing boats. Why? Because Rusul Alharb uses fishing boats. Without our fishing boats, we cannot trade. We cannot feed our cattle. We have nothing to eat. We have nothing to drink. We can only waste away and wait to die.'

As he spoke, I took in the small fishing village. The straw hut directly in front of us looked like something drawn by a child. Like a bundle of pick-up sticks had been dropped randomly from the sky and bound together loosely only at the very top. Life here was like an unfunny parody of what we in the West imagined it was. Coupled with the Rusul Alharb threat, life in the Lake Chad region was worse than I ever envisioned.

I finished my water rations but remained so damned thirsty that I considered risking the worm. But no. Dying of thirst *had* to be the far better fate, hadn't it? It couldn't be worse, I was sure.

The chief went on to tell us that Chad's humanitarian situation was further complicated by the major armed conflict in Sudan, which had been raging now for nearly twenty years. The War in Darfur, part of the Sudanese Civil Wars, gained international notoriety early on, when, in response to rebel groups accusing the Sudanese government of oppressing Darfur's non-Arabs, the government commenced a campaign of ethnic cleansing against those same non-Arabs, a move that resulted in the deaths of hundreds of thousands of civilians. The genocide in Darfur naturally chased hundreds of thousands of Sudanese refugees on to Chadian lands. Refugees who competed for Chad's scarce resources.

In the meantime, Chad was enduring a civil war of its own. The Chadian Civil War pit the Arab Muslims of the north against the Sub-Saharan Christians of the south. For years, power swung between the two sides like a pendulum. Once one side gained leadership, the other side started an armed revolution to counter it. Further fueling the conflict was a proxy war between Chad's neighbor to the north, Libya, and Chad's former colonial power, France. And while the Chadian government aided neighboring Sudan's rebels, the Sudanese government propped up Chad's rebels, making all but certain that the only real winners in the region were the international arms merchants.

'The end of your Cold War,' the chief said, 'created many opportunities for illegal weapons dealers. After politics and technology made nations' arsenals outdated, they brought those weapons to Africa. And Africa – all too ready and willing to part with its people's money and natural resources – could not get enough of them.'

TWENTY-SIX

L ater in the evening, I stared into the yellow, red-rimmed eyes of a thirteen-year-old boy and for a moment thought I understood how joining Rusul Alharb might be an option for those who had no other options.

In the light of the fire, I could see that the boy's dark skin was taut; his jaw muscles were protruding. His face was badly scarred; a deep cut ran down the center of his nose and a pair of diagonal lines were slashed into each sunken cheek.

The chief placed his arm around the boy and said, 'The government must be made to understand that force alone will not defeat Rusul Alharb. Not when they are able to recruit so easily. Chop off one of its arms and another grows back. Everyone knows you cannot defeat a monster like this.'

I thought of Danjuma. Hoped he was by now safely at the US Embassy in Abuja. That American personnel had seen to it that he received a hot meal and a warm, comfortable bed. Undoubtedly the first real bed he'd ever see, let alone sleep in.

'This boy, Isa,' the chief continued, 'he went with Rusul Alharb for six months, then returned home to his village, sick and hungry. Angry that he was lied to. Isa knows things about the terrorists that no one outside of the group could possibly know. So why does the government of Chad not give to this boy a voice? Why do they not listen to him? If Isa were to go to the Chadian army with this information to try to help them defeat the terrorists, the soldiers would most certainly torture and kill him. So he cannot go. He does not go. Instead, he hides. He watches other boys be tricked into joining Rusul Alharb. And he waits for them to come home. But very few ever do. Isa himself was lucky just to get away with his life.'

'Do you receive any humanitarian aid?' Jadine asked.

'Our government, they chase away humanitarian aid workers by trying to utilize them as slaves of the state. They try to

direct what the humanitarians do and how they do it. They try
to control which areas and which people receive aid in the
first place. Once they do this, humanitarians are no longer
neutral. No longer impartial. No longer are they independent.
They are no longer humanitarians; instead, they are pawns of
the state, moved around the chessboard by government leaders
in order to play and win at their political games.'

'Until they solve the humanitarian crisis,' I said, 'the Rusul
Alharb mess is only going to get worse.'

The chief nodded his head. 'You would think that it is only
common sense that instead of trying to kill every fighter in
Rusul Alharb, the government of Chad should address the
reasons boys like Isa join these groups in the first place. Until
they stop recruitment, they will not stop the attacks. And they
will not stop recruitment until they give these young boys a
choice. A chance at a different life. A *better* life. Offer them
something more. Something Rusul Alharb is not offering them.
Offer them a future. Do not just tell them; *show* them how
this will be done. These children, by the time they join Rusul
Alharb, they are not stupid. Some are less easily fooled than
their elders. They are smart; they can make good choices.
These children, they are not something to be exterminated like
bugs. These children are the region's future.'

That night, Jadine and I bunked in the hut belonging to the
chief, who slept outside. Although we initially pushed back
on the offer, the chief eventually insisted in a way that made
us realize we would be insulting him if we slept anywhere
else.

Over the course of the next few hours, I twisted and turned
and suffered terrible dreams.

In the years following college graduation, I thought it was
strange that I was still having night terrors about being
unprepared as I sat down to take a major exam. Although I
eventually realized the images were merely representative of
a broader anxiety issue, I'd wished that just once the Simon
Fisk of my dreams would stand up and say, 'I already got my
degree. I'm not taking any more of your goddamn exams.
Now I'm going across the street for a drink.'

I didn't want to do any more public speaking either. Early in my career, when I was tasked with giving a PowerPoint present-ation at a single meeting with the Marshals, I'd nearly shit my pants. But at least I was wearing them. In my dreams, I never once spoke in public with clothes on. In my dreams, for some deranged reason, I'd have to make every big speech buck-ass naked.

Once Hailey went missing, I longed for those being-unprepared-for-a-test nightmares of the previous ten years. Unsurprisingly, in the following months, Hailey's absence haunted me every time I lay my head down on the pillow. It got so that the emotions in the dreams were just as powerful as those when I was awake. But at least while I was awake, I could control some facets of how I responded to them. In my sleep, I had no such luck and unfailingly made the situa-tion even more dire by acting in a way inconsistent with my waking self.

For so long, I hated sleep.

After I found Hailey in London, I was sure those dreadful dreams would stop. Surely my mind would spare me the horror of the previous twelve years now that I was back with my daughter. After all, there was plenty else to worry about. Hailey was badly hooked on heroin and constantly suffering. I wasn't sure she'd ever fully recover. And just when I thought I'd gone to Moldova to retire, I met a mother whose daughter was in the possession of sex traders in Ukraine. Retirement was no longer an option for me.

Still, the Hailey-is-missing nightmares continued. As soon as I entered REM, Hailey was gone all over again. In some night terrors, I'd never found her. In others, I'd found her and already lost her again. For me, there seemed to be no reprieve, certainly not in sleep. If I lived to be an old man, those terrible memories, I was sure, would survive even the worst of senility.

And tonight's night terror was one of the most distressing I could remember. In the dream, I was with Tasha, who I'd just cheated on with my old college flame, Jadine. We were in the master bedroom of our immense DC home, and Tasha was packing to leave me. I stood in the doorway, asking her forgiveness, begging her to stay, pleading with her not to take

Hailey away, when the phone on the nightstand next to our bed rang like a train whistle.

Instinctively, I answered it. It was Alden, my father.

'I'm a little busy now, Dad, what do you need?'

'I need you to find the keys.'

'What keys? Whose keys?'

'The keys to the store.'

I became irritated, as I often did during conversations with my father, only for different reasons than speaking cryptically. 'What store? You're making no sense, Dad. I don't have time for this. Tasha's leaving me. I need to go.'

'She's missing, Simon.'

'Who's missing?'

'Hailey.'

'My daughter's home, Dad. She's here, just downstairs, playing ping pong in the basement with Ana.'

'She isn't, though.'

With those three words, Alden hung up the phone. I stood there, confused, as a bawling Tasha slipped out the door. As soon as she was gone, I knew that, as crazy as it had sounded at the time, what my father had told me over the phone was true.

Hailey *was* gone. She'd been taken. Of that I was suddenly sure. I just didn't know by whom. In other words, it was fourteen years ago all over again.

Christ, I thought, waking in a cold sweat next to Jadine in the chief's tiny hut. What I wouldn't do for a nightmare about a goddamn sociology exam. Even one in which I had to speak publicly, with my clothes off and my bare ass hanging out.

TWENTY-SEVEN

The next morning, the chief loaned us a small boat and pointed us in the direction of Bol. With us, he sent a shy young man to return with the boat once we were safely ashore. The young man's name was Sulayman. He was Isa's older brother, son to one of their father's four other wives.

As we passed other inhabited islands, we remained as quiet as possible but still drew the attention of dozens, maybe scores, as though we were the main attraction in the world's sorriest floating parade. Jadine and I kept our rifles nearby but out of sight. We had no intention of starting a fight, but we didn't intend on dying in one either.

Meanwhile, lingering in the back of my mind was the question of whether we'd inadvertently ingested copepods in the pitch-black waters the previous night. If so, had the copepods been dissolved by our stomach acid? Were the larvae already migrating through the walls of our intestines as we paddled east? A year from now, would a blister appear? And when it did, would my humble doctor in Moldova have the proper stick to coax a three-foot guinea worm out of my swollen scrotum?

Thinking about it nearly caused me to lose my sausage-and-egg breakfast rations, which we had shared with Sulayman minutes before we departed.

Once we reached Bol, we thanked Sulayman and sent him back to his village with the boat. Then we trekked in the direction of the airport, where a small plane owned by a Chadian businessman who owed a significant favor to the Secretary of State would be awaiting us on the tarmac.

First, we had a job to do. We needed to chat with nearby residents who might have seen the plane that met al-Haggi approaching the airport (which, according to our intel, was a rare occurrence). If we could determine from which direction the plane had flown, we might be able to identify the airport at which al-Haggi's message had originated. As far as leads went, it was thin. But we had been following meager threads from the moment we arrived in Abuja.

If we could extract the necessary information from the locals, we'd order the pilot to take us to the first airport in that general direction. If we failed, we'd move on to Plan B and order him to fly us into the Cameroonian city of Banyo. From there, we would advance west toward the Nigerian border in the hope of getting the drop on Rusul Alharb militants hiding in the Gwoza Hills and Mandara Mountains.

As we walked, Jadine and I – once again, partly out of our extraordinary fear and partly out of straight-up boredom – continued the conversation we'd started in the truck.

Jadine said, 'The operation – and our relationship – went completely sideways after Ahmad witnessed Mohammed Yakubu's execution by police. His friend of seven years, gunned down by law enforcement, murdered without charge or trial. It was more than he could take. It changed him in ways I wouldn't have thought possible.'

Yakubu's successor as leader of Rusul Alharb was his deputy Abubakar Shagari. Although his close relationship with Yakubu gained him some legitimacy, from the beginning Shagari was a divisive leader, whose fragile power hung tenuously on the ruthlessness he showed to those who were disloyal to him.

Like Yakubu, Shagari was an ethnic Kanuri who spoke Hausa, as well as Fulani, Arabic, and English. He was said to possess a photographic memory. He was also said to be immortal, this latter claim made far more credible by the Nigerian and Cameroonian security forces who repeatedly declared him dead.

Shagari was first reported killed shortly after Yakubu's execution by Nigerian police. Months later, he appeared in a video boasting about his accomplishments as Rusul Alharb's new leader. The Nigerian army would kill Shagari three more times over the next five years, the Cameroonian military only once (but with convincing photographic evidence).

The most plausible reason for these errors was the terror leader's liberal use of body doubles.

In any event, Shagari persistently returned to the screen to mock the declarations of his death and to further taunt the forces said to have killed him. The new Rusul Alharb leader appeared in videos with other messages as well. One in which he showed off weapons and vehicles stolen from government security forces. One in which he claimed responsibility for the abduction, rape, and killing of a Nigerian policewoman. One in which he claimed responsibility for the Chibok girls' kidnapping.

Dressed in full camouflage, with an AK-47 in each hand, Shagari cut a strange figure. 'I enjoy killing,' he said publicly on more than a single occasion. 'I enjoy killing anyone whom God commands me to kill, the way I enjoy killing chickens and rams.' No one doubted Shagari's sincerity on the matter. Psychiatrists working closely with intelligence officials had, however, consistently questioned his mental health. So had many of Rusul Alharb's semi-autonomous commanders.

This, in the minds of US intelligence analysts, made the terror group a fragile organization. Over the past ten years, weak central authority had undermined many of Shagari's triumphs, including his declaration of a caliphate in all areas Rusul Alharb controlled. Unfortunately, anyone in the organization who questioned his legitimacy was immediately shot, hanged, or beheaded, making it nearly impossible to turn someone close to him into a defector.

Enter again Ahmad Abdulaziz. Ahmad knew Shagari well; before the uprising in Maiduguri, he'd described Shagari to Jadine as a cold-blooded, battle-scarred version of Mohammed Yakubu.

She said, 'All those years, Ahmad despised Shagari. He had to keep himself from shaking every time Shagari walked into the room. He told me you never knew what Shagari would do. He could be smiling at you one minute and slitting your throat the next. Ahmad believed the only thing keeping Shagari from killing him was his close friendship with Yakubu. Which was why once Yakubu was dead, even my superiors agreed to pull Ahmad out.'

But Ahmad had been so profoundly affected by Yakubu's death that he refused to cooperate.

'He blamed himself. He blamed the Nigerian government. He blamed the State Department. He blamed me. The day Yakubu was murdered, something in Ahmad changed. Something broke, Simon. Irreparably. Suddenly, he didn't *want* out. Suddenly, he wanted to do everything in his power to give us Shagari.'

But even stranger than Ahmad's behavior was Shagari's. He not only let Ahmad live, he not only didn't push Ahmad out – he brought him in closer. It was as though Ahmad had somehow gained Shagari's trust overnight. Maybe it was simply that, with Yakubu dead, Shagari no longer saw Ahmad as a threat to his advancement in the organization.

'Within months, our analysts concluded that Ahmad had started feeding me false intelligence after Yakubu's death,' she said. 'That's when my superiors at State discovered the affair. Or, at least, that's when they say they did. I'm inclined to think they knew about it all along. They kept silent as long as it served their purpose. But once Ahmad went rogue, they used it to push me out.'

It was around that time that Jadine left the US Embassy in Abuja and set her sights on acquiring a teaching job at the University of Cape Town.

'I continued to reach out to Ahmad, but . . .' She paused as her eyes misted up. 'He'd left the university, and I think he feared he was wanted by US intelligence. And he was probably right. But I think he also feared that if he communicated with me, I'd set him up. I'm sure he thought my leaving Abuja was all for show. That I'd try to arrange a meeting and he'd wind up in the rear of a van with a hood over his head.'

I didn't point out the irony, but a slight twinge suggested it wasn't completely lost on her either.

'So,' I said, 'you think Ahmad turned to the dark side following Yakubu's death.'

'All evidence seems to indicate that. I wasn't entirely sure until we watched that video in Maiduguri. I've been out of the loop with respect to intelligence for years. I didn't know whether Ahmad really joined the cause or just escaped the continent. I didn't know whether he was captured by Nigerian security forces or killed by Shagari and his men. I didn't think

I'd ever know what fate befell him. And there was a certain comfort in that. During the day, I'd imagine him sitting in a café in Brussels. But once the sun fell, I'd become equally certain he'd been murdered in the desert. Whatever had happened to him, I only knew that it was all my fault.'

'He made his own decisions, Jade. He was a grown man.'

I immediately thought of the bullshit poster in Ndulue Balogun's bullshit real estate office back in Abuja.

> I am *not* a product of my circumstances;
> I am a product of my decisions.

Maybe there was something to it after all. For some people. In some situations. Still, it was hardly a truism worthy of poster form.

'He made decisions, Simon, largely on *my* lies.'

Yet that fact hadn't prevented Ahmad from falling in love with Jadine. After all, he'd known she was with US intelligence by their third date.

TWENTY-EIGHT

From the beginning of his tenure as Rusul Alharb's leader, Shagari personally led raids into remote villages, where he and his fighters slaughtered men, raped women, and kidnapped children, many of whom were later used in suicide bombings.

'Shagari quickly gained a reputation for being a barbarous commander,' Jadine said as we continued our trek in the direction of Bol's airport. 'And his recruitment methods were every bit as abominable as his battlefield tactics.'

When his numbers were down, Shagari sent young Rusul Alharb members back to their respective villages to recruit their fathers and brothers as soldiers, their mothers and sisters as wives. 'If your family refuses to come,' he told them, 'you *must* kill them, for they have chosen to live as infidels.'

So vile was Shagari's behavior that even ISIL eventually began distancing themselves from him.

Roughly two hours into our trek, we reached the top of a sandy hill as steep as a mountain. At the bottom stood hundreds of reed huts, each just large enough for maybe two or three people to lie down. We saw no roads. No hospitals. No schools.

'If anyone saw that plane,' Jadine said, 'it'll be someone down there.'

'Whoever talks to us will be putting themselves in grave danger.'

Jadine said, 'Stay at the top of this hill. Watch for trouble.' She placed a bud in her ear and attached the small, wireless mic to her shirt. 'If you see any suspicious activity . . .'

'And if you find yourself in any trouble, work in the codeword.'

'What's the codeword?'

'Help.'

She smiled at me weakly and started down the hill.

* * *

Ninety minutes later, she finally found someone willing to speak to her. Through my binoculars, I watched the hut she had entered on the edge of town. As I attempted to calculate how long it would take me to reach her if she required my assistance, the conversation, which had begun in Arabic, turned to English.

'I saw this plane, yes,' the woman said with an Arabic accent. 'I worry when I see these planes come. Always, I think, this could be the start of a raid by Rusul Alharb.'

'Why do you think that? Do Rusul Alharb leaders frequently land at that airport?'

'That I do not know. But their couriers fly into Bol often. These messengers exit the plane and go straight to the lake. A day or two later, we might hear news that an entire island of civilians has been wiped out.'

'Has Bol itself ever been attacked?' Jadine asked.

The woman sobbed, said, 'Here in Bol, we did not expect Rusul Alharb. So, when the chief's friend from a jihadi-held island alerted him that terrorists were intending to attack our market, he did not believe him. Because he did not want to spark the panic, the chief told no one but those closest to him.'

Some civilians, the woman told Jadine, heard news of the warning and that night stood guard on the shore watching for Rusul Alharb boats. After a few hours, they identified a canoe filled with women and children. Not soldiers carrying black flags and yelling, '*Allahu akbar!*' The good men standing watch helped the canoe on to the shore, then helped the women and children out of the boat.

'As soon as they reached the beach,' the woman said, 'two or three of the boat's passengers detonated suicide vests. Killing our villagers *and* their passengers.'

Only one passenger survived. Ironically, she had been wearing one of the vests that exploded. In the hours that followed, she lost both legs.

'In hospital, she tells doctors that she had been held by Rusul Alharb for many months. That they drugged her all day, raped her all night. This night, though, they told her to wear the suicide vest. They said the explosives could not hurt her. And if she killed some people on the shore or, even better, in the market, they would pay her riches when she returned to them.'

Jadine asked, 'Has Abubakar Shagari ever been here himself?'

'Of course. He comes to the islands to recruit our children. He promises them that any boy who joins the cause will receive buckets of money and he will be assured his rightful place in paradise when he dies.'

'And the children believe him.'

'Even some of the grown-ups, they believe him. They see first-hand his savagery, yet many in the islands still welcome him when he arrives. Still they support him after he leaves. They take him at his word that, as leader of the new caliphate, he will fulfill our people's basic needs like food and water, education and sanitation. He pledges everything to those who have nothing. Some insist they have no choice *but* to believe him. Otherwise, they would lose all hope and die.'

Twenty minutes later, Jadine left the town and returned to the top of the hill. She wasn't followed. But the weather had taken a turn for the worse. The rains were coming down hard and the accompanying lightning and thunder appeared close.

'You all right?' I asked her once she reached me.

'Fine.'

'You don't look fine. You look pale. Like you just received news you've got a guinea worm in your intestines.'

'It's nothing. It's just . . .' She held her arms tightly but still shivered in the deluge. 'It's just all these stories I've heard these past few days.'

'What about them?'

'Simon, you need to make me a promise.'

I half smiled. 'Oh, I owe you one, do I?'

'I'm serious. If something happens to me . . .'

'Nothing's going to happen to you, Jade.'

She smartly ignored me and continued. 'Simon, if I'm killed or incapacitated at some point during this mission, I need you to go on to achieve our objective.'

'Your daughter's hardly just an objective, Jadine.'

'*Promise me.*'

As the rains pounded the hill, I gave her a harsh look. 'You claim to know me so well, Jade. But if that were true, you wouldn't need to hear me make that promise.'

'I *don't*,' she cried. 'I just . . .' She quickly gathered herself. 'You're right. I only said it for the sake of comfort. I'm sorry I—'

'I promise,' I said, taking her hands in mine. 'I promise, Jade. If anything happens to you, I'll find Kishana and bring her home to your father.'

'Thank you, Simon.'

She reached up and kissed me, on the lips but without passion. We still had a job to do. The woman in Bol had been a treasure trove of information. In addition to learning a bit more about Rusul Alharb's courier system, Jadine also obtained an answer to our most pressing question.

'The plane you saw,' Jadine had asked the woman, 'do you know which direction it flew in from?'

'For sure,' the woman said, 'from the south, yes. From the capital. From N'Djamena.'

TWENTY-NINE

Jadine and I breathed a simultaneous sigh of relief as we touched down in N'Djamena. Following a fifteen-minute zombie-walk through the airport, we breezed through customs with bribes and stepped outside under the hot Central African sun and on to the hotel shuttle. We leaned back on our headrests and closed our eyes, content in the glorious knowledge that we were each only fifteen or twenty minutes away from the longest, hottest shower of our life.

Roughly twenty minutes later, the shuttle passed between two armed guards at the gated entrance and dropped us at Hotel N'Djamena, which appeared from the outside to be every bit as luxurious as any luxury hotel in the West. The interior didn't disappoint either. When we stepped into the lavish two-story lobby, our jaws dropped in unison. Neither of us had expected such opulence. Because to say Chad entertained very few travelers was one hell of an understatement.

The Republic of Chad was as landlocked as Kansas, but instead of having innocuous neighbors like Colorado, Nebraska, Missouri, and Oklahoma, she was fenced in by six countries constantly in violent crisis, namely the Central African Republic, Cameroon, Nigeria, Niger, Libya, and Sudan. Because of its distance to the sea and its harsh desert climate, Chad was commonly referred to as the 'Dead Heart of Africa.'

Not exactly your optimal tourism slogan.

And transportation in Chad was beyond rough. Years of conflict had left the roads in shambles, and the security situation remained dodgy, to say the least. Rebel activity was rampant in the south of the country, and the capital city of N'Djamena was a frequent target. So, despite the hotel's heavy security presence, the posh accommodations seemed to exist in an entirely different dimension from the outside world.

We went to the front desk and, under the name Patrick Bateman, checked in with a delightful young desk clerk named

Sylviane, then (escorted by a charmingly enthusiastic bellhop named Kosso) rode the elevator to the seventh floor, where we key-carded our way into a sumptuous suite with two separate bedrooms, two separate baths, a living room, dining room, and a wrap-around balcony with a stunning panoramic view of the Chari River.

As Kosso showed us around the suite, pointing out the various amenities as if reading from a script, I opened every closet, looked behind every curtain, checked under every bed. *No monsters here.* Each room possessed its own squeaky-clean ivory marble floors and was extravagantly appointed. In the master bath sat a tub that could easily fit four people. In the master bedroom stood a desk large enough for any Fortune 500 CEO. In the living room, Jadine sat on what was surely a six-figure sectional, positioned in front of a flatscreen television that could have passed as the Jumbotron at Nationals Park.

I promptly tipped Kosso, who bowed graciously and took his leave, closing the door behind him.

'Not bad,' I said. 'Deputy Secretary Jeffries is to be commended.'

'Believe me, he's just kissing my father's ass. My father is about to retire, and Jeffries wants to make sure my father recommends his loyal Deputy Secretary for the open cabinet position.'

'Your dad must have a lot of sway with the President.'

'More than any of his other advisors. More than his Chief of Staff, more than the Vice President. Maybe even more than the First Lady.'

'They go back a long time, don't they?'

'They served as freshman congressmen together. Became fast friends, then best friends. They voted alike, campaigned for one another. Traveled on fact-finding trips together. The President was even with him when my father first met my mother in Johannesburg. He's my godfather, in fact. They've been as close as brothers ever since. The President's children still call my father Uncle Jimmy.'

Jadine stepped into the second bedroom and gently closed the door behind her.

In my room, I stripped out of my rancid clothes with the intention of burning them. I placed them in a small biohazard bag that I found stuffed in a side pocket of my pack. I tied it at the top and tossed it underhand in the general direction of the waste basket. After which, my arm felt as if it had been wrenched from its socket. I was sore, I was broken, I needed rest.

Following a long, hot shower, I settled on to the master bedroom's queen-size bed still dressed in a towel. I leaned over and, with my semi-revitalized right arm, reached for the phone to call Moldova.

Immediately frustrated by the complicated instructions, I nearly slammed the phone against the wall and went to sleep. Instead, I took a deep breath and afforded my tired mind the opportunity to peruse the instructions once more and, by the third line, I realized I could simply dial zero for the operator, who'd connect my call.

The operator spoke fluent English. I told her I needed to make an international call. Pleasantly, she asked me for the number. I recited it from memory and listened to her dial. Then heard the gentle tone that served as the ringback in Eastern Europe. It repeated three times before my heart leapt at the soothing sound of Ana's voice.

'What do you *mean* you are in Chad?' she shouted lovingly in my ear thirty seconds later.

I heard the keyboard going again.

'US State Department warns to *reconsider* any travel,' she said before I could answer her. 'Due to crimes like armed robbery and carjacking, frequent terror attacks targeting foreigners, and . . .'

'What?'

'Oh, my God, Simon. *Minefields.*'

'Not to worry, baby. Jadine's got a device that detects—'

'Jadine? Who is this *Jadine*?'

Shit. I'd broken another of my fundamental rules. The tired mind shouldn't make sensitive phone calls. When you're tired, you're unfocused, you're irritable, you're damned. Tired-dialing was drunk-dialing's evil twin brother. And I'd just invited him inside my world with open arms.

I had previously convinced myself that Ana's jealousy was justified. She'd been badly screwed over by her previous lover (and employer), the Warsaw defense attorney Mikolaj Dabrowski, who had towed her along for more than ten years. In the end, Dabrowski turned out to be worse than the worst criminals he represented. He'd had Ana kidnapped. He was implicated in the abduction of six-year-old Lindsay Sorkin and discovered by police to be in possession of more than 30,000 images and videos depicting child pornography. He was currently serving a decades-long sentence at Mokotow Prison in Warsaw, a horrific place which, in my opinion, was still too good for him. According to Ana's brother Marek, given the nature of his crimes, Dabrowski had a bullseye on his back and spent most of his days in solitary in order to avoid being butchered by his fellow inmates. Which, in my estimation, made the sentence of incarceration at least somewhat more fitting for him.

To Ana, I said, 'Jadine is . . .'

(a) the mother of the girl I've been searching for;
(b) the daughter of the Secretary of State;
(c) a former elite operative from a top-secret US intelligence agency;
(d) a woman I dated briefly in college;
(e) all of the above.

I went with: 'Look Ana, I can't really discuss it over an unsecured line. I'll share the entire story with you once I'm back in Moldova.'

'When will that *be*, Simon?'

'Soon. I have a feeling the young lady we're looking for is somewhere here in N'Djamena. I don't think I'll be taking any further excursions into rural territory. We're on my turf now. We're in a city. Where I can ask questions. Where I can buy information. Where I can better see what's coming at me. This is where I thrive.'

It was true. As much as I loved nature, I didn't fare terribly well within its domain. The forest, the desert, the jungle, the plains – I disliked working in them all. I needed to be surrounded by concrete or else I'd go crazy.

I sighed inwardly. If I was going to be honest with myself, Moldova was driving me crazy as well. I'd tried and tried to persuade myself that I was happy because I honestly thought it was best for Hailey. But I was every bit as restless as Ana. We both needed to return to urban – or at least *sub*urban – life. And we needed to do it soon.

Just then, Jadine stepped into the doorway of my room in nothing but a fluffy white hotel towel. Her hair was still wet from her shower.

'Food?' she said. 'Or sleep *then* food?'

Through the phone, Ana cried, 'Who *is* that?'

'Sleep then food,' I said to Jadine.

'Good,' she said, 'that was my preference as well. I'll make reservations for Le Studio at nine. See you in a few hours.'

She walked out of my room and into hers, gently closing the door behind her.

'Simon?' Ana said.

I quickly recovered. 'That was just the woman next door. She wanted to know if I wanted to order some food.'

'How did she get into your hotel room? I heard no one knock on your door.'

'Baby, I'm so tired. I'll explain everything when I get home.'

'Explain it *now*, Simon.'

'Ana, please. You have nothing to worry about. I just need to get some sleep.'

'Call me as soon as you wake up.'

She killed the call. I returned the receiver to its cradle, rolled on to my back, closed my eyes, and settled the base of my head back into the contours of my soft, cool pillow.

Thirty minutes later, I still lay in that position, eyes wide, staring up at the ceiling, entirely unable to so much as nod off.

THIRTY

We dressed in fresh clothes left for us at the front desk by Deputy Secretary Jeffries and the Nigerian intelligence agent, whose name was now at the tip of my tongue. I stood in front of the mirror in the crisp white shirt and navy sports jacket and imagined for a moment that I was back in the States, twenty years younger, readying myself for a night out in the district with Tasha.

Jadine exited her bedroom in a simple black blouse and slate gray pants. It was hard to believe that she'd been dressed in a Kevlar vest and fatigues just seventy-two hours earlier. That she'd stowed away in a trailer hijacked by Rusul Alharb just yesterday. That she'd swum for her life in guinea-worm-infested waters just the previous night. It was almost impossible to believe that her beloved sixteen-year-old daughter Kishana was being held captive by one of the world's most barbaric terrorist organizations. That her daughter could well be in this very city, considering blowing herself up alongside her biological father as early as tomorrow morning.

Make no mistake: the pain in Jadine's eyes was evident. But she concealed it well enough that you'd need to know what you were looking for in order to discern it. At that moment, I wanted to take her in my arms, to assure her everything would be all right. But I couldn't risk complicating our relationship during this mission. Nor could I know for certain, under the circumstances, that everything *would* work out for the best, that her daughter *would* be hers again when all this was over.

'Ready?' she said.

The hotel offered several dining options and, admittedly, room service was the most tempting, but we both needed to see friendly, healthy, well-fed human faces other than our own or else we'd risk losing what remained of our sanity. The suffering in this part of the world was just too gut-wrenching for either us to spend another full night stuck in our own heads.

Minutes later, Jadine and I headed downstairs in the glass elevator for Le Studio, the hotel's casual dining restaurant.

For a moment in the lobby, I allowed myself to fantasize that Jadine and I were at Hotel N'Djamena for an entirely different reason. I took in the promise of a sparkling outdoor pool as though, after a good night's sleep, Jadine and I would jump right in, maybe knock back a few cocktails at the swim-up bar before lounging poolside with a good crime novel. Tomorrow morning, we'd stroll outside and take photos of the hotel's lush gardens, then relax on our private lanai as we watched the rushing Chari River from a safe distance. Later, Jadine would probably go off to the spa to keep that flawless skin flawless. I'd head down to the fitness center, hit the treadmill and lift some weights because, in this fantasy, I hadn't just trekked for days through the Sambisa forest and Lake Chad Basin. Instead, I'd been eating well, even putting on weight. Afterward, I'd hit the sauna or the steam room. When I finally returned upstairs to the suite, I'd find Jadine making use of the free Wi-Fi and I'd jokingly scold her for being on Facebook again. We'd climb into bed and watch a pay-per-view movie that was still in theaters. After the movie, or perhaps even during, we'd kiss, we'd undress one another, we'd make love. We'd fall asleep in each other's arms because for tomorrow we'd already scheduled a great big day of doing nothing but the same.

Then I felt guilty, even ashamed.

Ever since I'd found Hailey, the *shoulds* and *should nots* had re-entered my life. And by then, I'd lived so long without them. Not just with respect to my actions but my very thoughts. It somehow felt wrong to cheat on Ana, even if it was just in my head. This despite the fact that I didn't have much more control over my thoughts than I did my feelings. And I sure as hell didn't have much control over those.

We were, I supposed, a product of our circumstances *and* our decisions, and in the realm of sexual morality, it was our decisions that counted most. Yet, without question, our circumstances affected those decisions. And here, the intimate relationship – that unbreakable bond – between intense fear and hypersexual urges couldn't be ignored. For days now, we'd both been one minor mistake or a bit of bad luck from death. And now that we'd survived the trailer hijacking, our adrenaline was ebbing and all the blood that was earlier diverted from our organs to our muscles was returning home.

Outside the restaurant, an armed Chadian soldier stood guard. I stared at him harder than I intended to. Thinking about how the amped-up security presence in DC following 9/11 made Tasha feel *less* safe, *less* secure.

'Did you ever think of joining?' Jadine asked me after following my gaze to the soldier.

'The military? Not seriously. Too much testosterone for a sensitive gent like myself. Plus, I don't like carrying shit.'

'Oh, sure, the carrying shit.'

'Speaking of which,' I said, 'I highly doubt I could go number two in a latrine, let alone dig one myself.'

'Or clean it.'

'*Clean* it? That's a thing?'

'A pretty important thing if your unit wants a clean latrine.'

I nodded to the soldier who didn't acknowledge me back. Maybe he was bored. Maybe he was afraid. Maybe he was a bit of both. If so, I knew the feeling.

The most recent major terror attack on the Chadian capital occurred only five years earlier. Over the course of three days, before and during Ramadan, Rusul Alharb insurgents perpetrated three suicide bombings against two police targets and N'Djamena's main market. The attacks killed roughly fifty people, including a half-dozen policemen. Hundreds were injured, dozens severely.

The hostess searched for our reservation under the name Patrick Bateman, the alias I'd used for years, ever since my friend, Berlin private investigator Kurt Osterman, dubbed me an American psycho. She gathered two leather-bound menus and asked us to follow her as she slowly navigated past a few patrons to seat us in the far corner at an intimate table for two.

'So,' Jadine said once we'd settled, 'there must be *something* I don't know about you. If you had to guess, what would that something be?'

I pretended to think on it, then said, 'Well, I'm not a big fan of conversation during meals.'

'No, I'm pretty sure I knew that about you by our second date.'

Jadine looked incredible in the candlelight. Incredible in any light in that simple black blouse. Jeffries or what's-his-name had superb taste in clothes.

'My father was recently diagnosed with dementia,' I said.

'Oh, I'm sorry, Simon.'

I glanced outside the floor-to-ceiling window, at the Chari River rushing past. Unfortunately, the full beauty of some things could only be appreciated behind the protection of glass.

'I don't know how to feel about my father's illness,' I admitted. 'I don't know how to feel about *him* anymore.'

'Has he mellowed any in the past twenty-five years?'

I hid my bitterness behind a mirthless smile. 'Not in the slightest.'

A young man named Casimir walked up to our table. Introduced himself as our server and apprised us of the evening's specials. While he spoke, it seemed clear to me that he took great pride in his uniform, such as it was – a heavily starched white button-down shirt beneath a satiny maroon vest, straight black pants, and sharp black shoes polished to a shine.

'Something to drink, madame?' he asked.

'Just a soft drink, no ice.'

'Sir, something to drink?'

'I'm fine with water.' As soon as I said it, I heard Jimmy Carter describing the onscreen images of the guinea worm as it was being coaxed from the flesh of a screaming human being. 'Actually, better make it a bottle of Gala Ambrée.'

'Very good, sir.'

When the waiter stepped away, Jadine said, 'You know that beer is brewed right here in N'Djamena, right?'

'Well, I figured if I'm going to catch a guinea worm, I might as well catch a good hearty buzz while I'm at it.'

'Smart thinking.'

'Had you come to expect any less from me?'

She smiled as though she were keeping a secret.

'What?' I said.

'You realize we're flirting, don't you? Didn't you tell me in Abuja that your girlfriend Ana was the jealous type?'

'Well,' I said, 'she's a big flirt herself. Back in Abuja, I just thought you had much more on your mind than flirting.'

'Oh, really.'

I knew I was drifting into dangerous territory. And that this part of the continent was dangerous enough as it was.

I attempted to ease us out of there by asking about Kishana.

Jadine rested her elbows on the table and leaned forward. Her eyes lit up in a way that made it obvious that, prior to the kidnapping, her teenage daughter was easily her favorite subject.

'It may sound insincere under the circumstances,' she said, 'but I can only tell you what I would have told you days before Kishana was taken. She is the *perfect* daughter. Even while she was a baby, she never gave me or any of her sitters any trouble. I waited for the terrible twos and thrashing threes, but they never arrived; if anything, she became even *more* loving and understanding and obedient as she grew older.'

Jadine wiped away a rogue tear. 'She's always been a brilliant girl, no problems in school. When she was just twelve, she decided she wanted to make full use of her dual citizenship and went to live part-time with our cousins in Maryland. Over the next four years, she charmed her way into her grandfather's life, even legally changed her name to Coleman.'

'How did you feel about that?'

'What's in a name, right? *She* didn't know Luan Visser. And it wouldn't have mattered if she had. I was happy to give my consent when she asked for it.'

Our drinks arrived.

'Anyway,' Jadine continued, 'while she was Stateside, she developed a fervent interest in politics and public service. When she asked me for permission to join the Peace Corps, how could I say no? She was as mature as a woman twice her age. Never had any interest in drugs or alcohol. *Plenty* of interest in boys the past few years.' Jadine laughed despite herself. 'But even the boys she dated, Simon, they were boys I would have taken home to meet my own mother when I was her age.' She winked mischievously. 'Not one boy remotely like you.'

I smiled, softly shot back. 'Hey, I was a catch.'

'You were, Simon. A catch and *release*, that is.'

'That's harsh.'

She shrugged her left shoulder. 'I guess I figure you can't hate me any more than you already do.'

'Hate you? Why would I possibly hate you?'

'Because it's my fault, Simon. All this. You think I don't realize that?'

'I don't hate you.'

'I tricked you, I lied to you. I manipulated you and there's no excuse for it.'

'I know all about it and I'm still sitting here, aren't I?'

She reached over the table and took my hand, rubbed her thumb gently over the top of it, causing the fine hair on my arm to stand on end.

'You *feel* real enough,' she said quietly. 'But it's still kind of hard to believe you stuck around after all I've done.'

'We all do things we're not proud of, Jade. Some of us, almost exclusively.'

She pulled back slowly and covered her eyes with her palms for several seconds before lowering them. 'I'm worried about the girl we're going to rescue, Simon. She's not going to be the same Kishana she was when she was taken.'

'Don't jump to conclusions,' I said. 'She's much older than Hailey was. And she's not going to be with her abductor for a dozen years. She's not going to be with him for more than another few hours, if I have anything to do with it. And she's strong, I'd bet. Like her mother. Like her grandfather. She'll recover from this, Jade, I'm sure of it.'

'What if she meant what she said in that video, Simon?'

'She didn't. You said so yourself. She was clearly reading from cue cards behind the camera. The girl you just described, Jade? She's not going to be brainwashed over a few days. She's not going to become a terrorist overnight.'

'I would've said the same thing about Ahmad.'

'Ahmad was inside for years, though. He lost his shit – simple as that. And keep in mind, he was a devout Muslim *before* all this happened. All Yakubu or Shagari had to do was convince him that his god wasn't the all-loving, all-forgiving, peaceful deity he thought he was. Once you truly believe in a creator, what *wouldn't* you do for him? If you genuinely believed you could escape this shit life for paradise, why *wouldn't* you join the jihad?'

'You make it sound as though religion is a mental illness.'

'It can be, can't it? Not just Islam but virtually every organized religion. If you become convinced that there's an almighty who will reward you in the afterlife by spreading his word through the use of force in this life, that's a powerful delusion. Whether it's killing infidels or homosexuals or abortion doctors, anyone who can justify murderous behavior by reciting cherry-picked lines from a two-thousand-year-old text is demonstrably not right in the head.'

'By that logic, patriotism can be a mental illness as well.'

'It can be. It's called nationalism. And much of the West is suffering through its repercussions right now.'

When Casimir the waiter returned, we both ordered traditional Chadian dishes off the menu – omelets, salads, kebabs, and stew – along with a second round of drinks.

'So, tell me about Hailey,' she said once he left. 'Tell me about the last couple years.'

'Hailey's a different story altogether, Jade. The Hailey who was taken was *not* the Hailey who came home. She'd been through far too much for far too long. When we first arrived in Moldova, she was battling a terrible heroin addiction. Breaking it was much harder and took much longer than I ever imagined.'

I paused, drew in a deep breath, again wondering if I was to blame for Hailey's slow recovery.

I said, 'I don't know what I expected to happen once she was out of heroin's clutches. I suppose I pictured her smiling all the time, putting her arms around me, showering me with affection to catch up on all the time we missed together. But as the weeks and months wore on, it became agonizingly clear that heroin addiction wasn't the only affliction we'd have to contend with.'

Jadine waited as I gathered myself.

I said, 'It wasn't that Hailey wasn't *always* smiling following her recovery. It was that she *never* smiled. Seemed completely incapable of it. As for affection, she hardly came near me. I don't think it was out of any animus; it was just that that was the person she'd become after twelve years in captivity. She was – she *is* – angry all the time.'

'At what? At whom?'

'At the world.' I lifted the beer to my lips. 'And given the circumstances, we were limited in what we could do for her. I couldn't exactly take her around to see a number of psychiatrists in Moldova; it would have left a trail. Moldovans are good people, but they're as susceptible to bribes as anyone else. So, with the help of my friend Kati Sheffield, I managed to mask our IP and connect her via Skype to some prominent shrinks back in New York and London.'

'What have they said?'

'She's been repeatedly diagnosed with post-traumatic stress disorder, which wasn't very surprising. The extent of the PTSD, however, was. In my ignorance, I assumed that simply because Hailey was spared any sexual abuse, any psychiatric disorders she suffered would be mild or temporary. But I couldn't have been more wrong. Even now, she constantly experiences these intense negative emotions; they give her nightmares, cause her to become detached. She jumps at the slightest noise, the faintest touch.'

Jadine reached across the table and took my hand again. Only then did I realize I'd been avoiding her eyes while I spoke. Gazing at my empty beer bottle, staring through the full glass of ice water I'd set at the edge of the table to keep myself from taking a sip.

I said, 'In the beginning, I thought the negative emotions she was experiencing were about her kidnapper, about me, about Tasha – even about Ana, who maybe came on a bit too strong in her new role as a surrogate mother. But then I realized that all these emotions – the fear, the sadness, the rage – were directed inwardly. She was mad at *herself.* She felt guilty and ashamed. And she either couldn't or wouldn't explain why.'

'I'm no psychiatrist,' Jadine said, 'but I'd guess *couldn't* is more like it. It's going to take time.'

'I get that. And I'm trying to remain patient – not a typical Fisk trait, as you're probably aware. But I'm worried that, in the meantime, these potent feelings are going to cause her to do something that will result in our losing her all over again. Because during these outbursts, she's reckless, she's self-destructive. She runs out of the house and holes up in the nearest pub. She goes home with different men every night. Strange men. Men she's never met before. Without a second thought. And she fights. Other girls, guys. It doesn't matter who – she seems to want a piece of everybody. All of which is made a thousand times more impossible when we're doing our damnedest to keep a low profile so that Hailey and I aren't discovered by bounty hunters who'll see that one or both of us answers charges of murder.'

'Is she on medication?' Jadine asked.

'We've been going through the process. I know from experience that psychiatric treatment includes a lot of trial and error. So far, we've tried all kinds of antidepressants – SSRIs, SNRIs, atypical, tricyclic, MAOIs. She takes tranquilizers, does some sporadic talk therapy online but gets frustrated very easily and usually logs off before the end of the session.'

I flashed on the buffet of prescription medications that Tasha's doctor laid out for her soon after Hailey went missing. Pills she ultimately used to take her own life.

I turned away and watched the people at the table closest to us – a handsome man with a heavy Australian accent and a beautiful Asian woman, neither yet middle-aged. Maybe they were missionaries, maybe educators. Maybe they were in the Chadian capital for business. Or maybe they were on the world's most hazardous honeymoon. Whatever else they were, the couple was so obviously in love that it caused me to ache with envy.

Because I knew that, under her usual sunny disposition, Ana was back in Moldova questioning her decisions. She'd had a promising legal career in Warsaw. She had friends, she had family. She'd had a life. And she dropped it all to come to Moldova to help me with Hailey's recovery. At first, she'd said she'd stay for a few weeks; then weeks became months, and before either of us knew it, months had morphed into nearly two years.

And what had Ana gotten in return? A brooding middle-aged man wanted in Europe for murder and a recovering teenage addict who was mad at the world and had every right to be. Poor Ana. She loved two severely wounded people who, no matter what she did, no matter how much she loved us, would never fully heal.

I tried to surface from the murk of my mood by altering the topic of discussion again. I said, 'I thought you had to be at least eighteen years old to join the Peace Corps.'

Jadine nodded. 'Ordinarily, you do. Kishana was granted an extremely rare waiver on the grounds that she'd already earned enough credits for high school and even some college.' She stared blankly into the candleflame. 'She's such a smart girl.'

'I don't doubt it,' I told her, taking her hand in mine this time. 'And I very much look forward to meeting her.'

Jadine absently nodded her head just as Casimir returned with our entrees. He carefully set our dishes in front of us, then took a step back and asked if there was anything else that he could bring us. As he said it, he smoothed down the front of his satiny maroon vest. Pride in his uniform, pride in his work. I'd make certain the State Department tipped him especially well when the bill came.

Once Casimir left us, we quietly picked at our food.

Although we'd both professed to being ravenous when we first arrived at the restaurant, neither Jadine nor I seemed to have very much of an appetite anymore.

THIRTY-ONE

'You hear that?'

I didn't hear anything, and I told her so.

'Really?'

'Hey, you're the one got me hooked on music festivals back in college.'

Before Hailey, Tasha and I had done all the big ones: Lollapalooza, Coachella, Summerfest, even Burning Man, though I didn't much enjoy the latter because I spent most of the nine-day festival deep in the Nevada desert making sure no one slipped anything into our drinks, a task that became increasingly difficult the more I jammed to my favorite bands while getting smashed on Cuervo.

'There,' she said. 'Hear that?'

I shook my head. 'Damn this fancy hotel's thick walls.'

We'd just returned from the restaurant and I was still in the process of checking the suite for monsters. In the closets, under the beds, behind the curtains.

No monsters here.

Outside, I'd already hung the *Do Not Disturb* sign on our door.

'Simon, I think it's gunfire.'

'Can't be,' I said.

But it could be.

And it was.

And it was coming closer.

'Shit, Simon. We're blind in here,' she said.

While our room offered an exquisite view of the muddy banks of the Chari River, we couldn't see a damn thing that was happening at the front of the hotel. Without eyes, we couldn't know if we were facing off against a couple of crazed gunmen or whether the entire Chadian capital was under siege. Perhaps by Rusul Alharb, perhaps by rebels.

Jadine, still adorned in the clothes she wore to dinner, kicked off her shoes and threw open the closet door. She threw me my go-bag, then dug into hers.

I removed my sports jacket and tossed it on to the sectional. Over my shirtsleeves, I slipped into the Kevlar vest. I strapped my go-bag on my back and readied my assault rifle. Then I made for the door.

There, I stopped and took in the layout of the hotel on the *In Case of Emergency* sign.

Jadine said, 'We should split up.'

'Split up?' I said. 'I'm not sure that's wise.'

'Simon, we're countering a terrorist attack, not investigating a spooky seaside resort with Scooby-Doo.'

'Glad you can make jokes at a time like this.'

'I learned from the best,' she said, cocking her weapon. 'Now, let's move. You take the east stairwell. I'll take the west. We'll converge on the second floor. From there, we'll have the high ground just above the lobby.'

'Is our objective stopping every last one of these bastards or getting the hell out of here?'

'Do you know your basic military hand and arm signals?'

'Yeah.'

'Then let's see what we see and go on from there. Whatever this mission is, it's not a suicide mission. We both need to get out of this hotel alive.'

'You'll hear no objections from me.'

I turned back to look at her. Wrapped my hand around the door handle, and said, 'Right, then. We go on three.'

With my rifle on my shoulder, I descended the cement stairs, cautiously, listening for the footsteps of gunmen, hotel staff or civilians. In the stairwell, the sound of the gunfire was tremendously amplified. Yet, unlike yesterday, I felt focused. Afraid but calm. I recalled that my favorite FLETC instructor Dale Butler was fond of repeating what I think was an old Eastern proverb: *The tiger of the mind is more ferocious than the tiger of the jungle.*

Fear is like fire, he often told us. If you can control it, you can use it to defeat your enemies. If you can't control it, it will consume you completely.

Tonight, fear, as I charged down the stairs, felt more like a friend. It made me alert instead of hysterical. Tonight, it fueled instead of froze me. Drove me rather than stalled me. Tonight, adrenaline was an asset, an ally. The sudden rush of epinephrine had once again diverted energy from my organs to my muscles, increased my heart rate, and expanded my airways. The result was a surge in strength and a burst of acceleration. My senses became heightened, while the pain I'd felt in my bones over the past couple of days faded completely out of existence.

I suddenly felt twenty years younger. Not invincible but phlegmatic. As unflappable as I'd been a few years ago in Paris, Berlin, Warsaw, Kiev, and Minsk.

At the door to the second-floor lobby level, I stopped. Listened for the gunfire, the screams from staff and guests. The sounds made it clear that there were at least two separate gunmen. Both downstairs in the first-floor lobby, which meant chancing a look was relatively safe. With my arm, I nudged the door open slightly to see. I could make out a clerk and a bellhop huddled behind the front desk. On their faces were masks of pure terror. I was relieved to see that neither of the two was Sylviane. Neither was Kosso. Perhaps both had gone home in the hours since we checked in.

The gunmen were young. Teens or early twenties. Mid-twenties at most. They were dressed in dark T-shirts and gunmetal-gray sweatpants. They carried AK-47s with additional magazines hanging from multiple fanny packs secured around their waists.

For a few seconds, I watched them operate. Their approach was chaotic as opposed to methodical, which meant they hadn't been trained for this. Which meant the attack was very likely spontaneous. Which meant that it was probably in reaction to something. Quite possibly, our presence.

I pushed through the door and bolted behind a tall ivory pillar supporting the bannister that ran in a semi-circle around the second-floor lobby. Across the way, Jadine had just done the same.

Bullets suddenly sprayed the second-floor walls well above our heads. Which meant one of us had been seen. Fortunately, the shots were far too wild to know which one of us it was. It was possible that the gunmen had simply perceived movement and didn't know we were armed. Possible that they thought we were hotel staff or just a couple of guests come to see what all the commotion was about.

I risked a glance at the first floor. With the gunmen distracted by us, the clerk and the bellhop were making a mad dash for the restaurant. Only they didn't get far. The nearest gunman swiftly spun and fired in their direction, creating a hideously violent sound that shook me to the core. One went down instantly. The other released a brief scream that trailed him as he ran. A second spread of gunfire followed. And the scream was cut off as abruptly as a stereo with a yanked plug.

Meanwhile, Jadine seized on the opportunity. Materializing from behind her pillar, she fired at the preoccupied gunman.

Enveloped in a thick crimson mist, he crumpled to the marble floor quick as a collapsible ironing table.

The other gunman turned and fired in Jadine's general direction as she regained cover behind the pillar. His rounds seemed endless and he had another four mags, at least.

Finally, a small mercy, a brief silence signaling he was out of ammunition.

I rose, tried to get off a shot but froze. Because in the moment he took to replace his spent magazine, I heard rapid fire coming from a distant floor overhead. Jadine heard it too. Which meant there were more than just the two gunmen in the lobby. From the sound of the upstairs gunfire, there were four gunmen, at least. Maybe five or more.

I signaled to Jadine that I would go upstairs while she took down the lone gunman left in the lobby.

As I moved back toward the stairwell door, I caught sight of a corner of the lower lobby that had been obstructed from my vision before. There lay at least a half-dozen bodies. Most face down on the marble in sizable pools of blood.

Suddenly, my stomach fell. From this vantage point, I could make out the corpse of our charmingly enthusiastic bellhop Kosso, as well as our delightful desk clerk Sylviane. I could even see our waiter Casimir, whose body was positioned nearest to the front door, as if he had been departing the hotel at the end of his shift when the first shots were fired. Tourists and businessmen were also hit. One was crawling along the wall toward the body of a bloodied woman. Squinting, I recognized the Australian man we'd seen in the restaurant, desperately moving toward his lover, the beautiful Asian woman. A moment later, following another round of fire, both were unquestionably dead.

The longer we waited, the more innocent people these bastards were going to kill, so I waited until the lower-lobby gunman still standing had his back turned, then yanked open the door to the stairwell. Just before I slipped inside, I caught sight of Jadine once again rising from behind the bannister.

Aiming.

Firing.

I swung around to catch the outcome.

The first bullet struck the gunman's right shoulder, spinning him around. The second caused his head to vanish behind another scarlet fog.

As soon as she was sure he was down, Jadine turned and made for her own stairwell.

I heard the heavy metal door click shut behind me as I raced back up the stairs, my heart thudding nearly as loudly as my footfalls.

THIRTY-TWO

As I raced up the stairs, I heard voices. One man's and one woman's, each with a heavy Scottish burr. I slowed and lowered my weapon so as not to frighten them. I threw my empty hand in the air and yelled, 'Hotel security.'

The middle-aged couple were huddled in the corner of the stairwell on the fifth floor, both in hotel robes over colorful pajamas.

'They're on seven,' the man said. 'They're going door to door. Room to room. We bailed out of there just in time.'

'How many did you see?'

'At least two. Maybe more.'

'They're shouting in Arabic,' the woman said. 'I speak it a little. They seem to be searching for someone.'

I figured I had a pretty good idea who that someone was.

'Our room faces the front of the hotel,' the man said. 'We just heard sirens and saw flashing lights coming from the paved circle just outside. The police are here but they seem in no rush to come indoors.'

'Head downstairs,' I said. 'The pair in the lobby are down. Just be careful. Keep your eyes and your ears open until all this is over.'

'Are there other security officers to be on the lookout for?'

'In the opposite stairwell, there's a woman with an M27 who's about to meet me on seven. Assume everyone else is dangerous.'

'Godspeed, mate,' the man said.

The woman touched my arm as she started past me down the stairs.

I raised my rifle to my shoulder and continued my swift ascent.

*　　*　　*

Just as I approached the door to the seventh floor, the power blew out and the emergency lights kicked on, dimly illuminating the vast stairwell.

Gently, I leaned against the push bar, ready to pull back and fire if the door suddenly swung open from inside the hallway.

I leaned in a little farther, listened for the gunfire I'd heard less than a minute earlier. But now complete silence filled the length of the hall.

They're going door to door, the Scotsman in the stairwell had said. *Room to room.*

They seem to be searching for someone, the woman had added.

Which left little doubt in my mind that they were searching for me and Jadine. And they seemed to know we were on seven. Which meant someone at the front desk had given them our floor number, probably just before being executed. Or else the gunmen knew our floor coming in. Which would mean they were receiving up-to-the-minute intelligence.

We'd just gotten back to our room when the gunfire started.

Downstairs, I hadn't seen the body of the Chadian soldier stationed in front of the restaurant. But then, that evidence was only circumstantial. Besides, it didn't matter. Not now. Now the only thing that mattered was stopping these gunmen before they murdered every man, woman, and child in the hotel. And it didn't matter how. All that mattered was that I capture one of them alive. Because he would be our best shot at learning Kishana's location before it was too late.

In the darkness, I watched a gunman exit one room at the opposite end of the hall and move to the next. He seemed to be carrying a master key card that unlocked all the doors on the seventh floor. Maybe all the doors in the entire hotel. I waited but didn't see the second gunman. Could be he went off to search another floor. Could be he was sitting in one of the rooms watching the latest Natalie Portman film.

From my vantage point, it appeared that several doors stood open, but the door to our suite near the center of the hallway remained closed. Which meant the gunmen might not have been given our specific room number. Maybe not even our specific floor. I'd been downstairs for a while. The gunmen could have started on ten and been working their way down. Maybe there were even a couple of men per floor. Hopefully, though, it was just the single pair, both still on seven.

The same gunman exited another room and tried the next door. The darkness allowed me to advance far enough into the hallway that I could see how the gunman was entering. Quickly and carelessly. Bypassing the first few closet doors and instead starting at the rear of the room and moving frontward. Bad technique. Bad training. Possibly no training. This operation had been thrown together at the last minute, no doubt about it. These men were clearly used to searching the African bush, not ten-story hotels or apartment buildings in major cities.

Advantage Fisk.

As soon as he was out of sight again, I raced toward our suite. I key-carded my way in, hoping the gunman couldn't hear the faint beep signaling the unlocking of the door. Given that he was busy utterly thrashing the room three doors down, I highly doubted it. I ducked inside and gently closed the door behind me.

I lifted my sports jacket off the sectional. When I did, a button flew off in the opposite direction. A button or something else. Whatever it was, it rolled under an anachronistic radiator and out of sight. I briefly scanned the nearby floor but heard the gunman out in the hallway getting closer. I needed to hide. I needed to retain the element of surprise.

I slipped into the closet nearest the door. The closet that would be behind the door the moment he opened it. As soon as he stepped through, I'd jump him from behind. Knock him down with the butt of my rifle.

But I wouldn't shoot him.

Because we needed him alive.

Tucked away in the closet, I drew a deep breath. Adrenaline had once again taken over my body, extinguished the five-day build-up of fear and replaced it with something else. Something indescribable. A powerful mix of righteousness and rage.

Fewer than thirty seconds later, I heard the key card in the lock. Through the slit in the closet I watched the hotel room door swing open.

A moment later, the young gunman was sauntering past me, moving toward the back of the room.

As I leapt out of the closet, I raised the butt of my M27 and kicked the room door closed with my heel. Said, 'Maybe you missed the *Do Not Disturb* sign,' as I drove the weapon home into the back of his skull.

THIRTY-THREE

I didn't care for the crack I heard when the butt of my rifle connected with the back of his skull. I needed him alive. And knocking him unconscious wouldn't do either.

The gunman hit the floor hard.

Thankfully, the little bastard popped right back up again.

He spun around to face me.

I caught him with a vertical buttstroke, this time at only half strength. He stumbled sideways into Jadine's room but stayed on his feet, punch-drunk.

I followed his every step, so that once he finally righted himself, I'd be standing straight in front of him again. Then, with the business end of the M27 over my shoulder, I drove my arms forward and smashed the butt of my weapon up under his chin.

His head snapped back hard enough to take him off his feet and land him flat on Jadine's bed, the AK-47 he was holding now dangling by the strap.

I swiftly relieved him of it.

Then jumped on top of him, pressing the length of the M27 into his throat. Trying to quell the inferno that tonight's attack had ignited within me. I felt it in my throat, I felt it in my gut, I felt it in my chest.

I had the upper hand and was about to begin my questioning when the son of a bitch reached down into one of his fanny packs, came up with a penknife, and jabbed the blade into my right side.

Hurt like hell but didn't go in very far. Didn't penetrate any vital organs, I was sure of it.

I pushed down on the stock of the M27 hard enough that he had to bring both hands up to his throat. Then I dislodged the penknife from my side and plunged the blade deep into his left bicep.

He tried to scream but wasn't getting enough air into his lungs.

As I held the rifle down hard against his throat, I reached down and ripped off the rest of his fanny packs. *No more surprises.* Tossed them over the side of the bed.

'Are you with Rusul Alharb?' I shouted.

I pulled up on the M27 to allow him to speak. Instead, he used the opportunity to nod his head.

I started at the sound of gunfire in the seventh-floor hallway, then returned my attention to the man underneath me.

'Are you here looking for me and my partner?'

Another nod.

I was making it too easy for him to evade my questions, but the next one required more than a yes or no answer.

'How did you know where to find us? Who's the leak?'

'*La 'adri,*' he managed as he gulped for more air, '*la 'aerif.*'

Arabic.

'How did you know where to find us?' I shouted again.

'*La 'adri, la 'aerif.*'

I heard the electronic key unlock the outer door.

'English!' I hollered.

Jadine called out, 'It's me! Friendly! Don't shoot!'

'*'Ana la 'atakalam alanjilyzih, al'ahmaq!*'

I felt Jadine's presence behind me. I glanced over my shoulder as sweat streamed from my forehead into my eyes.

'What did he say, Jade?'

'He said, "I don't speak English, asshole!"' Jadine came around the side of the bed. 'Simon, you're bleeding!'

'It's not deep. Ask this bastard what we need to know, so we can get the hell out of here.'

'*Ayn alhujum?*' she said to him. 'Where is the attack?'

He shut his eyes tight and shook his head back and forth.

Jadine jerked the penknife out of his arm and pressed the point just below his left eye. '*Ayn alhujum?*' she repeated, gradually applying pressure.

A newfound fear ran through him like an electrical current.

'*Majmae tijariin! Majmae tijariin!*'

'*Ayn?*'

'Abuja!' he shouted as blood trickled from the small cut forming just below his eye. 'Abuja! Abuja!'

She turned to me. 'A commercial complex in Abuja. A shopping mall.'

'When?' I said.

'Mataa?' she cried.

'Ghadaan sabahaan!'

'Tomorrow morning,' she said.

Then to him: *'Aya mwl? Aya mwl?'*

'La 'adri, la 'aerif!'

'Aya mwl?' As she pressed the knife deeper into his skin, his eye bulged from its socket. 'Which mall? Wadud Plaza, *maratan ukhraa?'*

'Nem fielaan! Nem fielaan! Wadud! *Nem fielaan!'*

She pulled the penknife back from his eye. Then, as effortlessly as cutting the tags out of a new pair of underwear, she sliced the flesh across the left side of his neck, slashing with a surgeon's precision both the jugular vein and carotid artery.

'They can't know what we know,' she said calmly, as blood spurted and the life drained from his face.

THIRTY-FOUR

'This was no random terror attack, Jade. This was a hit.'
'Then we need to escape this hotel without being discovered by police or else they'll strike at us again while we're being questioned at headquarters.'

'They knew how to find us,' I said. 'Someone gave up our location. Which means we need to go even one step further.'

'Meaning what, Simon?'

'We need to let everyone think they succeeded. We need to let them think we're dead.'

'Just how are we going to pull *that* off? All the terrorists are dead. If they hit their target, who took out the last gunman?'

'There won't be any shortage of people trying to claim credit for killing four members of Rusul Alharb,' I said, contemplating the body on the bed. 'You read the intelligence. For every incident of mass violence in this region, there are at least a dozen official accounts, none of which come remotely close to the truth. By the time everything gets sorted here, we'll be long gone. By morning, we'll have your daughter and whether we're dead or alive won't matter to anyone but us.'

'And our families,' she said. 'Simon, what about Ana and your daughter back in Moldova? This attack will hit the international news within hours, if it hasn't already. What happens if Ana and Hailey hear there was a major terror attack at your last known location?'

'It's a chance we'll have to take. Now that we know there's a leak, we can't risk anyone in Nigerian intelligence finding out we're alive.'

'So what if they do? They won't know where we are or what we've learned.'

'Sun Tzu, Jade. "All war is based on deception. Hence, when we are able to attack . . ."'

'"We must seem unable."'

'Precisely. Now, how long do you think we have before the police move in?'

'They won't move in until they're sure of one of two things. One, that there are no live gunmen with hostages. Or two, that back-up security forces are about to arrive from Moundou.'

'Which is how far from here?'

'Seven and a half hours by auto.'

'Which means that, even if they left Moundou at the sound of the first shot, they're still a few hours away.'

'What are you thinking?'

'Did you see any victims on or near this floor? Maybe a white man? A black woman?'

'A few doors down I saw a white guy who I think was here on business. And just next door is a black woman, who was shot in bed beside her husband.'

'We need to get those two bodies into this room. We'll dress them in our clothes, place our IDs in their pockets, and toss a grenade in their laps, so that police will need dental records to make a positive identification.'

'We're going to mutilate their corpses?'

'This world belongs to the living, Jade. I promise, they won't feel a thing. The question is, what happens then? How the hell do we get out of here?'

'If police see us attempting to flee, they'll assume we're Rusul Alharb and start shooting at us.'

'All the more reason to make sure they *don't* see us.'

'Some of the fancier hotels in African countries with civil strife have underground bunkers and tunnels so that the threat of a rebel uprising doesn't drive away their wealthiest and most high-profile clients. I'd bet this hotel is one of them.'

'Check it out,' I said. '*Carefully.* I'll fetch the bodies and begin setting the stage up here on seven. Then we'll need to find someone willing to accept payment in return for feeding our names to a few of the journalists outside.'

Sixty minutes later, after trekking through the narrow, dusty underground tunnel beneath the hotel, we were standing in an empty alley half a mile away. I'd bribed one of the massacre's survivors – a young bellhop who had barely escaped with his life – to tell authorities that he'd been on seven delivering room service to an American named Simon Fisk and his guest Jadine Visser when the attack kicked off. And that he'd seen us both gunned down.

'We don't have much time, Simon. We may *need* to alert the Nigerian security forces. Maybe they can find Ahmad before sunrise. Maybe they can stop him before he reaches Wadud Plaza.'

'He's bound to have a back-up plan. If he sees any unusual activity in the area, he'll move on to another target. And we can't risk any more leaks.'

'We can trust Jeffries. He's a suck-up, but if I forbid him to share something with Nigerian intelligence, he'll keep silent.'

'The *name*,' I said. 'What was the name of the Nigerian intelligence agent we met in Maiduguri?'

'Ikenna Orji,' she said.

I repeated the name aloud. My mind went right back to the place it went when I first heard the name spoken in Maiduguri.

Well, I'll be damned, I thought. *Ikenna Orji. I didn't forget the agent's name because I'm getting too old. I forgot his name because I never fucking grew up.*

'All right,' I said, suppressing the grin trying to gain control of my lips. 'Call Jeffries. He can at the very least get us back to Abuja before sunrise. And once we're there, we're going to need a way to get around the city, fast.'

'Let me guess,' she said. 'Boys and their toys. You're still just one big kid, Simon.'

I allowed myself to smile. 'Have him meet us somewhere neutral near the airport. Tell him to make sure he isn't followed. If he sees a tail, he needs to abort.'

'And if he does, what then?' she said.

'In that case, we're better off just stealing a car.'

PART III
The Battle of Abuja

THIRTY-FIVE

In a half-empty warehouse, a half a mile from Nnamdi Azikiwe International Airport in Abuja, we met with Deputy Secretary John Jeffries for the third time in six days. He was alone, as we'd instructed. His expression, as usual, was stern. Yet he appeared exceedingly uncomfortable. Restless. Fidgety. Downright nervous. Though it wasn't clear whether his apprehension was over Rusul Alharb, bent Nigerian intelligence agents, Secretary Coleman, Kishana, or yours truly. Back in N'Djamena, after Jadine tended to my minor hip wound, I'd personally thought we'd shared a highly efficient and pleasant phone call.

'I need a bike,' I'd told him when Jadine handed me the phone.

'A bike?'

'A motorcycle.'

'We can transport you anywhere—'

'Thanks, but we've already flown coach on Kenya Airways, jumped out of a military helicopter, and rode for hours in the back of a sweltering trailer only to have it hijacked by Rusul Alharb. No more whirlybirds, no more taxis, no more anything where I'm not behind the wheel and can control every acceleration, deceleration, and turn.'

'All right. What kind of bike are we—'

'Ducati 959 Panigale.'

'That's awfully specific. I don't know exactly what we'll be able to—'

'Arctic white.'

'I see, but as I was saying, I don't know exactly what we'll be able to *find* on such short notice here in Abuja. Bikes like that—'

'Are sold roughly six and a half blocks from the US Embassy. Right off the expressway on Independence Avenue, a hop and a skip from your Korean counterparts. I saw one right outside on the lot. Arctic white with Ducati red rims. Expensive but worth every naira.'

'I'll see what I can do.'

Less than an hour after the call, Jadine and I boarded a private jet owned by the French business magnate Bernard Marchand, heading west from N'Djamena to Abuja. As anticipated, we were the Gulfstream IV's only passengers. The flight damn sure beat all previous modes of transport provided to us.

'OK, where's the bike?' I said as Jeffries reached out to shake my hand in greeting at the warehouse.

He motioned toward the rear of the building, then led us past several rows of boxes to a large blue tarp. He motioned toward it. As though he expected me to hop on top of the tarpaulin cover, rev the engine, and drive right out of there.

'Is there something underneath this tarp?' I said.

He rolled his eyes but reached out, grabbed a handful of royal blue tarpaulin, and tore it off.

And there it was. The Ducati Superbike 959 Panigale.

Lightweight. Powerful. Fast enough for the racetrack yet street legal. The perfect balance of performance and control.

Arctic white. A paintjob to die for.

Ducati red rims on Pirelli tires.

'You were right, Mr Fisk. It was . . . expensive.'

'Worth every naira,' I said.

Beneath the low persimmon sky of the West African dawn, the Ducati superbike raced along the airport expressway in the direction of downtown Abuja. Although Wadud Plaza didn't open until nine, our hope was to locate Ahmad and Kishana before they ever reached their target. Preferably before they even strapped on their vests.

It wouldn't be easy. Thanks to my friend, computer guru Kati Sheffield, we knew that no one under the name Ahmad Abdulaziz was registered at any Abuja hotel. Of course, that didn't mean he wasn't staying at one. More than likely, Ahmad possessed at least one alternate identity, with papers to match. Or, failing that, he would have bribed a desk clerk to check him in at the hotel without seeing his passport.

Still, the area we needed to search wasn't terribly large. How far, after all, would Ahmad want to travel wearing a suicide vest? And if, as we strongly suspected, Kishana remained highly uncooperative, he'd want to be as near to his target as possible to decrease the risk of a mission-ending incident. Once she was dressed in her suicide vest, Ahmad would need to gag her in order to prevent her from warning innocent bystanders to flee.

There was also a good chance that Ahmad and Kishana were holed up in a Rusul Alharb safe house. Fortunately, Wadud Plaza was located in a heavily commercial area. So, if Ahmad had wanted to be within spitting distance of his target, he would have likely needed to lease an office rather than a flat. An office, where there was far less of an expectation of privacy. Where people were more likely to talk.

As I leaned into the turn, Jadine squeezed her arms tighter around my upper abdomen. Both of us were now dressed neck to ankle in my favorite fashion designer – Miguel Caballero of Bogota, Colombia. I'd originally requested the full black biker armor days ago when I'd first met Jeffries, but because of the ticking clock, I was sure I'd never see it. In fact, I'd even failed to mention it over the phone from N'Djamena, because I was sure there was nothing Jeffries would be able to do about it at that late hour. For once in this mission, I was confronted with a decidedly pleasant surprise.

'What's this?' I said when Jeffries handed me the heavy box back in the warehouse.

'The clothes you ordered.'

My jaw nearly dropped when I punched through the packing tape and opened the box.

Dryly, Jeffries said, 'These clothes were also . . . expensive.'

Of course, they were expensive. I had been introduced to the brilliant fashion designer's work only two years earlier by a Scottish gangster known as the Chairman. Gerry Gilchrist of Glasgow. 'Not just to spare you from road rash either,' Gilchrist had said to me with his heavy Sean Connery accent. 'It's bloody bulletproof. Can withstand a fifty-caliber round, if I'm not mistaken.'

Caballero had designed clothes for former President Barack Obama, for Prince Felipe of Spain, President Uribe of Colombia, even the late Venezuelan dictator Hugo Chavez. In addition to motorcycle gear, he designed topcoats, blazers, even tuxedo shirts. 'I think it's safe to presume,' the Chairman had said, 'that were James Bond not merely a fictional character, Miguel Caballero would be his personal tailor.'

After being shot in the chest with a .45 in the kitchen of a cramped flat just outside Liverpool, I was inclined to agree.

No doubt Duncan MacBride, the pockmarked punk who fired the bullet into me, would also endorse Caballero's designs. Were he still among the living, that is.

As we crossed Mohammed Buhari Way, I couldn't help but picture the girl in the video and wonder where she was, what she was thinking. Had she lost all hope of rescue? Was she resigned to her fate? Or was she the type of individual who'd fight her captor right up until the last breath, as I imagined her mother would? Did Kishana suspect that her mother was in Abuja searching for her? Or did she think her mom was back in Cape Town, strategizing with her grandfather's people about how to help Nigerian security forces find her before it was too late? Or had she too heard the news reports from N'Djamena? Did she think her mother was dead?

And what if Jadine and I failed to reach her in time? In her final minutes, what would go through Kishana's head? How do you reflect on a life merely sixteen years old? Would she think about the experiences she had had or the ones she would never have? She would never go to college, never fall in love, never get married or have children, never start and build a business or career for herself, never amass a collection of personal or professional accomplishments she could die proud of. What had been Kishana's plans for when she returned home from the Peace Corps? Had she chosen a four-year university? Did she want to work with an NGO or study law like her mother and grandfather? Was she interested in military service? Business? Science? The arts? The humanities?

Did she have any particular talents even Jadine didn't know about?

Did she feel as though she had a calling?

Did she have a boyfriend? A best friend? A father figure beyond Ahmad?

I thought then of Danjuma, who had indeed made it safely to the US Embassy here in Abuja. Jeffries had assured me that the boy was being well cared for and that he'd already made at least a dozen friends among the staff.

Back at the warehouse, Jeffries said, 'He actually walked right up to the US ambassador to Nigeria and asked him for a bottle of champagne. Told him he wanted to celebrate.'

'Celebrate what?' I said.

'That's what the ambassador asked him. The boy said, "We are all of us having lived for one more day."'

THIRTY-SIX

The Wadud Plaza shopping center wasn't much to look at. From the outside, the structure resembled a rundown Florida strip mall with a two-story fleabag motel sitting on top of it. It appeared particularly pathetic now, at roughly ten minutes before seven a.m., a full two hours before the mall was scheduled to open for business.

I pulled the Ducati over to the opposite curb and parked. With my helmet still on, face mask still down, I surveyed the buildings in the immediate vicinity.

From behind me, Jadine said, 'Isn't it a little careless for us to be sitting across from the mall on a shiny new motor-cycle, staring up at the windows in the surrounding area?'

'Nonsense,' I said, slightly lifting my face mask. 'Ahmad thinks we're dead. Our bodies were blown to bits by a hand grenade back in our hotel room in N'Djamena, remember. Besides, Ahmad's a smart guy. You said so yourself. Several times. He'd never suspect anyone to be dumb or reckless enough to attempt a rescue in a bustling African city on a sparkling new Ducati whose engine can be heard from thirty miles away.'

'You have me there.'

Once we dismounted, I retrieved our significantly smaller but bulletproof black packs and handed one to Jadine, who swiftly slipped into it.

'I can't walk around in this helmet, Simon.'

'No need to. Leave the helmet with the bike. Just put on your hat and sunglasses.'

'What if he's peering out the window with binoculars?'

'He's not. Is that how you'd spend your final few hours on earth? Besides, even if he is wasting his time at a window, he's not going to be looking for ghosts.'

'You're right. Only Jeffries and my father know we're alive. And your friend Kati.'

'And our pilots. But I suspect Monsieur Bernard Marchand pays them enough to ensure that they're bribe-proof.'

'The co-pilot seemed to have his eye on me.'

'Believe me, I caught that. But can you blame him?'

Jadine lowered the brim of her cap to the top of her sunglasses. It was hard to believe it hadn't even been a week since I went to her office at the University of Cape Town, seeking her help because I thought I'd been caught in the frame for first-degree murder.

If only things had been that simple.

She said, 'Tactically, it only makes sense to split up. We can cover twice as much ground in the couple of hours we have.'

This time I had no choice but to agree. I said, 'You take this street, work your way up. Then make a right at the corner. I'll start on the opposite side of the street and turn left. We'll meet in the middle, directly across from Wadud Plaza.'

'Keep your radio on.'

'Will do. And, Jade, don't you forget our deal.'

'Our deal?'

'Yell if you come across a lion.'

We worked methodically. Building to building. Door to door. Office to office. Doctors, lawyers, accountants, IT, small businesses of every sort. All of whom spoke at least enough English to tell me they hadn't seen the middle-aged man or teenage girl depicted in the photos I showed them.

Per our admittedly rudimentary plan, we stopped at each uninhabited space, picked the lock, and took a quick look around. The more doors we opened, the more discouraged we became. I could feel it in my bones and hear it in Jadine's voice through my earpiece. Both of us were fast losing hope that we'd find Ahmad and Kishana before the mall opened. Unlike the Stones, time was not on our side.

The operation was also taking longer than expected. We'd need to keep up the frantic pace at which we were going just to meet in the middle across from the front entrance to Wadud Plaza before the mall opened at nine.

'Have you seen this man? This young woman?'

The more negative responses I received, the more doubt in

my own decisions crept in. In the Sambisa forest, Jadine had been calling the shots. At some point, I'd taken over. I'd been the one to decide against contacting Nigerian security forces. Was that a mistake? I'd been so sure that they'd scare Ahmad away, but was that not the second-best outcome we could expect for today? It would keep Kishana alive just that much longer. It would at least buy us more time to find her.

Would we have been any closer to finding her if I had chosen to search the Gwoza Hills and Mandara Mountains instead of Maiduguri and the Lake Chad Basin? Without Harun al-Haggi's intelligence, we wouldn't know about Kishana's martyrdom video. But we also wouldn't have lost all that time in Chad. And if we hadn't accessed that website, Ahmad might still be unaware we were looking for him at all. As in all of life, there was no way to know what we would have found down the paths not taken.

And it pained me, in both instances.

THIRTY-SEVEN

At ten minutes to nine, Jadine and I stood together across the street from the entrance to the Wadud Plaza shopping center. Even ten minutes before the mall opened, the parking lot was a catastrophe. A seeming free-for-all, with most cars parked diagonally, some stationed lengthwise at the curb, others floating in some other dimension entirely. It was easy to see why the twin attackers a few years ago used car bombs.

'The plaza is already packed with people,' Jadine said. 'We need to alert the police so that they can initiate evacuation procedures.'

'This may be our last chance to find your daughter, Jade. If the police show and begin evacuation procedures, Ahmad's either going to move on to Plan B or go to ground. In either case, our odds of finding him and Kishana alive severely diminish. Our chances would dwindle to almost nothing.'

Jadine set her jaw. 'The last attack here killed twenty-one people, and the plaza wasn't nearly as crowded as it is now. I can't put dozens, maybe hundreds, of lives in jeopardy for one sixteen-year-old girl, even if she is my only child.'

'If we find them, we can stop him with a single bullet. And if you're right about Kishana: once he's dead, she's not going to be detonating any suicide vests. We can still complete this mission with no collateral damage. Just give us the chance. Give your daughter the chance.'

She stared at the building across the street as though she could see through its walls, to the scores of staffers already inside, setting things up for the customers about to push through the doors.

'I watched the aftermath of the last Wadud Plaza bombing live on the news, Simon. Witnesses heard the blast from miles away. The sky was thick with a toxic black smoke that could be seen two districts over. All the buildings we just searched, every one of them had their windows shattered from the force of the explosion. The news focused on those who lost their lives, but more than fifty were injured as well. Many of them with life-altering burns. Shrapnel buried deep in their flesh. Some lost arms and legs. The lucky ones, just fingers and toes. Two of the wounded eventually died excruciating deaths from infections.'

'One last scan of the area,' I said. 'This time out in the open, with our binoculars. If he sees us, maybe we get lucky and he rabbits like al-Haggi back in Konduga.'

'All right. One last scan and then I make the call.'

I dove into my pack and fished out the binoculars, which were smaller than my hand yet yielded extraordinary vision. I pressed them to my eyes and adjusted the focus as I surveyed Wadud Plaza one last time.

The signs over the stores were simple banners with large letters in dozens of different fonts. *Phonz*, one said. *Microfinancing*, read another. Electronics retail and repair. Women's clothing, shoes, jewelry, the selection in each very likely wanting.

'Something's not right about this,' I said.

'What do you mean?'

'This attack is supposed to be some grand gesture, right? Like when they hit the United Nations building here in Abuja, only a hundred times worse.'

'So?'

'The setting. *This* setting. It isn't grand enough. This isn't a grand place. Certainly not a place to win glory. Not to mention, Wadud Plaza's been bombed before. By a couple of nobodies. Is Rusul Alharb really going to blow up the grand-daughter of the US Secretary of State in front of the world and only take out twenty or twenty-five people in the process? And is the destruction of this building the image they want to portray? A shopping plaza that has been hit before? The new Rusul Alharb, the one that pledged its allegiance to ISIL, is media-savvy. They're going to be filming this. They're going to want CCTV cameras to show the carnage in order to bring the reality of it home on their websites and YouTube channels.'

'The gunman. He *said* the mall. Wadud Plaza.'

'In that order,' I said.

'What?'

'He said "the mall" at first. The first words you translated to me were "a commercial complex."'

'By which he meant a shopping mall.'

'You're sure?'

'I'm sure.'

'Then you asked him when.'

'And he said, "Tomorrow morning."'

'Then you asked him which mall was going to be attacked.'

'And he said, "Wadud Plaza."'

'Did he, though? No, not right away. He said something before that. The same words he'd spoken in response to one of my questions before you got there. Something like, *"La 'adri—"*'

'La 'adri, la 'aerif.'

'That's it. That's what he said. *La 'adri, la 'aerif.* What does it mean?'

'It means, "I don't know."'

'Then you pressed him.'

Her face rapidly melted into a mask of grim realization. 'I *led* him.'

'You were tired, Jade. *We* were tired, dog-tired.'

'I wasn't thinking. *I* mentioned Wadud Plaza. With a knife to his eye! Wadud had been hit before, like you said. I asked him if it was Wadud Plaza. Was Wadud Plaza the target *again*?'

'And he said, "Yes. Yes, Wadud, yes."'

'You think he was lying?' she said.

'Not about the first part. Not about the attack going down in Abuja. Or even a mall.' My voice picked up some urgency. 'But this one isn't the *right* one. It can't be. What are the other shopping plazas here in the capital?'

'Novare Apo, along the Murtala Mohammed Expressway, in the Gudu District.'

'How many stores?'

'Not so many. There's a Shop Rite supermarket there. A chain bank, a hair salon, a food court. Some of the stores have been vacant for quite a while.'

'That doesn't sound like our place either. What other malls are there in Abuja?'

'Dunes Center. But it's sort of high end. Not many shoppers walking around, especially in the morning. They get more of a night and weekend crowd.'

'Where else, Jade?'

'Jabi Lake Mall. It's large. Aesthetically pleasing. It has a cinema. A Shop Rite supermarket. Lots of stores. Some brand names.'

'Let's put a pin in it. What other malls are there?'

'There's Reddi Plaza.'

'I've heard that name before. Tell me about Reddi Plaza.'

'It's an indoor mall with dozens of stores, a food court, and a movie theater. It's very modern. It's very—'

'Western.'

'Yeah, Western.' She paused as she searched her mind for something. 'The shopping plaza also leases office space. It's a commercial complex in every sense of the word.'

'And if he leased even a small space, he could have spent the night. So that in the morning, they'd be right there, already at their target.'

'We need to get there, Simon.'

'How far from here?'

'In this traffic?' she said.

'In this traffic, on a Ducati superbike, with a driver who truly knows how to maneuver her.'

THIRTY-EIGHT

As the Ducati sped toward Reddi Plaza, a terrible guilt washed over me. This was my fault. I'd known that Jadine had never interrogated anyone before. Despite her earlier tough talk, she hadn't been assigned to a black site. She was running a few spies, that was all. I'd stepped back – out of the picture even – not just because I didn't speak Arabic but because I'd come to trust Jadine's judgment more than my own. Which didn't mean I had nothing to offer. Two heads were always better than one. But I had just wanted to tap out, to not be responsible for the outcome, regardless of whether it succeeded or failed.

Granted, I *had* been tired too. Exhausted even. And the pain in my hip where the bastard stabbed me had probably been diverting a few million brain signals. Yet still, this error was amateurish, and I'd missed it completely. Because I didn't ask Jadine to translate what the gunman was saying word for word, as I would have in nearly every other situation. Under any other circumstances, I would have made the decision to verify exactly what was being said so that I could interpret every word independently. Even if I'd gained no additional information, it was just as Jadine had said about the State Department's Bureau of Intelligence and Research: 'We all had the same intelligence on WMDs in Iraq. We just came to the correct *conclusions*.' Here, I didn't even bother issuing a report.

As I leaned into the next turn, the wide, four-story shopping mall came into view.

Reddi Plaza was located on Tafawa Balewa Way, a few blocks from the main branch of the Central Bank of Nigeria and the National Christian Center. The stores here were considerably larger than the ones at Wadud Plaza, some even with familiar names. Like Nike, Nokia, and Virgin.

Here, the names of the stores facing the parking lot weren't

printed on banners as they were at Wadud Plaza. These stores
displayed tall and expensive signs over their businesses.
Recognizable fonts with raised lettering. All of which clearly
lit up the parking lot long after dark.

This was a grand place. Grand for West Africa. Grand for
Nigeria. Grand for Abuja. Grand even for some of the more
rural parts of the United Kingdom and the States.

This was the place. I felt it in my gut. I felt it in my bones.
This was where we'd find Ahmad Abdulaziz and Kishana
Coleman.

I parked the bike. We swiftly dismounted, removed our
helmets, and slipped into our bulletproof packs.

Jadine said, 'This place is just as bustling as Wadud Plaza
this morning.'

'Have you been here before?'

'Of course.'

'Ever been here with Ahmad?'

'Just once, I think. The first time he secretly visited me in
Abuja.'

'Where did you go?'

'We never made it past the food court.'

'Why not?'

'Because he sort of . . . Well, he sort of proposed to me.'

'He proposed *here*?'

'The first time, yeah. But only very informally. Came off
more like a suggestion than a question. I told him no. He got
upset and stormed outside to the parking lot. Went back to his
hotel. We made up hours later when I finally went after him
and apologized.'

'Where's the food court located?'

'Third floor, almost directly in the center below that sign
that says Reddi Plaza, Shopping and Entertainment.'

'Then that's our first stop.'

Years ago, during the Lindsay Sorkin case, I'd been involved
in a shootout at a shopping mall in Minsk. Ana and I had been
the target of a Syrian assassin who'd been tasked with finding
Lindsay Sorkin before we did. Lindsay's father had developed
a weapon that could potentially replace soldiers in the

battlefield. Rebel groups and nation states alike saw an opportunity, and the Syrian had been an experienced mercenary hired to grab it.

I killed him in a near-empty candy store. But not before Ana was shot. In the ambulance on the way to the emergency clinic, I was sure I was going to lose her, and I knew that I was fully to blame. Now, I wanted to tell Jadine to remain outside in the parking lot. But how could I? It was *her* daughter's life on the line. If it had been Hailey's, would I have been denied? Besides, in many ways, she'd led this mission from the start. And we wouldn't have gotten this far without her. In truth, I doubted I would have survived that first night in the Sambisa forest.

'Let's go inside,' I said, as we crossed through the Reddi Plaza parking lot. 'Let's find your daughter and give this story a happy ending.'

'There *are* no happy endings in Nigeria,' she said. 'The best we can hope for is to ease some suffering, to take away some pain.'

I took her hand in mine. 'Let's do that, then, Jade.'

As soon as we entered the mall, she said those magic words again. 'We'll cover more ground faster if we split up.'

Again, she was right, without question. Yet again, I didn't feel good about it.

'I'll start at ground level,' she said. 'You go up to the food court. Maintain radio contact.'

As I watched the glass elevator descend, I made for the escalators. On the second floor, I immediately saw a coffee shop and considered grabbing an espresso. I'd been running on fumes since yesterday's brief nap at the hotel in N'Djamena, and I could feel myself slowing down. My head felt sluggish and my legs were screaming out in revolt.

Just a little longer. Let's see this thing to the end.

I ascended another escalator to the third floor.

As I moved through the mall, Kishana's image was burned into my mind, but I repeatedly lost Ahmad's. Which was dangerous, because many of the women in the mall wore traditional Muslim hijabs that concealed their faces. So I mentally ran through the list of the telltale indicators that security experts used to identify suicide bombers.

I watched people's body language. Searching for someone who looked uncomfortable. Restless. Fidgety. Downright nervous. Like Jeffries looked this morning. I watched for sweat, for repeated licks of the lips, a stiff gait. For someone dressed in baggy clothes, something wholly unsuitable for the weather.

As people shuffled past me, I sniffed the air for the chemical scent of perfume or cologne, which many suicide bombers wore to prepare for their ascension into Heaven. For their seventy-two virgins, I supposed.

But mostly I watched people's eyes. Not just for anger but fear. A blank stare. A pair of eyes that blinked so much you'd think they were silently communicating in Morse code. I looked at lips. Not just for repeated licks but for the biting of them or a twitch. Lips that were moving without saying anything because they were muttering prayers.

I watched the way people walked. Not just for a stiff gait but for someone who looked as if they weren't going anywhere. As if they'd just bought a one-way ticket and didn't anticipate leaving the mall in one piece.

I looked for bulging bodies with skinny faces. For hands in pockets, for fingers wrapped tightly around cell phones.

I looked for a middle-aged man with a teenage woman, but I didn't dismiss the chance that they could be separated. If Kishana was indeed brainwashed, the pair could be moving in separate directions with the intention of causing maximum damage.

Once I was convinced neither Ahmad nor Kishana was in the food court, I started back downstairs.

At the bottom of the escalator on the second floor, I saw a man. Tall, slim, clean-shaven. Dressed in baggy denim jeans and a jet-black windbreaker zipped up to the throat. He wore his hood like a teenager but was clearly an adult. My age, maybe. Give or take a few years. With the hood on, it was difficult to discern his features. But since he was staring off into the distance, he gave me all the time in the world to look at him. To study his face. A face I'd seen in photographs all week long but never before.

Slowly, I reached into my go-bag. Gripped the stock of the SIG Sauer M11 that Jeffries had given me at the warehouse. And began to pull it free and out in the open. My index finger already inside the trigger guard, relaxed and ready to squeeze.

THIRTY-NINE

A young woman in a black hijab stood a few feet away from him on his left.

This was the tricky part.

If I shouted, either at him or at Kishana or at the innocent bystanders, I could spook him, push him into a panic that would force his hand and have him reaching for the detonator.

Right now, his left hand was at his side. His right was clinging to the pocket of his windbreaker by a thumb. It would take under three seconds for him to reach inside and set off the bombs presumably strapped around him and Kishana.

If I shot him, I had better kill him. Because if I injured him, he could still set off the bombs. Killing him, killing me, killing Kishana and dozens of others, at least.

The largest and safest target was always center mass. But positioned right in front of Ahmad's heart could be a bomb. Which meant I needed to take a head shot.

From this distance, it would be difficult. It would take perfectly steady hands. Frankly, I wasn't sure I could pull it off in this depleted condition.

I placed my chin against my left shoulder and spoke quietly into the microphone. I gave Jadine our location. Cautioned her not to run. Not to start a panic that could cause Ahmad to act.

'Take the escalator up,' I said. 'Approach him from the opposite side. One of us will need to get close enough to him that when we make our move, he won't have time to go for the detonator.'

At that moment, Ahmad Abdulaziz turned his head. Just thirty degrees but enough for his gaze to fall right on me. Before I knew it, his eyes had gone wide. He reached out for the young girl in the hijab with his left hand. His right sunk deep into his windbreaker pocket.

I drew my weapon.

Aimed. Instinctively at center mass.

And fired.

The bullet tore through his chest, sending his body soaring several feet into the wide stone pillar behind him.

The sound of the shot reverberated throughout the mall, launching a panic. Shoppers and retail staff scattered clumsily, some knocking into each other so forcefully that they fell straight to the hard marble floor. Screams seemed to come from everywhere. Men, women, and children. Voices in a state of sheer terror.

The girl in the hijab scurried away and was quickly lost in the throng. Meanwhile, I darted toward Ahmad, taking the last ten feet, sliding on my knees. From there, I gently tugged Ahmad's hand free from his windbreaker pocket, which indeed contained the phone I assumed he was using as a detonator.

Seconds later, Jadine was at my side, staring into the hazy eyes of her former lover, her former husband, her former spy, Ahmad Abdulaziz, who lay bleeding from a gaping hole on the left side of his chest, likely just above the heart.

'Where *is* she?' she said, as she knelt at my side.

'Ran off,' I told her. 'In the direction of the department store.'

Ahmad suddenly gripped me by the wrist. For a moment, he looked up at me, then his gaze slowly shifted to Jadine.

'She is . . . not here,' he said, as blood bubbled atop his lips and spilled over on to his chin.

'Then where is she?' Jadine shouted, as I carefully unzipped the windbreaker. 'Where's Kishana now?'

He tried to speak between quivering lips, but the words failed to come out.

Carefully, I opened his jacket.

Inside his jacket I found a holster with a loaded handgun but no suicide vest.

'She—' he started again.

'She *what*?' Jadine thundered.

The young woman in the hijab suddenly ran up to us. She uncovered her face, which was drenched with a clinging mix of sweat and tears.

'I'm Kishana's friend Zahra from the Peace Corps,' she

cried. 'Kishana's father and I have been searching for her for more than a week now.'

On the floor below us, police and security forces were entering the mall en masse.

'*Searching* for her?' Jadine shouted. '*He* took her.'

The girl shook her head frantically, sweat and tears now coming off her like a wet pup shaking herself after a bath. '*Rusul Alharb* took her. They kidnapped her. I was there.'

'They kidnapped her because she's *his* daughter,' Jadine spat back.

'Yes, in order to get to him. To punish her father for *betraying* them.'

Ahmad again tried to speak to no avail.

We were going to lose him and soon.

'Betraying them *how*?' Jadine said.

Zahra drew a deep breath. 'How do you not *know* any of this?'

'Any of what?' I tried softly, hoping to calm her down.

She drew a deep breath to compose herself. 'After Mohammed Yakubu was murdered, Ahmad tried to get away from Yakubu's followers. But he was stopped. Someone in Nigerian intelligence threatened to out him to Shagari if he tried to walk. In the meantime, he made Ahmad feed you false information, so that US intelligence would drop him. So that he could run him on his own.'

Police and security forces were starting up the escalators on either side of the mall.

Zahra said, 'Shagari didn't trust him at first, but Nigerian intelligence worked Ahmad. Helped him burrow his way into Shagari's inner circle the same way he had into Yakubu's.'

Jadine looked to be in shock. 'You're saying Nigerian intelligence has been running Ahmad these past *ten years*?'

'Until only recently. When Ahmad tried again to bow out. His handler supposedly planned an escape for him. But when the time came, nothing panned out. Suddenly, Shagari became suspicious of him. Ahmad had no choice but to flee and hide. Then somehow . . .'

'What?' I said.

'Somehow Shagari discovered that Kishana was his

daughter. So he led a raid to kidnap her. *Not* knowing she was the granddaughter of the US Secretary of State. That, I don't know *how* they found out. When they took her, it was just to get at *him*.'

Ahmad squeezed my wrist with what little strength he had left.

'Shagari,' he managed, as more blood rose up and out of his mouth, causing him to cough and shudder.

He tried to lift his head and blood streamed down his neck.

With tears streaming down her face, Jadine said, 'Shagari? What about him, Ahmad?'

'Has.' He swallowed hard and coughed. 'Has. Her.'

And then Ahmad was gone.

I turned back to Zahra and asked, 'His handler, do you know his name?'

'Balogun,' she said. 'Ndulue Balogun. Ahmad told me he's based at a real estate office here in Abuja.'

FORTY

'Goddammit, I'm so sorry, Jade.'

'I would have done the same thing,' she said quietly. 'It's not your fault. We've been operating in the dark. Worse than that, we were misled and straight-up lied to from the beginning.'

We were seated in the US Embassy, waiting to see the chief of station. The time for going it alone was over. We needed help, and we needed it fast. The clock continued ticking, and we didn't know which part of Abuja to search next. We were running out of time, running out of options, and the fear and anger and self-doubt that Jadine had been able to conceal so well over the past six days finally showed on her face.

'I was so sure it was him,' she said. 'The martyrdom video we saw in Maiduguri left no question mark in my mind.'

'Because it's what Shagari *wanted* us to believe. Harun al-Haggi was the only breadcrumb he left for us and it led us straight out of Nigeria and into Chad, where he'd hoped to assassinate us.'

'He failed at the assassination, but he succeeded in wasting our time,' she said. 'What if we'd never set out for Maiduguri and never went to Konduga? What if we'd gone east toward the Gwoza Hills and Mandara Mountains instead?'

'I think he would have had men in the hills with sniper rifles trained on the edge of the forest, ready to take us out the moment we cleared the trees. In case we survived, he'd probably left another breadcrumb waiting for us in the first village we searched. A breadcrumb which would have also led us straight into Chad.'

'We underestimated them.'

'Everyone does. That's how they've survived as long as they have.'

'What's worse,' she said, 'is that I completely misjudged Ahmad. Personally, professionally. In every way possible.'

Zahra, who was currently in the embassy speaking to Nigerian authorities with a State Department lawyer at her side, had already spent a significant amount of time speaking with us in private. I had first asked the question weighing heaviest on my mind.

'Why did Ahmad react when he saw me?'

Zahra said, 'He saw your picture on the news. Police refused to offer the names of the victims of the hotel massacre in N'Djamena. But a pair of journalists somehow learned that an American by the name of Simon Fisk had been killed along with a South African college professor named Jadine Visser.'

Zahra proceeded to tell us everything she knew about Ahmad and the search they had conducted over the past nine days.

Apparently, Ahmad had been run by Nigerian intelligence for the past decade, ever since the end of the Maiduguri uprising, which had resulted in the extrajudicial killing of Mohammed Yakubu by police.

'He blamed himself for Yakubu's death,' Zahra had told us in the conference room, where she'd sat with her hands in her lap, nervously twiddling her thumbs. 'The agent who was running him, Ndulue Balogun, had once been introduced to Ahmad by Kishana's mom.' Here she motioned with her chin to Jadine, who silently acknowledged the statement with a slight dip of her head. 'Ms Visser had apparently used Balogun for brief meetings and for what Ahmad called "dead drops." Passing on information under the radar or something. He said Ms Visser used Balogun in order to conceal their romantic relationship from her superiors at the State Department.'

Jadine nodded but said nothing, though her nostrils flared and her chest expanded with air each time Zahra referred to her in the third person. Clearly, Jadine wanted to correct the record, or at least tidy it up, but the information Zahra possessed about her search with Ahmad was too crucial to our own to disrupt.

Zahra, speaking more to me than Jadine, said, 'So, when Ndulue Balogun approached Ahmad at the university in Maiduguri during the uprising, Ahmad immediately trusted him. Balogun told Ahmad he was there on Ms Visser's behalf and that they had to act in order to save Mohammed Yakubu's life. He assured Ahmad that he would get Yakubu to a safe house outside the country, where he would use the incitement charges already filed against him to try to flip him in return for full immunity. He said that Yakubu's son could act as the figurehead and that Yakubu himself could run Rusul Alharb in exile until things calmed down.' She finally glanced at Jadine. 'So, Ahmad – thinking it was the only chance he had to save his friend – told his new handler where he could find Yakubu.'

'That's how they found him so quickly,' Jadine said, almost to herself. 'And why I lost contact with Ahmad during the uprising and its immediate aftermath.'

There was still so much we didn't know about Ndulue Balogun, who'd evidently cleared out of his bullshit real estate office at some time over the previous six days. Had he been working with Shagari? Was he taking money from him? Had he believed in Rusul Alharb's cause all along? Or were his actions all somehow in furtherance of his career in Nigerian intelligence? Had his incentive been not money or ideology but power?

Had Balogun sent us into the Sambisa forest, knowing that Rusul Alharb had just vacated the underground facilities under and around Camp Zero? Had he been responsible for planting the name Umar Okafor in our intelligence reports, hoping we'd take the bait? Had Okafor been paid to turn us on to the messenger Harun al-Haggi?

If all that were true, I suspected that misdirection was the only reason Shagari had kept al-Haggi alive in the first place. The whole message may have been a set-up. Not necessarily meant for me and Jadine, but for Ahmad. Shagari had wanted him to suffer.

What seemed clear was that by the time Shagari forced Kishana to make the martyrdom video, he'd discovered Kishana was also the granddaughter of the US Secretary of State. Assuming Balogun was bent and working with Rusul Alharb, Shagari would have received that pivotal intelligence shortly after our visit to Balogun's bullshit real estate office on day one.

Jadine asked Zahra a question I didn't quite hear.

Zahra said, 'Ahmad didn't know Kishana was in Nigeria with the Peace Corps. He had no idea. They'd been estranged for over ten years. He was sure Kishana wouldn't even recognize him if she saw him. Which was true; Kishana had told me that herself during our first week in Adamawa State, when everyone was getting to know one another.'

'Before you arrived in Nigeria,' Jadine said, 'were all of your colleagues aware of Rusul Alharb's sustained presence in the northeast? Particularly in Borno, Yobe, and Adamawa?'

'We all knew the risks, which was why we'd all been given fake identities. As far as the locals knew, we were Muslim aid workers. From Ethiopia and northern Sudan. We were all fluent in our respective languages. We were all provided intricate backstories.'

I sensed we were drifting from our primary focus and tried to pull us back. 'What happened that led to the mass kidnapping in Adamawa?' I asked Zahra. 'Do you know?'

'Ahmad had been trying to get out from under Balogun's thumb. Shagari was becoming increasingly erratic. He was killing his own men at even the slightest whisper of betrayal. But Balogun said his superiors wouldn't budge. They needed Ahmad where he was. Ahmad pushed back, which only angered his handler more.'

'What did Balogun do in response?'

'First, he threatened to charge Ahmad with crimes committed by Rusul Alharb. Everything up to and including murder. Ahmad didn't care so much about that. He'd been documenting everything for the past ten years. And if he went off to prison, his lawyer would automatically receive everything. Ahmad said he'd arranged it.'

'Did he tell Balogun about the lawyer?'

'Unfortunately, yes. And that got Balogun even angrier. Next, he threatened to out Ahmad to Shagari. He said if Ahmad tried to run, Nigerian intelligence would hunt him down and bring him right back to Shagari. He'd watch him be burned alive or beheaded in the next viral video.'

'Did Ahmad have the impression that Balogun was working *with* Shagari and Rusul Alharb?'

'Not working with them, no. But Balogun obviously knew

how to pass information to them without becoming implicated himself.'

'I'm sure you've already relived that night too many times,' I said, 'but I need you to do it once more. Because Kishana's mother and I clearly can't trust the intelligence we've been provided. What took place during the mass kidnapping in Adamawa State?'

Zahra nodded her head, in agreement that she'd already relived the night of the mass kidnapping too many times, and in resignation that she was about to do so again.

She said, 'The militants were dressed as Nigerian security officers. They entered our camp and said that they'd received news of an imminent Rusul Alharb attack and that they were there to get us to safety. The girls from the Peace Corps suspected right away that it was a trap. But we couldn't just leave the local girls to be taken. Not after what had happened in Chibok. So we fought back. Kishana fought back.'

'The kidnappers were armed?'

'They were carrying guns but seemed too reluctant to use them at first. Instead, they wielded knives and other types of blades like machetes. Once things truly got out of control – I don't think they had expected any of the girls to fight back – they unholstered their weapons and started firing.'

'Some escaped but most were taken?'

'I barely got away and only because of the total chaos the Peace Corps girls created. Kishana didn't go easily, but she was taken. It was only afterward that I pieced together that she might have actually been a target of the assault because of the way the kidnappers were preoccupied with her and because of what they were saying.'

'What were they saying?'

'Something like, "This is the one. This is the one he wants. This is the one he needs."'

'What happened immediately after the kidnapping?' I asked Zahra.

'We gave statements to the police and the *real* security forces. We were all devastated. And when we asked the officers about the chances of getting our friends back, they appeared grim. They told us over one hundred of the Chibok schoolgirls were still missing after several years. They told us that neither the Nigerian nor the United States Government would negotiate with terrorists, making a trade for the girls impossible. They basically told us not to hold our breath.'

'How long after the attack did you meet Ahmad?'

'The very next day. He had a photo of Kishana, and he asked around about who knew her best, and the girls pointed to me because we'd been so close. He pulled me aside and told me the whole story of how he'd been a spy for Nigerian intelligence and how he'd been betrayed. He told me that the leader of Rusul Alharb – this Abubakar Shagari – had sent him a message, saying he had his daughter and that he would kill her and send her body to him in pieces.'

'He asked you to help him find Kishana?'

'No, he only asked me questions that might help *him* to find her. When we finished speaking, I was the one who asked to go with him. He was reluctant. He told me it was too dangerous. But I insisted. I told him I love Kishana like a sister and that I would risk everything to bring her home.'

Jadine placed her hand on the table, seeming to want to reach out to Kishana's friend for her caring and loyalty. But she also no doubt perceived the resentment Zahra felt for her. Maybe Ahmad had been poisoning his companion against Jadine all week. Or maybe Kishana and Jadine didn't have the perfect relationship Jadine had led me to believe. It was impossible to know. And it sure as hell wasn't the time to ask.

'How did you begin your search?' I said.

Zahra tilted her head skyward and stared at the ceiling. 'It began with Shagari. He'd told Ahmad that he would *personally* kill Kishana, so Ahmad reasoned that if we found Shagari, we'd find his daughter. The problem was, as well as Ahmad knew Shagari, the chances of finding him were slim.'

'Why is that?'

'Ahmad told me that Shagari moves from one place to another every day, without ever announcing where he's going, even to the militants he's bringing with him. He trusts no one. He loves to hear himself talk but never gives away any important information. And he never sleeps two consecutive nights in the same place.'

'How did you finally go about searching for Shagari?'

'We went to a hotel with free Wi-Fi and began downloading every available video Shagari made over the past ten years. There were hours of footage. Ahmad didn't know for certain, but he feared that Balogun knew Kishana was the Secretary of State's granddaughter. He said we needed to think like Shagari. If he knew about Kishana's relationship to a US cabinet member, this would be his biggest, most memorable attack ever.'

'What did he think Shagari would do?'

'He was sure that if Shagari knew about Kishana's family relationship with Secretary Coleman, he would take his time and plan it out. He'd want to pull off something more serious than any previous Rusul Alharb attack – even the Chibok schoolgirls kidnapping and the United Nations bombing. That first day, we went through hours of footage and assembled a reel of everything Shagari said on tape that Ahmad and I thought might be relevant to his plans for Kishana.'

Given the ludicrous topics Shagari liked to rant about in the videos he released to the world, this was no small feat. Zahra and Ahmad had to root through a two-ton pile of shit just to discover a few potential gems.

'Do you still have this reel?' I asked her.

'It's in the cloud.'

'Which means you can access it from anywhere, right? If we get you in front of a computer, could you show it to us?'

FORTY-ONE

The image of Abubakar Shagari onscreen was now more disturbing than ever. I pictured him standing behind Kishana, just as the executioner had in the video Secretary Coleman played for me in Cape Town. I envisioned him suiting her up in a suicide vest, with that batshit grin wide on his face. And all of us, helpless to wipe it off him.

Onscreen, Shagari stood tall in a clearing, dressed in his usual garb. Full combat fatigues with a camouflage scarf wrapped around his head and hanging down, opposite a weathered AK-47. He was clean-shaven above the lip but had a thick two- or three-inch beard running along his chin.

Although he went by a number of aliases, here a somewhat younger Shagari introduced himself as the leader of Rusul Alharb. He greeted his 'dear brothers in the mighty name of Allah,' then promptly took credit for the two dozen deaths that resulted from the devastating car-bomb attack carried out on the United Nations building here in the Nigerian capital several years ago. His message to his Muslim brethren was that they should know that this war was a war between Muslims and infidels. That this was a religious war.

As the video played, the Shagari onscreen gradually grew older. His rants, meanwhile, became longer and even more preposterous. In one breath, Shagari would profess that Rusul Alharb did not want to hurt anyone. That they had not forbidden anything. In the next breath, he would declare that democracy was unholy, that the Nigerian constitution needed to be burned to ashes. That many things forbidden in the Quran and the *hadith* were taught in Western schools and, therefore, Western education itself must be outlawed throughout the country.

After roughly twenty minutes, Jadine shot up from her chair. 'I can't watch any more of this,' she said, storming out of the room.

As badly as I wanted to go after her, I forced myself to

remain in front of the monitor watching Shagari pontificate on the peaceful religion he had wholly debased and distorted. Because the cuts were seamless, and because Shagari seemed to have only the one outfit, it was difficult to discern where one speech ended and another began. But the themes remained consistent, if not the facts.

He repeatedly proclaimed that he and his followers had decided to fight and go to paradise. That they sought martyrdom. That they wanted to do battle. That they wanted their blood to flow. That they *wished* for death yet would wage war on the infidels until their dying breath.

At times he raised his Kalashnikov and fired it into the air, then threatened the lives of political leaders from the US President to the UK Prime Minister to the Sultan of Kano, a man by the name of Ibrahim Jaja, for whom Shagari reserved some of his most venomous and over-the-top hate speech.

Finally, just as I decided I couldn't bear to watch any more, he looked into the camera and – with his uncanny ability to make you feel as if he were speaking to you and you alone – stated, 'I am waiting for you. I am going to kill you. I am going to slit your throat. Whoever you are, wherever you are. That is what I am going to do. And I am going to enjoy it.'

'How did you end up in Reddi Plaza this morning?' I had asked Zahra.

'We simply started in Adamawa,' she told us, 'and went village to village, looking for information. Ahmad was convinced that even those loyal to Rusul Alharb would tell us what they knew for the promise of enough money. And he was right. We learned nothing in the first few villages we visited. Then, all of a sudden, it was as if someone turned on the spigot. We started picking up names and places and rumors at every village we went to. Each piece seemed to lead us to another state. We bounced between Yobe, Adamawa, and Borno like pinballs, until Ahmad finally realized that Shagari was sending us on a wild goose chase. Through his men, he was feeding bits and pieces to residents he knew would talk. But everything was false. Every road led to nowhere.'

'How long did this go on?'

'Four or five days, I guess. Then Ahmad took what we both knew to be a serious risk. He reached out to one of his friends from the Yakubu days. This friend was no longer a member of Rusul Alharb, but he was still plugged in, so to speak. Ahmad and I tracked him down in Maiduguri. We followed him to a café, where I volunteered to pass him a message, asking him to agree to a meeting with Ahmad. In the message, Ahmad conceded that it was regarding extremely sensitive information and said I should return in an hour for a response. When I came back to the café, the man simply nodded his head and handed me an address.'

'Were you with Ahmad at the meeting?' Jadine said.

'Yes. Ahmad's friend said that he had heard about the mass kidnapping and that it involved the daughter of someone who had betrayed Shagari. He didn't know who that someone was. But he *had* heard Shagari's plans for her.'

'Which were?'

'When the abduction first took place, its objective was merely personal revenge. Like so many of the girls he'd abducted, he intended to use her as a suicide bomber. He even had her make a martyrdom video in which Kishana was forced to implicate Ahmad as the influence behind the bombing.'

'Where was it supposed to take place?'

'Originally, there in Maiduguri. Somewhere near the university. But as of that morning, the plan had changed. Shagari had learned that Kishana was the granddaughter of the US Secretary of State. He forced her to make a new video acknowledging that fact yet still implicating her father. Meanwhile, though, he was apparently acting more oddly than ever. He seemed to be preparing for his own martyrdom, which he'd often spoken about but never made overt steps to go through with. So, Ahmad's friend was convinced that Shagari intended to use Kishana's relationship to the Secretary to make himself into a legend. He'd heard whispers that Shagari and Kishana were already on their way to the capital. So, Ahmad and I hopped on the next flight to Abuja.'

'Take a sip of water,' I said.

She did and it seemed to calm her. 'We think Shagari must have dispensed lookalikes around the city. Because we have followed at least a half-dozen dupes over the past couple days. Some that looked so clearly like Shagari they could have played him in a movie, maybe even a documentary. Always this look-alike would be traveling with a young girl in a hijab. They had us running around the city in circles. Finally, Ahmad decided to try his friend one last time. Which he knew was even riskier over the phone. But he wanted so badly to get Kishana back and sensed we were running out of time.'

'Did his friend have new information?'

'Not much. But he had heard secondhand rumblings that there would be a major attack on a shopping plaza in the next couple days. So Ahmad and I printed out a list of malls and began to search every last one. This morning, after searching Jabi Lake Mall, we drove to Reddi Plaza. We were there only fifteen or twenty minutes before . . .'

Zahra paused, wiped each eye with the back of her hand. Took another sip of water. Parted her lips to speak, but the tears began flowing again.

I swallowed hard, my own eyes misting up.

'I know,' I told her softly. 'I know.'

FORTY-TWO

'**M**r Fisk, Ms Visser, my name is Laken Varem, chief of Abuja Station.'

Laken Varem was an extremely tall man, maybe six four or six five. Well built. Two hundred and twenty pounds, perhaps two thirty. With a voice that fit his stature, both physically and professionally. His English was more British than American, and he spoke with a Nigerian inflection.

He shook my hand, which felt insubstantial in his catcher's mitt. Then he settled himself into the plush chair behind his desk.

'I understand this has been a most difficult week for you both.'

Neither Jadine nor I said anything.

Laken said, 'There is an expression often used in this country. *Nigeria na war o.* It means, life in Nigeria is war.'

'Having been here for six days, I can tell you visiting is no prize either.'

'I am very sorry that I was out of the country and unable to greet you personally when you arrived. But now that you are somewhat familiar with our country and the workings of Rusul Alharb, perhaps we can share a dialogue that will prove useful in getting Kishana home. Most Americans know Nigeria only by our four-one-nine scams.'

'You mean there's no Nigerian prince trying to transfer ten million bucks out of country?'

'To most of us, it's nothing more than a laughable hoax. But millions of dollars are lost to these schemes each year. And the Nigerian government openly states that they have no sympathy for victims of these scams. Since the victim technically conspires to illegally remove funds from Nigeria, the government says these so-called victims get exactly what they deserve.' He folded his mammoth hands atop his neatly arranged desk. 'And the pain doesn't necessarily end with the victim's last voluntary payment. Once the victim catches on and stops paying, the thieves use their personal information to drain their bank accounts and max out their credit card balances. Some victims have even been lured to Nigeria. Once they get here, they are imprisoned against their will. Then they are sold for ransom or they are sold into slavery. Most of these victims are never seen or heard from again.'

Jadine leaned forward in her seat. 'No offense, gentlemen. This is all very fascinating. But may we discuss Nigeria's crooks and conmen at a separate meeting? Kishana is running out of time.'

'Of course,' Laken said, nodding his head, straightening himself in his chair, and clearing his throat in a single fluid movement. 'The chatter we have picked up suggests a major attack, maybe today, maybe tomorrow. Perhaps in the morning, perhaps in the afternoon. But we haven't seen or heard anything both credible and specific enough to act on. We don't know their target. But we think it is definitely *not* a shopping plaza. The excitement this attack is generating is far too great for that.'

'Which is suggestive of a landmark,' I said. 'Or a government building. Or both.'

'Indeed. That was my thinking as well. Only two buildings, I think, meet both criteria. The first is the Ship House.'

'What's the Ship House?'

'It's the iconic building that houses the Nigerian Ministry of Defense.'

'Why is it called the Ship House?'

'Because of its architecture. The structure is built in the shape of a ship.'

'In the shape of a ship?'

'Its style is controversial, to say the least.'

'But you think it's a potential target,' I said.

'The Ministry of Defense consists of Nigeria's Army, Air Force, and Navy. And Rusul Alharb has been known to strike military installations. The Ship House is a popular tourist spot. People like to take photographs of it. But access to the building itself is very limited. It would be difficult to pull off a successful suicide bombing.'

'Where are Nigeria's politicians during the day?'

'The National Assembly is where debates take place and laws are passed. The building itself is the one with the imposing green dome. I am sure you have seen it from the expressway. It was built twenty years ago at a cost of thirty-five million dollars.'

'How large is it?'

'Roughly forty thousand square meters. It houses both the Legislative and Senatorial Chambers. But only the lower chamber is in session this week and security is tight. So I think the National Assembly can be dismissed as a potential target.'

'What other potential targets are there here in Abuja?'

'There is the National Christian Center, which is located right near us. It's only fifteen years old. Neo-gothic architecture. Pivoted arches leading to a centrally placed altar that makes a complete rotation every ten or so minutes. A booming pipe organ situated near the choir. Simple yet beautiful stained-glass windows. The cathedral is open to tourists, so it would make a soft target. But casualties at this time of year would be minimal.'

'How about that extraordinary mosque we keep passing?'

'Rusul Alharb has attacked many mosques before, so it can't be ruled out as a target. The Abuja National Mosque is world-famous for its golden dome and four minarets. It's open to Muslims and non-Muslims alike, except during prayers.'

'How about that monstrosity on Tafawa Balewa Way?'

'That is the Central Bank of Nigeria. The building is over three hundred feet tall. One of the tallest buildings in the entire country, if I'm not mistaken.'

'How well is Rusul Alharb doing at fundraising these days?'

'Financially,' Laken said, 'Rusul Alharb is hurting. Even though they run a relatively low-cost operation. What are their overheads? They steal their weapons and vehicles from the Nigerian military. They pay local children pennies to work as spies. Most of their fighters aren't paid much more. They live off the land. They have slaves to gather berries, to cook, and to serve. Still, Shagari has difficulties paying his militants' salaries.'

In the beginning, Laken told us, Mohammed Yakubu received millions in funding from Osama bin Laden. After Yakubu's death, Rusul Alharb still received training and financial support from al-Qaeda in the Islamic Maghreb and al-Shabaab in Somalia. When they had money, they were able to pull off complex operations. Assaults on police facilities. Raids on large villages. Even more suicide bombings, because the families of the martyrs were being paid so well.

He said, 'When the African Union finally stepped up to back a coordinated effort from Niger, Benin, Chad, and Cameroon, Rusul Alharb lost most of its territory in Nigeria and had to retreat into the Sambisa forest and a few friendly villages in the northeast. Shagari had no choice but to pledge loyalty to ISIL. But a major problem occurred. Mohammed Yakubu's son, Mustafa Uthman, disagreed with Shagari just slightly on ideology. They had a falling out. And Rusul Alharb broke into two factions. One led by Uthman and one led by Shagari. And ISIL only backed one.'

'Mustafa Uthman's.'

'Correct. Which is why other sources of funding became so critical.'

Originally, he said, Rusul Alharb was primarily dependent on smuggling and human trafficking. They smuggled all types of contraband – arms, drugs, gold, diamonds, even migrants. They kidnapped girls and women and sold them into sex slavery. To supplement this income, they levied taxes on locals. They got into the microfinancing business, and when debtors could not pay up, they were forced to join Rusul Alharb.

They also robbed banks. When they were flush with cash, they distributed stolen money to the community to gain their favor and ensure their loyalty. When they were at their strongest, they forced governors of some Nigerian states to pay them extraordinary monthly fees in order to avoid their attacks. They took over farms. They took over the cattle and fish trade. But just like any other business, they remained vulnerable to local economic distress. Which was ironically accelerated because Rusul Alharb themselves so disrupted the economy.

During the dire financial times, they relied on kidnapping

for ransom. They relied on extortion. Ransoms were paid anywhere in the range of ten dollars for locals to three million dollars for a family of French nationals. They kidnapped dozens of mid-level Nigerian officials. They kidnapped the wife of Cameroon's deputy prime minister. They kidnapped wealthy Nigerians, the release of whom required one million dollars each.

'Kidnapping for ransom, extortion, they are lucrative businesses,' Laken said. 'But for that revenue, they rely on cooperation from the banking system. At the behest of the Nigerian government, the Central Bank had consistently helped to facilitate these large monetary exchanges. And this is where the US government finally intervened.'

The US State Department designated Rusul Alharb a foreign terrorist organization several years ago. Which meant that State's Counterterrorism Finance group could provide Nigerian authorities with extensive training to interdict Rusul Alharb's finances. When Nigeria faced the crisis of mass kidnappings, the United States offered to provide search-and-rescue operations only on the condition that Nigeria refuse to pay any further ransoms. Soon, *any* assistance from the United States was contingent on Abuja's demonstrated commitment to prevent such payments. Even at the expense of hostages' lives.

'Finally,' Laken said, 'the Central Bank of Nigeria was pressured to block the accounts and transactions of any customer reasonably suspected of being linked to Rusul Alharb or any of its members.'

'That sounds like something that would really grind Shagari's gears.'

'Indeed. Shagari has had what you might call a "beef" with the Central Bank for years. Its former governor, Ibrahim Jaja, had called publicly for Nigerian residents to take up arms and defend themselves against Rusul Alharb.'

'Ibrahim Jaja,' I said. 'Why does that name sound familiar?'

'He is a man who is very well known in Nigeria. He previously served as the Emir of Kano.'

'The "Sultan of Kano,"' I said quietly. 'Shagari railed against him in one of the videos we just watched.'

Laken nodded. Then his eyebrows shot up and he turned to

his computer. His enormous fingers raced across the keys as he fixed his gaze on the screen.

'What is it?' Jadine said.

'It's Ibrahim Jaja,' Laken said with a newfound urgency. 'This afternoon, there is a formal celebration of the day the Central Bank commenced operations seventy years ago, after Nigeria gained its independence.'

'Is Ibrahim Jaja scheduled to make an appearance?' I asked.

'It appears from my invitation that *all* of the Central Bank's former governors will be in attendance, as well as some prominent Nigerian politicians and businessmen.'

Jadine and I simultaneously leapt from our chairs.

I planted my hands firmly on Laken's desk, leaned in, and said, 'Ms Visser and I are going to need a change of clothes for the event.'

FORTY-THREE

I pulled the Ducati on to Independence Avenue and accelerated in the direction of Tafawa Balewa Way. The navy suit I wore wasn't designed by Miguel Caballero but by Brioni, and therefore wasn't bulletproof. But then, I didn't necessarily need to concern myself with being shot at so much as getting myself blown up.

For some reason, though, I wasn't scared. Maybe it was because of the power of the bike beneath us. Maybe it was having Jadine's arms wrapped tightly across my chest. Maybe it was because I knew that what I was doing was bigger than both of us.

In any case, my mortality over the past two years was becoming less abstract and more concrete. Partly, I thought, because I had completed my life's mission. I'd finally found my daughter. I'd exacted revenge on her abductor. Of course, the work of saving Hailey was far from over. She was still struggling in so many ways and could relapse into a deadly drug addiction at any given moment. I just wasn't certain I was the right person for that part of the job; in some ways, I thought, I was making Hailey worse.

Hailey left no doubt that she was grateful for my rescuing her. But beneath that appreciative veneer, I could sense a deep resentment. Like, where were you all those years? How could you have allowed my abduction to occur in the first place? Why, if you loved Mom and me so much, did you request a position that would keep you overseas more than a third of the year? Why did you have to befriend my kidnapper when you were a college student and remain friends with him as an adult? Why were you in Bucharest when he took me? Why – how – knowing him as well as you did, didn't you suspect him when I was taken?

I never fooled myself into thinking this resentment was undeserved. Hailey had every reason to hate me. I'd failed her in a father's most fundamental job: keeping their child safe. All the 'but it wasn't your faults' in the world wouldn't change that. So maybe my part of the job of saving Hailey *was* over. Maybe I *had* completed my life's mission. And I didn't have the energy to begin a new one.

I passed several slower-moving vehicles to the protest of horns.

Another reason I'd been obsessed with thoughts of mortality was my father's rather rapid decline. No matter how old you are at the time, when the last of your parents goes, there's no fleeing the fact that you're next.

Knowing that every man and woman went through this at some stage in their lives was of no comfort. Others' suffering rarely was, yet it was still often used as an assertion to make people feel better.

'You think you got it bad,' they would say, 'look at what's-his-face.'

'Eat what we give you; there are children starving in Cambodia.'

'At least we don't live in a Third World country.'

Maybe I was more aware of my mortality simply because the actress who played Princess Leia died. Because Han Solo got old. Maybe it was because I didn't recognize the music on the radio anymore. Maybe it was because Facebook was showing me how badly my high school and college friends had aged. Maybe it was because I discovered a few white hairs in my whiskers. Maybe it was because I felt so sure I had fewer years ahead of me than behind me. And even if that wasn't true – if I didn't love forty-four, I doubted very much I'd enjoy ninety.

But then, maybe it was because my doctor in Moldova told me I needed to lower my cholesterol.

'But I'm fit,' I'd argued.

'It does not matter, my friend. It's genetics. You said your father always had high cholesterol, yes? There you have it.'

'Well,' I mumbled, 'isn't my father the gift that keeps on giving.'

And yet I wasn't just more *aware* of my mortality; I was angry at it. At times, I wanted to grab it, to shout in its face,

This wasn't how things were supposed to go! My daughter shouldn't have been abducted. My wife shouldn't have committed suicide. The Twin Towers shouldn't have fallen. *I was robbed!*

So, over the past couple years, I'd spent an inordinate amount of time peering down the paths not chosen. Rewriting brief passages to determine how much of a difference each small turn of events made on my life, and what my life could have been – if only. I began mentally listing my regrets but became too depressed when I realized I'd eventually run out of brain space.

I started thinking of my obituary. That it might not even be printed in a language I could read. Not that I'd get to read it. But I could see it pretty clearly by now. Something like:

> Simon Fisk, retired private investigator who briefly became a person of national interest after his six-year-old daughter Hailey was taken from the DC home he shared with his wife Tasha, died yesterday in Chisinau, Moldova. Fisk was born in London but spent his childhood in Providence, Rhode Island, before traveling south and earning his bachelor's degree from American University. After graduation, he married his college sweetheart, Tasha Lynn Dunne, and gained employment with the US Marshals. Following a few years on the job, Fisk's daughter Hailey was kidnapped from the couple's Georgetown home. For the next fourteen years, he worked as a private investigator specializing in parental abductions, cases in which the non-custodial parent kidnapped and transported the child overseas to a country that doesn't recognize US custody decisions. Fisk is survived by his daughter Hailey, whom he successfully recovered following a harrowing international abduction that lasted more than twelve years.

I finally turned into the shadow of the behemoth that was the Central Bank of Nigeria. More than twenty floors and what would appear from above to be four separate buildings merged into the shape of a cross with a central pyramid joining them all.

The building was constructed of solid granite columns, which reached all the way to the sky. Between the columns were contemporary windows, blackened to thwart the worst of the midday sun. From one angle, the structure looked eerily like the United Nations building in New York. From all other angles, it looked like six or seven of them.

Images of the World Trade Center and the Pentagon flashed in my mind. Images of the USS *Cole*, of the American embassies in Nairobi and Dar es Salaam. Of the aftermath of terror attacks in London, in Paris, in Madrid, in Brussels, in Istanbul.

Thousands dead. Among the wounded, tens of thousands more.

I pulled the Ducati into the Central Bank's parking lot knowing damn well that we might never leave it.

FORTY-FOUR

Laken had agreed that a heavy police presence in sight of the Central Bank could cause Shagari to panic and detonate his and Kishana's suicide vests. He also agreed that a call to either the Abuja police or Nigerian security forces could result in a leak that alerted Shagari, thereby causing him to panic and detonate his and Kishana's suicide vests. Thus, we were right back where we started. We'd come full circle. A single man and woman hoping to succeed where an army would fail.

We weren't completely without help. Laken had contacted his friend at the Central Bank and had my and Jadine's pseudonymous names added to the celebration's guestlist. Unfortunately, we'd still have to pass through metal detectors, which meant if we wanted a firearm, we would have to take it off one of the building's private security guards.

I parked the Ducati far away from the building. Jadine and I removed our helmets and swiftly crossed the lot. This time, there would be no backpacks, bulletproof or otherwise.

As we walked, Jadine said, 'If Shagari recognizes us, he's going to detonate.'

'There are over four hundred and fifty guests. And he's not going to be looking for us. He thinks we're dead.'

'Maybe he won't get past security.'

'I'd like to believe you're right. But something tells me he has inside help, and that he may well have been inside the gargantuan bank building for days.'

We stepped through the door into the lavish lobby and were immediately greeted by a metal detector. Followed by a handsy security officer wielding a wand.

Another uniformed guard stood at the opposite end and asked for our names.

'Bateman,' I said handing him my spare passport. 'Patrick and Justine.'

He checked us off the list and told us to enjoy the afternoon.

'You do realize Justine Bateman is Jason Bateman's sister,' I said as we moved through a small crowd near the elevators.

'Jason Bateman, the actor? The funny one?'

'She played Mallory Keaton on *Family Ties*.'

'The show with Michael J. Fox? I loved that show. I just chose a first name close to my own. I didn't anticipate being married to you when Laken asked for it. Why do you use Patrick Bateman anyway?'

'Long story,' I lied.

We fell silent as we stepped on to the elevator. It wasn't the time to mention that Kurt Osterman had once called me an American psycho. Particularly with such a gruesome task ahead of us.

First step was to sneak into the executive kitchen on the second floor and swipe a pair of knives, strong enough to pierce through human flesh yet small enough to conceal. Given Jadine's sleek black dress, she would obviously have more difficulty with the concealment aspect than I would.

Once we were armed, we'd move straight into the party, which was being held in the Central Bank's main ballroom, just off the kitchen. The second step would be to identify Shagari and Kishana. Which could offer more difficulty than it initially seemed. Because we likely wouldn't find Shagari dressed in his usual fatigues. He'd almost certainly be wearing a suit to blend in. And he had most likely shaved.

I remained confident I would recognize that batshit gleam in his eyes, and I doubted he could conceal that shit-eating grin for very long. After all, Shagari had repeatedly said he wanted to die in this war. He *wanted* martyrdom. He didn't see himself exploding into pieces or burning in hellfire this afternoon. As far as he was concerned, he was heading to the top floor, where a grateful deity would be waiting for him with his prize.

Step three was where we would get our hands dirty. We'd agreed that the only way to stop Shagari without a gun would be to sneak up behind him and execute a silent blade kill. If we were lucky, he'd be standing toward the back of the ballroom, where the kill, if made carefully, might go unobserved. If we found him in the center of the ballroom, however, we could expect pure chaos in the immediate aftermath, even if our plan went smoothly. But it would be nothing like the bloodbath that would have resulted from Shagari's detonating the vests.

While Jadine and I agreed on the silent blade kill, we differed on how to go about it. I preferred the more conventional method. Most special forces units were trained to make the kill by stabbing the kidney through the lower back. The extreme pain rendered the enemy mute and paralyzed as he slipped into death. Jadine preferred the Hollywood version, which reportedly remained the method of choice with the US Army Rangers. This required reaching around and placing a hand over the enemy's mouth, while using the other hand to slash his throat with a blade.

Admittedly, both methods had their merits. The bottom line here was that Shagari would die in different ways depending on which of us found him.

Slipping into the kitchen proved fairly simple. After all, the Central Bank's guests were multimillionaires in a country where seventy-five percent of the population earned under one thousand dollars a year. Simply put, no one here was slipping into the executive kitchen to pilfer a few high-end steaks or some expensive cutlery.

In the kitchen, I chose a simple yet sturdy paring knife. Jadine chose a boning knife.

We both acknowledged the grim fact that if there were other suicide bombers besides Shagari and his hostage Kishana, the mission would end in catastrophe. But we'd also agreed with Laken Varem that Shagari wouldn't risk smuggling in additional bombers. Not just because of the difficulty, but because he wouldn't be interested in sharing the glory.

After grabbing the knives, we moved out of the executive kitchen and into the grand ballroom.

Thanks to online photos from previous events, we knew precisely what to expect. Which was a massive 8,600 square

feet and a towering twenty-foot ceiling, appointed with magnif-
icent crystal chandeliers. The west wall was accented by
heavily tinted floor-to-ceiling windows draped in swanky
fabric. All in all, the ballroom presented a palatial space that
would form a weighty backdrop for a terror attack that could
potentially kill many of Nigeria's wealthiest and most powerful
residents.

'We've come to your favorite part,' Jadine said.

'I know, I know,' I said. 'Here's where we split up to cover
as much ground as fast as possible.'

FORTY-FIVE

The eyes. Even in the best disguises, the eyes never change. Sunglasses could hide them. Contacts could color them. But in the end, the eyes were always a dead giveaway.

Which made ruling out large numbers of guests with a single glance much easier than it sounded. Particularly given the eyes in this room. The eyes in this room hadn't seen real-world bloodshed. The eyes in this room hadn't seen true terror in the eyes of their adversaries. The eyes in this room weren't hard.

The people in this ballroom hadn't witnessed the things Shagari had witnessed. They hadn't committed the horrific acts of violence that Shagari had committed. And they weren't in this ballroom with the expectation of meeting their maker today.

I surveyed the room while moving in concentric counter-clockwise circles. It wasn't twenty seconds before I completely lost sight of Jadine. Now, as I approached the ballroom's dance floor, I started to feel discouraged. Had I made the wrong call again? Were Shagari and Kishana in a building across town? In the Ship House? In the National Assembly? In the National Christian Center? In the National Mosque?

I suddenly felt faint. My vision went blurry. I staggered and nearly lost my footing.

A small gentleman clasped me by the arm and helped me stand straight.

I shook my head and the fog immediately dissipated.

I was hungry. Too hungry. I should have grabbed something edible from the executive kitchen after all.

'Thank you,' I said to the middle-aged man who'd helped me. Although he looked vaguely familiar, I couldn't place him.

'You are very welcome,' he said with a thick Nigerian accent. 'Something seems to be going around today.'

With a thin smile, he motioned with his chin to a young woman who appeared to be extremely, even dangerously, intoxicated. Her legs swayed. Her eyelids dipped shut every other second. She was dressed in a bulky outfit and was being propped up by two men in catering uniforms. Only she wasn't drunk. She was . . .

'Drugged,' I said softly.

The gentleman asked me a question, but I was already in motion, already pushing through the tremendous crowd. I couldn't come at Kishana from the front in case those caterers were Shagari's men. Which, as I watched them, seemed more likely than not.

As I moved, I searched the room for Jadine. Scanned the crowd for Shagari himself.

The two caterers were now gently pushing Kishana forward, toward the center of the room, toward the dance floor, which was virtually unoccupied given the elevator music that had been playing throughout.

I watched the mouth of one of the caterers. His lips were moving, yet no one seemed to be listening to him. I searched the other's eyes, which were glazed and locked in a hundred-yard stare.

The caterers, I determined, were Shagari's men. Thus, I needed to eliminate them before I could help Kishana to safety.

Once I had moved past them, I turned and started in their direction. Slowly, cautiously, I stepped up to them from behind.

Their white pants and jackets were form-fitting, so they weren't strapped with suicide vests. But they could still be armed.

Kishana stumbled, causing one of the men, the man on the right, to drop back slightly, while the other continued forward.

It would be my best, maybe my only, opportunity.

I reached into my jacket and gripped the handle of the knife.

As I slid up behind the man on the right, I removed the knife from my jacket. Lowered my eyes on my target and stabbed him hard through the lower back.

He didn't make a sound. And by the time he was falling to the ground, I was already behind the other one.

As I stabbed the man on the left through his right kidney, I spotted Jadine across the dance floor.

I caught the gleam of her blade at her side and saw where she was heading.

A moment later, I locked on to Shagari's eyes with my own.

As the second man fell, I came up behind Kishana and caught her. Then I briskly used the knife to tear the back of her dress. Then to rip through the fabric on the back of the suicide vest she was wearing.

People all around me suddenly started screaming. One of the fake caterers had fallen on to his stomach so that the massive blood loss he had just suffered was visible on the back of his white jacket.

I pulled Kishana away just as Shagari's eyes fell on the caterers.

I caught the gleam of Jadine's blade as she reached around Shagari's neck.

I watched Shagari reach into his pocket as a thin red line formed across his throat.

Then the entire world exploded.

FORTY-SIX

The force of the blast shredded the guests immediately surrounding it, propelling blood and body parts in every direction. I'd snatched Kishana and turned my back to provide her cover an instant before the explosion.

The impact to my back was worse than any blow I'd ever taken before. Bodies and glass and shrapnel bombarded me, throwing me hard to the ground, slicing through my jacket and pants, ripping every piece of exposed flesh from my calves to the top of my head.

An impossible heat instantly followed, singing my limbs and searing the flesh on my back.

I attempted to rise but couldn't. Through the blinding smoke, I looked back to find a heavy table pinning my left leg. In my shock, and concerned more about Kishana than myself, I had hardly noticed the pain. But I knew the situation was dire, that my leg being pinned could easily lead to our deaths.

I screamed out, knowing damn well that any sound I made would be drowned out by the bedlam.

Then I felt a hand resting firmly on my shoulder. Heard a man's voice say in a deep Nigerian accent to be still while he lifted the table from my leg. A moment later a great weight rose off me.

My relief was immediately followed by a surge of panic as I realized that I hadn't yet tested the leg, that it could be every bit as useless to me now as it was pinned under the table. I concentrated all my strength and pushed up, my left leg weak and trembling with pain but strong enough to support my weight.

I bent over and placed my fingers on Kishana's neck. Thought I felt a pulse but couldn't be sure, and there was no time for further examination.

I turned to the man who'd helped me, only to discover it

was the same small man who'd pointed Kishana out to me earlier. The same small man who had greeted us six days earlier at the airport. Who had driven us to Mama Cass near Balogun's real estate office.

'Rashidi,' I shouted. 'Help me lift her on to my shoulder.'

Barely able to see him through the haze, I couldn't know if he heard me. But when I attempted to lift Kishana, at least half her weight had vanished. Carrying her on my shoulder, I turned to Rashidi.

He yelled, 'There's a stampede at every door. People are being trampled.'

I motioned with my woozy head. '*This* way, then. Through the kitchen.'

The kitchen was another catastrophe – pots, pans, cutlery and dishes littering the floor, fires ablaze in every corner – but it appeared navigable even through the thickening smog.

Over the blare of the fire alarms, Rashidi shouted, 'Follow me. I'll lead the way.'

Just as I stepped back to let him past me, we heard another explosion. Sections of the ceiling above us cracked and began falling all around us.

'Quickly,' he cried.

As loud and nerve-wracking as they were, I knew that I'd later come to appreciate the alarms. Their incessant peal was all that was muffling the wailing of the fallen, who were everywhere we turned.

With Kishana on my shoulder, I knew there was nothing I could do for any of them. And I would be useless to everyone, including Kishana, if I were dead. And I *needed* to save Kishana. I'd made Jadine a promise atop that rainy hill in Chad. If anything happened to her, I would go on to achieve our objective. I would return Kishana safely home to her grandfather.

We exited the kitchen and bolted toward the nearest stairwell, only to find it blocked by debris.

'There's another around the corner to the left,' Rashidi shouted.

I followed him, my left leg growing weaker and weaker with every step. There was a bone broken somewhere, but there was no time to determine which one. The leg would either be strong enough to carry us out of here or it wouldn't.

Rashidi slammed into the crash bar, opening the heavy maroon stairwell door. In the stairwell, the alarms sounded even louder, the bells ricocheting endlessly off the concrete like an infinite round of bullets.

As we descended, my left leg protested with agonizing pain. Pain so great I was sure I would pass out. I considered urging Rashidi to take Kishana and run without me, but he was too far ahead, and I knew I couldn't gain enough ground to catch him.

I was all she had.

I had to get her out of there.

I had promised Jadine.

The last glimpse I'd caught of her rumbled around in my head. Jadine coming up behind Shagari, Shagari reaching into his pocket, the glint of the knife . . .

Now wasn't the time.

Halfway down the stairs. Then three-quarters. About to reach the door when we heard another explosion from overhead.

Rashidi had waited for me at the bottom of the steps.

'More bombs?' I said.

'Probably just secondary explosions,' he told me as he opened the door.

The door opened only halfway, clearly blocked by something large and heavy outside in the hallway. Rashidi motioned me forward. I thanked him and poured through the opening with Kishana.

He followed immediately behind.

As I ran, I gazed forward. The lobby was devastated. What had looked so lavish only an hour ago now looked like a Hollywood hellscape. A scene shot immediately after a nuclear blast that wiped out millions. The lobby looked like the end of the world.

The black glass from the shattered windows was everywhere.

The east wall had completely collapsed.

Light fixtures had fallen. Exposed electrical wires shot out from everywhere like hissing cobras.

People, dead or barely alive, lay on the ground, some no doubt dropped through the fractured ceiling overhead.

Rashidi and I moved forward together without looking at one another. Because both of us knew that all we could do was avoid the obstructions and make for the streaks of daylight at the front of the building. Moving forward was our only hope of survival.

FORTY-SEVEN

Outside, replacing the acrid smoke in our lungs with bottled oxygen, Rashidi and I stood side by side. Kishana was being treated nearby by first responders.

'No signal,' Rashidi said, staring helplessly at his phone.

I remembered the frustration I had felt as I tried to get in touch with Tasha from Pentagon City on the morning of September 11, 2001.

All circuits are busy now. Please try your call again later.

My suit was in ribbons. Blood and soot and powdered concrete covered every inch of my body.

As the adrenaline ebbed, the pain in my leg came on in full force.

'You need treatment,' Rashidi said, observing my distress. 'I'll get one of the medics.'

I laid my hand on his shoulder. 'There are worse off. Let them get treated first. This hurts like a bitch, but it isn't life-threatening.'

I wanted to go back in, to aid the fallen. But I knew that if I went inside, I wouldn't make it back out. With Rashidi's help, I lowered myself on to the concrete and sat.

Hell, with my leg as bad as it was, I might not have even made it back inside the building to begin with.

My head suddenly started swimming again. I lay back on the concrete. Just for a moment to gather myself.

When I finally came to, it was in a private room in the infirmary at the US Embassy.

Laken Varem was seated across the room, reading one of Africa's greatest pieces of literature, *Things Fall Apart* by Nigerian author Chinua Achebe.

I mumbled the chief of station's name.

'Good morning, Mr Fisk,' he said with no hint of a smile.

'Morning?' I said.

He dropped the book on his chair and approached the bed I was on. 'Afraid so. You have been out cold for about eighteen hours.'

'Head injury?'

'Head injury.'

'Serious?'

'Serious enough. But you'll live. The doctor is next door treating Kishana. He'll explain your injury when he comes in.'

'How is Kishana?'

'Alive. Thanks to you. There are still drugs in her system, and she inhaled a good deal of smoke. Otherwise, there's barely a scratch on her. The Secretary is currently meeting with the ambassador. He asked me to alert him as soon as you woke up so that he can extend his gratitude to you personally. Shall I get him?'

I pictured Jadine's final moments and felt short of breath.

'Not just yet,' I said.

I'd only spent a single week with her in the past two and a half decades. Only four weeks of my entire life. Yet she had made such an impact on me. I couldn't believe, couldn't bear, that she was gone.

'Is there anything I can get for you?'

'Just a phone. I need to call Moldova.'

Ana was apoplectic when she picked up. 'I heard nothing from you these past two days. I thought for certain that you were *dead*.'

'I know, baby. I'm sorry. We maintained radio silence hoping for a tactical advantage. I knew you'd panic when you turned on the news, but there was nothing I could do about it.'

'Turn on the news? Has something happened?'

'You mean, you haven't been following the news?'

'There was *no* news these past two days. We suffered a terrible storm. The entire village is completely without power. I was afraid to death that my mobile would run out of charge before you called.'

I sighed. Deeply. And it hurt. A harsh pain somewhere in my chest. My back felt as though it had been baked.

'Did you find the girl, Simon?'

'I found her. She's safe in the room next door. We're being treated at the American Embassy.'

'Treated? You as well? Has something happened to you? Are you hurt?'

'I'll be OK.' There was a knock at the door to my room. 'Hey, this is my doctor at the door. I'll call you back in a little while and brief you on what he says.'

'Simon, my mobile may run out of charge by—'

'I'll be home soon, baby. I should be on a plane tomorrow. I'll try reaching you every few hours until then. Give my love to Hailey.'

I waited for her to respond, but the call had been cut off. Whether by choice or charge, I didn't know.

'Come in,' I called out.

The door opened slowly. Danjuma tentatively stepped inside. The boy was as clean as can be. He was wearing a championship shirt from this year's winner of the Super Bowl. He even appeared to have gained some weight in just the few days since Jadine and I left him in Maiduguri.

'You look like the shit,' he said to me.

'Them's the breaks, kid. But you look a whole hell of a lot better.'

'Mr Orji says I look like a Nigerian prince.'

'Yeah, well. Just don't send out any emails making the pronouncement.'

'Emails? What is this?'

'Never mind. I got socked in the head, so I'm not thinking straight. They're treating you well here?'

'Very well.'

'Has anyone talked to you about what's next?'

He smiled. 'Many people, yes. They say the streets in America are no longer paved in gold. But that I am welcome there.'

I tried to nod but felt a sharp pain toward the back of my head.

'So,' I said, 'are you going to accept asylum in the United States?'

Danjuma shook his head decisively. 'This, I cannot do.'

I watched him, waiting for a punchline, given the brilliant

smile on his face. But he said nothing more without my prompting.

'Why not?' I finally asked him.

His demeanor became more serious. 'Nigeria is not perfect,' he said. 'But Nigeria is my home.'

It was only in that moment that I could truly appreciate the power behind those words. *My home.* It wasn't necessarily where you came from, where you were born. But where you made your life. Where you wanted it to continue. For me, it wasn't London. It wasn't Rhode Island. And it wasn't Moldova. My home was where I'd spent the best twelve – then the worst twelve – years of my life. My home was Washington, DC.

It was where I went to college, where I met Tasha, where I met Jadine. It was where Hailey was conceived, where she was born. And if I came through this alive, I decided – and assuming the Secretary kept his word – Washington, DC, was where I would return.

FORTY-EIGHT

Abubakar Shagari wasn't dead.

Sitting up on the bed, I watched Deputy Secretary John Jeffries deliver the news with his usual flintiness.

'He posted a video to YouTube first thing this morning, taking credit for the bombing of the Central Bank and taunting police and security forces.'

'A lookalike,' I said.

Jeffries nodded.

Secretary James Coleman had just left. He'd visited, thanked me profusely, and informed me that any outstanding warrants for me or Hailey would be dealt with by him and the President within the next forty-eight hours.

He'd started to say something else but was visibly broken up.

'It's all right,' I told him. 'I understand.'

Visibly shaking, he thanked me again and left the room just as tears began to fall from his eyes.

'How many dead?' I asked Jeffries.

He hesitated, then said softly, 'One hundred thirteen. That number is expected to rise over the next few days and weeks.'

I closed my eyes, gently massaged my temples.

'Leave me,' I said.

My next call surprised even me. I found myself dialing the number to my father's medical practice.

'Is Dr Fisk available?' I said when the receptionist answered.

'I'm sorry, he isn't. However, Dr Kessler is filling in for him. Are you a new patient?'

'I'm his son.'

'Oh.'

'Do you know when he'll be back?' I asked.

'I'm not sure,' she said carefully. 'But I have a number where his caretaker can be reached.'

'Caretaker?'

She read off the number. It had a North Carolina area code.

Forty minutes later, I set down the phone. According to the woman with whom my father had been having an affair, Dr Alden Fisk wasn't just forgetting names anymore. Wasn't just misplacing his keys or walking into a room without remembering why. All of which had happened to me over the past several months.

No, Alden was far worse off. His personality was changing. He'd never been sweet, but now it seemed he had no filter whatsoever. And when he did misplace things like his keys, he didn't find them beneath piles of paper on a disorganized desk, or in the living-room couch cushions, or tucked away in the front pocket of a pair of pants already consigned to the wash. He didn't find them outside sitting in his door lock. He found them instead in the oven, in the freezer, in the microwave. In the medicine cabinet next to the toilet.

'He's been asking for you,' she said.

'You don't have to blow smoke. I'm under no illus—'

'I'm telling you the truth, Simon.'

She had no reason to lie to me. She didn't know me. And what she knew *of* me had been told to her by my father. So, presumably, what she knew about me was horribly distorted. In other words, she wouldn't like me and certainly wouldn't make an effort to spare my feelings by telling me that my father had been asking for me after all this time.

I had already told her I'd visit as soon as I cleared it with the State Department. And I'd meant it. I would bring Hailey, too. I'd bring Ana, if she wanted to come. Maybe give them a taste of what life would be like if we returned to the States to live.

Afterward, maybe a trip to Hollywood. Exceedingly brief, so as not to spoil Ana's illusion of the place. Anyone who spent any significant amount of time there knew that it was such a steep cliff to fall from.

Maybe Hailey could start thinking about colleges.

Maybe I *would* return to the Marshals.

Maybe Hailey and I *could* live the life Tasha had imagined

for us. Even in her absence, her dreams could live on. Hailey could be reintroduced to her grandparents, who I was certain would want to spoil her rotten, which could be just what she needed right now.

Of course, there was the immigration issue. I didn't want to get married just so Ana could remain in the States. And right now that would be the only reason I *would* get married.

I could probably work something out with Secretary Coleman, but I'd have to make it clear to Ana that our situation might be temporary. I wanted her to be secure in the knowledge that she could stay forever in the States. But whether we would be together till death was a question I couldn't yet answer.

I had one last call to make for the time being. This one to my dear friend Kati Sheffield in Connecticut.

'Breaker, it's me. I need a favor.'

'That's what I'm here for.'

'Before you say yes, I'm going to warn you. This one may be a bridge too far. Even for you.'

'After the way the State Department fucked with us with the Ryan Cochran case? I don't think there *is* a bridge too far, Finder.'

'This is a bridge past State,' I said. 'Same branch of government, just one level up, I'm afraid.'

'Tell me what you need.'

I told her.

FORTY-NINE

'Ndulue Balogun is dead,' Laken Varem said from behind his desk at the embassy the following morning. 'His body was found in the bush outside Madagali by Nigerian security forces on a routine patrol. He was shot twice in the back of the skull from point-blank range, but we don't know by whom. His disappearance this past week had obviously set off all kinds of alarms with Nigerian intelligence. It may well have been one of his colleagues who did the deed.'

'Or,' I said, 'it may have been Rusul Alharb.'

'Right. If Balogun *was* in league with Shagari, once he was outed within the intelligence community, he would be of no more use to them. He'd be only a loose end. And Shagari doesn't like loose ends.'

'Neither do I,' I said.

Which was why I had demanded one last face-to-face meeting with Deputy Secretary John Jeffries before I left the embassy.

'Rashidi,' I said. 'The man who helped me. One of yours?'

'Not one of ours. I inquired with my Nigerian counterpart. He's not one of theirs either.'

Yet it was no coincidence that he was there at the beginning and at the end. First as a man who hung around the airport, willing to do anything for a buck. Then as an invitee to the Central Bank's extravagant seventieth birthday bash. For the first time I wondered whether Jadine recognized Rashidi back at the airport when he offered to stamp our passports. Maybe that was why she hadn't expected him to demand a bribe. Maybe he was with the State Department's black-ops intelligence service. If so, he was damn good at his job.

'I am very sorry about your friend,' Laken said. 'I did not know her personally, but from what I know *of* her, she was an incredibly impressive woman.'

'She was,' I said.

'I am pleased she will live on in her daughter.'

When I said nothing, Laken filled the uncomfortable silence. 'She did not die in vain,' he said without conviction.

'That remains to be seen,' I said.

A few hours later, I was seated across from Jeffries at the table in the conference room. He had just gone over the details of what he repeatedly referred to as my reward. Any and all charges against me and Hailey would be dropped in all jurisdictions in the US, Great Britain and Ireland. Red flags would be removed by Interpol. By the end of the week, he would provide me with a new US passport for Hailey and a tourist visa for Ana. When we arrived in the United States, the federal government would pay for any psychological or psychiatric treatment we needed. Hailey would be offered tutors to earn her high school diploma. She could then begin applying to the universities of her choice.

'We can assure her acceptance anywhere,' Jeffries said as though I had any doubt.

I stared at him. I liked to stare at him because it was now clear that my presence alone in the room with him made him extraordinarily nervous.

Once he completed his presentation, he sat back, asked if I had any questions about anything he had just gone over.

I shook my head.

Grateful, he said, 'Very well,' and stood from his chair before adding, 'The Secretary and I know that we can count on your discretion in all these matters.'

He gathered his briefcase and turned toward the door.

I said, 'Well, maybe you can and maybe you can't.'

The Deputy Secretary froze. Pivoted back to me and waited. Probably thinking, maybe it's a joke. Surely, he's not serious. This was all a done deal less than a minute ago.

'I'm sorry?' Jeffries finally said.

'Not yet, you aren't. But you will be. And so will your boss. Unless my demands are met.'

'Mr Fisk, we just went over—'

'Not what was already promised to me, John. That was for

bringing Kishana home. This is in addition. This is to keep my mouth shut.'

'May I ask. Why didn't you bring this up with the Secretary?'

'Because he may want plausible deniability. And that's just fine. So long as I get what I need.'

'And what is it that you need?'

'Just an elite special forces team.'

Jeffries laughed. Relieved, apparently. Ah, this was just a joke after all, he probably thought. That Fisk guy, what a sense of humor.

I didn't laugh. Eventually, Jeffries noticed I wasn't joining him in the merriment.

'I'm sorry,' he said. 'You're serious, aren't you?'

'I think you know I'm serious.'

'And what do you need these elite special forces for exactly?'

'They're coming with me to northeastern Nigeria,' I told him. 'We're going to search for the hundreds of kidnapped children who *aren't* related to one of the most powerful men on the planet.'

'This isn't—'

'This is something that can be ordered directly by the President,' I said. 'I assume you're familiar with the AUMF – the Authorization for Use of Military Force. Passed by Congress in 2001 following the terror attacks. Every president since then has decided to keep the authorization in his back pocket. Today, we're going to put it to good use.'

'The AUMF doesn't allow the President to employ forces in West Africa, nor does it—'

'The AUMF has been used by the Department of Defense to justify military actions all over the world. In fourteen countries, most of which had nothing at all to do with nine/eleven. Djibouti, Eritrea, Ethiopia, Kenya, Libya, the Philippines, Somalia, Syria, and Yemen, just to name a few.'

'I'm not sure the President will—'

'He'll go along with it. He and your boss are tight, right? Besties, even? Friends since they were both freshmen congressmen in DC.'

'Mr Fisk, I'm not sure I understand what you're—'

'Remember when the President was intent on releasing the

results of his ancestry test in order to demonstrate his genetic diversity ahead of his first presidential campaign? He even provided his DNA sample live on network television to his dear friend and billionaire campaign donor William Waterman, founder and CEO of the Double Helix biotech company in Sunnyvale, California.'

Jeffries stood silent, a perfectly blank look on his face.

He wasn't nervous anymore. Now he was shitting bricks.

I said, 'James Coleman didn't travel alone to Johannesburg all those years ago. He was accompanied on that trip by a fellow congressman. A congressman who, over the past four and a half decades, became a two-term governor, then went on to represent his state in the Senate before running for the US presidency. Twice. The first go-around he won his party's nomination. Second go-around he won the election. Starting to sound like someone you know?'

'How did you—'

'Does it matter?'

Kati Sheffield knew how to cover her tracks. Ultimately, all it took for her to break into Double Helix's system was some minor social engineering. In any event, my strong hunch had paid off.

'I suppose not.'

'My friend Jadine Visser died not knowing who her real father was. Kishana *will* know the identity of her real grand-father. The question is whether she and the world will learn the truth before the President's re-election campaign. Or after it.'

EPILOGUE

I t took a few months, but the President finally authorized the use of force in Nigeria, with the stated purpose of eliminating the terror group Rusul Alharb and rescuing the hundreds of children who had been stolen from their homes and schools over the past ten years.

After several weeks of training with them at Fort Benning, I was accompanying the US Army Rangers, the ultimate light infantry unit. The Defense Department had collected much of the intelligence we needed by debriefing two former child soldiers, Danjuma of Nigeria and Isa of the Republic of Chad.

As we flew over the African continent, we knew the kidnapped girls were somewhere below. In Nigeria or Niger, Chad or Cameroon. Some could still be in the Sambisa forest. In the Gwoza Hills or the Mandara Mountains. Some could be in the islands of Lake Chad. Wherever they were, they needed to be found. They needed to be brought home. And the 75th Ranger Regiment was just the elite special operations team to pull it off.

In the months since the bombing of the Central Bank of Nigeria, I'd healed in every physical respect. But in my heart, I remained deeply wounded. In the end, Jadine's death struck me nearly as hard as Tasha's.

Ana, of course, was less than thrilled that I was heading back to Africa. But to her credit, she understood.

Back in Moldova, our bags were already packed for when I returned. Hailey and I would be moving into a lovely three-bedroom brownstone in northeast DC. Ana would stay with us for at least a few months until we were settled. Then she and I would re-evaluate our relationship and living situation. Unsurprisingly, Ana sorely missed her friends and family still living in Warsaw. Especially her brother Marek. And she missed her legal career.

In an unexpected twist, Ana told me all this before I gathered the courage to explain to her that our arrangement in the States might not be permanent.

Equally unexpectedly, the news gutted me.

It was both terrifying and thrilling to not know what the future held in store. But when had it ever been any different? We often tell ourselves we know what our future will look like. But I, for one, have never once been proven right.

So, when I returned from Africa, I would take things day by day. I would contemplate how I wanted live and how I wanted to make my living. But whatever I decided, Hailey would come first. We didn't know what her future held either. But we did know that her prospects looked far rosier than they had at any time in the past fourteen years.

Even as we flew over Nigeria through the pitch-black of night, I looked forward to starting a new life in the States. Whatever hell the world could throw at us, I was confident that Hailey and I could overcome it. That we could be the father and daughter I'd always fantasized about. That I could watch her grow into the smart, strong woman I knew she was capable of being.

Jadine had given her that chance. In a way, she and I had saved each other's daughters.

'We're twenty minutes from our Damboa drop sight,' the Army Ranger next to me shouted. 'Get ready to rock and roll.'

I was ready. For this and whatever came after.

I was convinced I still had some good to offer the world. Whether it was as a US Marshal, a return specialist, or something else entirely.

'Ten minutes,' the Ranger next to me shouted.

I undid a buckle and rose from my seat. I still hated heights but was determined one day to get over it.

As I lined up for the jump, I thought, *Probably not tonight.*

That was all right. There was time.

'Five minutes,' he shouted.

I pictured Hailey. Not Little Hailey but nineteen-year-old Hailey. The Hailey I had left in Moldova. The Hailey I would be going home to.

We had a lot of catching up on life to do, Hailey and I, once we returned to the States. Lots of quiet restaurant meals and Netflix films. Lots of brief strolls through the park, lots of long days at the beach. Lots of smiles and selfies. Lots of chats over espressos. Lots of hugs and kisses and maybe even a few daddy/daughter dates at the pizzeria or the ice cream parlor.

'Two minutes!'

But first, I had something personal to take care of.

First, I had a job to do.

First, I had to end someone.

First, I had a date with a murderous son of a bitch, a child rapist who went by the moniker of Papa Truelove.

AUTHOR'S NOTE

*B*eyond Gone is a work of fiction. The characters, organizations, and events depicted in this novel are either products of the author's imagination or are used fictitiously. Unfortunately, an international terrorist group similar to Rusul Alharb *is* active on the African continent. At the time of writing, the protracted conflict with this group has resulted in the deaths of tens of thousands of civilians and the displacement of millions. More than five years after the notorious Chibok schoolgirls abduction that resulted in global media attention and the hashtag BringBackOurGirls, 112 of the 276 girls taken still remain missing.